EVERY SWEET
THING IS
BITTER

EVERY SWEET THING IS BITTER

A NOVEL

SAMANTHA CREWSON

CROOKED
LANE

NEW YORK

Copyright © 2025 by Samantha Bruce

Published in the United States by Crooked Lane Books, an imprint of The Quick Brown Fox & Company LLC.

Crooked Lane Books and its logo are trademarks of The Quick Brown Fox & Company LLC.

ISBN (hardcover): 979-8-89242-081-5

Cover design by Jocelyn Martinez

Printed in the United States.

Crooked Lane Books
34 West 27th St., 10th Floor
New York, NY 10001

For Dad
The real writer in the family

The full soul loatheth an honeycomb; but to the hungry soul every bitter thing is sweet.

Proverbs 27:7

Dear reader,

Every Sweet Thing Is Bitter includes depictions of violence, self-harm, suicidal ideation, and substance abuse, as well as references to physical and sexual abuse. Some readers may find these elements disturbing or distressing.

As much as I hope this book finds a home on your shelf and a place in your heart, I hope even more that you will prioritize your own mental health first and foremost. Protecting your peace is always the greatest priority. If any of the aforementioned topics will be triggering for you, it's within your right to pick up a different book.

Regardless of what you read next, I hope it touches your soul.

Samantha Crewson

CHAPTER

1

August 10th

1:36 PM

THERE IS NO sign welcoming you to Annesville. Blink and you miss it. The town begs you to forget it before you arrive.

Other tiny towns scattered across the Midwest comfort travelers with vestiges of a livelier past, like hollowed-out car factories, grain silos rusted from disuse, tracts of houses foreclosed upon during the recession. Annesville offers no such fragments of nostalgia. There are no restaurants, no parks, no schools, no doctors. Instead, there are three liquor stores lined up along the main road like unfelled dominoes, undistinguishable from one another but for the sun-faded signs in their windows, along with an abandoned gas station, a barber shop, and a mechanic's garage. The post office closed unceremoniously when I was fourteen. An errand as simple as a gallon of milk requires a fifteen-mile drive north to the Long Grass reservation, just over the South Dakota border, or south to the town of Tyre. On every side, Annesville is flanked by endless beige prairie. We are in the Nebraska sandhills. No crops can grow here. God himself has salted this earth.

Five unpaved side streets branch from the main road like trib-
utaries from their mother river. In a town of ninety-some people,
there are no city services to plow the snow or collect the leaves or
clean up the odd gutty mess of roadkill, which is often left to sup-
purate in the sun for weeks before someone is finally repulsed
enough by the stench to scrape the decaying creature from the
dirt. The lots are large, no fences between neighbors, the excess
spaces filled with trucks, trailers, RVs, and even a handful of tiny
fishing boats for catching walleye down at the Twin Lakes. Houses
range from rundown to dilapidated. Rusted swing sets and knee-
high grass decorate the front yards, along with a few signs urging
voters to reelect the local congresswoman. Everyone has an American flag. Most people have a Gadsden flag.

In Annesville, no one moves away. People die and pass along
their house to children who will also die there, a cycle spanning
generations. My family is no different. We are the fourth generation of Byrds to live in the saltbox house on Cedar Street—or
I suppose I should say *they* are the fourth generation of Byrds to
live there. It hasn't been my home in thirteen years.

In the paper on my dashboard, beneath a bold red title that
reads *MISSING*, is the reason I have returned: my mother. The
bullet points beneath her picture—shoulder-length brown hair,
brown eyes, five-feet-four, one hundred and ten pounds, birth-
mark above left eyebrow—suggest a softer, prettier woman than
the one pictured. She is all sharp angles and unforgiving edges,
her features carved from marble, her nose thin and severe like a
blade. The hollows beneath her eyes are deep enough to catch
rainwater. She looks older her forty-seven years. She was last
seen leaving the women's Bible study on Thursday night, three
days ago. The bottom of the page implores anyone with information about the whereabouts of Elissa Byrd to call the Tillman
County Sheriff's Department.

The saltbox house is frozen in time. I drive by with my head
ducked, in case my Missouri plates attract undue attention. I once

peeled swaths of blue paint from the same siding, reclined on the same lopsided porch swing, fled from snakes in the same over-grown grass. We always had a problem with eastern racers. They're as fast as their name suggests, long enough to rear up and peek their slender black heads above the grass. Fuel for night-mares. One even slithered into my bed once.

I drive to the southern edge of town, where the church cow-ers from the liquor stores to apologize for their indecency. The church is the closest thing Annesville has to entertainment, though it can only scrape together services on Wednesday nights and Sunday mornings. While every other building languishes in disrepair, the church is pristine. The empty bell tower reaches for the sky above stained glass windows. Behind the church, across a manicured lawn, are small portable classrooms for Sunday school and weekly Bible reading groups segregated by gender.

My sisters and I never missed a service growing up, not because we were devout, but because our father would berate us to the point of tears if we objected. Once or twice, when I was old enough to be properly punished for my insolence, he cracked me across the face. Spare the rod, spoil the child. The services imparted me with little spiritual guidance, only an encyclopedic recall of Bible verses I carry with me to this day. Most of them are from Leviticus.

If anyone curses his mother or father, he must be put to death.

When I pass the church, I notice an older man in a bathrobe milling around the parking lot. I dismiss it as a local drunk until I recognize the gleam of a prosthetic leg.

"Mr. Crawford?" I call from the car. He doesn't look at me, and the cold shoulder takes me aback. Gil Crawford is the only person who ever visited me in prison. He made the six-hour drive to York twice a year, once for my birthday in May and then the day after Christmas, always with a small stack of books as a gift. He sent me twenty dollars every month too. It was the difference between washing my hair with bar soap or with shampoo.

To everyone else in Annesville, I am persona non grata. But not to Gil Crawford—or, at least, I shouldn't be. Our contact since my release has been fleeting. I've been too busy surviving from one day to the next to maintain a close relationship. Perhaps I've spurned him without intending to.

I step out of the car and say his name again. The midafternoon sun blazes white above the prairie. Gil's hands cup into a visor over his eyes as he gazes into the distance. When I tap him on the shoulder, he jumps. His hair has turned white and his face sags with age like a bloodhound, but his enormous bell pepper nose remains comfortingly familiar.

"I'm sorry, Mr. Crawford, I—"

"Connor isn't here," he says. "He has baseball practice."

My mouth gapes, unable to form words, as if I've been lobotomized. All I can manage is, "What?"

"Coach Romanoff is pushing them hard. They need it. That team from Scottsbluff is a real juggernaut."

It dawns on me then. The bathrobe alone should have tipped me off. Is it Alzheimer's? Dementia? Was it not enough for him to lose a leg in Iraq and a wife to cancer? Life does not dole out suffering in equal rations, but knowing that makes the capriciousness of the universe no less painful. Gil pulls on the loops of his robe belt and tucks his hands into his pockets, his face angled toward the sun again with a serene smile, like a cat sunning itself in a patch of grass.

"Coach Romanoff canceled practice today." I stand close to Gil and weave my arm through his. He accepts the gesture, sighing deeply. He must remember me. He must know it's me. He's telling me about his son, my dearest childhood friend. He must know who I am. I want to tug on his hand and beg for reassurance. *Remember me? Remember me?* Like when I was a little girl, starved for affection. *Please remember me.*

"He never cancels."

"His appendix burst." That the lie is necessary does not ease my discomfort in telling it.

"I asked him to work on barehand throws with you. You have a hell of an arm, Providence, but you lose too much time collecting the ball on the throw to first." Gil makes my name sound lighter and airier than it has any right to be, its three syllables beautiful instead of cumbersome.

"My father says off-balance throws are amateur hour." If I threw without my feet set when we practiced together, an affair often stretching deep into the night, my father would pelt me with a softball right between the shoulders. The welts would sometimes be bigger than the ball itself. *Don't play like a fucking girl.*

Gil laughs. "There's a reason your father never got a scholarship to play ball."

"Why don't we go find Connor? Maybe he can practice with us too."

He blinks hard, skimming the surface of lucidity. His hands relax. "I think I should see him. Connor had something important to tell me."

Gil starts to walk toward the prairie, but I steer him toward the passenger seat. I'm about to head to his house on Maple Street when I notice the wristbands. Yellow: *FALL RISK.* Blue: *ALLERGY, AUGMENTIN.* White: *CREEKSIDE NURSING HOME.*

The drive to Tyre lasts twenty excruciating minutes. Gil monologues about a cherrywood table he's building for my father, which he really built years ago. (My father never paid him for his work. Instead, he agreed to stop hurling racial abuse at him every time their paths crossed at the Tyre poolhall. The Crawfords were the only Black family in Annesville. If my father had it his way, the town would be lily white.) Cherrywood, but strong as an oak, ha ha, little carpenter's joke. Gil thinks I'm a teenager. He asks how school is going this year, if that old fossil Mr. Keaton is still teaching American history. I smile and nod at all the right beats, ignoring the knot my stomach has contorted itself into.

A sheriff's cruiser is parked in front of the nursing facility. I don't recognize the deputy chatting with the nurses, half a dozen women lined up in a gradient of scrubs from navy to robin's egg blue, but I thank my lucky stars it's not the sheriff. Two nurses rush to my side and guide Gil into a wheelchair. They whisk him into the building before I can say goodbye.

"Where'd you find him?" asks the deputy. His lower lip juts with chewing tobacco. When the scent wafts toward me, my craving for a cigarette intensifies, an ache in the back of my mouth like a rotten tooth ready to be pulled.

"The church in Annesville."

"He took someone's car," offers a nurse with a matronly bob. The words are directed at the deputy, not me, but her defensiveness sets my teeth on edge. "It's not the first time he's made his way up to Annesville. Most of us," she says, glaring at a young, curly-haired nurse, "know better than to leave our keys where Mr. Crawford can find them."

"I've never had a patient *steal* my car before!" the other nurse protests.

The deputy lowers himself into the cruiser. "We'll have your car back shortly, miss. And as for the rest of you—eleven silver alerts in the county this year and they've all been from Creekside. Don't make me come out here again."

The remaining nurses nod their heads before ducking inside the building. The deputy's threat is a feeble one. Like most of the healthcare facilities in Tillman County, Creekside has a skeleton staff with dubious qualifications. You can't be picky out in the boondocks. Better to have an undertrained nurse than no nurse at all.

At the very least, my small act of heroism has earned me a visit with Gil. The nurse at the front desk cradles a phone against her ear with one shoulder, her fingers dancing across the keyboard in front of her. When I show her my ID, she takes a cursory glance before waving me down the hall. Her inattentiveness is welcome. I hate showing people my ID. I live in constant fear of an eagle-eyed store clerk or bartender recognizing my name. Around here, the name Providence Byrd only means trouble.

As I walk down the hallway, one of the nurses from outside recognizes me. She's petite, brunette, cute. There's something familiar about her—perhaps the younger sibling of a friend from school. She chews on a wad of cinnamon gum. "Did you want to check in on Gil, honey?"

I bristle at a girl younger than I am calling me honey. "He was kind of a surrogate father to me growing up."

"Of course, honey. Let me pop in and ask his son if it's all right."

"His son?"

But the nurse hurries out of earshot, peeking into a room at the end of the hall. She leans through the doorway on one foot, the other extended behind her like a figure skater who has landed a perfect jump. She turns back to say something to me, but Connor comes out before her words can.

He has finally grown into his long, lean body, a far cry from the lanky teenager who invited me to his house every day after school because he knew I wasn't safe at home. His hair is styled into cornrows and gathered into a small bun, leaving nowhere for the acne scars pocked along his cheeks and chin to hide. Last I remember, he wanted to be a teacher. With a button-up shirt and horn-rimmed glasses, he certainly looks the part now. My heart swells with pride. My childhood dreams have long slipped away, but it comforts me to know Connor didn't suffer similar misfortune.

He offers me the greeting I least expect: a hug. I am not a hugger. Hugs are chokeholds masquerading as gestures of affection. But I power through my unease and reciprocate, allowing a fragment of my resentment to melt away. While his father showed me extraordinary kindness during my stint in prison, Connor sent me just two letters before heading to Indiana for college, at which point frat parties and football games took precedence over an incarcerated childhood friend. I understand it and, at the same time, selfishly, I don't. I've never been able to cope with the pain of being forgotten.

"It's the third time this summer he's gotten up to Annesville," says Connor when we separate, like we're picking up a conversation from five minutes ago. He takes off his glasses and scrubs his hands over his eyes. "Like he always used to say, the lunatics are running the asylum here."

The nurse who fetched Connor glares at him from behind a cart of medical supplies. She brushes past him a little too close, just near enough to bump his shoulder.

"What is it?" I ask.

"Alzheimer's."

"But's he's only . . ."

"Sixty-seven," he supplies. "It's early onset."

"God, I'm so sorry, Connor."

We peer into the room at the same time. Without the handful of photos arrayed across the dresser, you could never tell who lived there. The room is all but devoid of personal touches. My heart breaks to think Gil will die in this husk, his only child the last family left to help him cross over to the other side. Gil sits upright in his bed with a plate of ketchup-soaked meatloaf before him, carving the meat with a spoon instead of the plastic knife they've provided. Something inside of me breaks, real as a snapped rib. My resolve to visit him breaks with it.

Connor leans against the wall. "I came to visit at Christmas. I knew something wasn't right. It got worse so fast. Damn near cut his hand off with his old carpentry saw while I was getting groceries one day. I had to move him in here, then I moved back so I can . . ."

"I'm sorry," I say again.

"I'm sorry too."

"For what?"

"Your mom."

My cheeks burn. "Yeah, of course. It's . . . well, I'm sure you know more than I do."

The warmth of our reunion is gone. Our relationship has been reduced to a spiritless exchange of condolences. The gap in the conversation stretches into a chasm, both of us unwilling to reach our hand toward the other. "I'll be at the search later." He registers my blank expression. "Sungila Lake, up on the reservation."

"I'm surprised the sheriff's department and the tribal police kept their teeth away from each other's necks long enough to organize a search party."

"Makes two of us," he says. "If my dad knew what was going on, he'd come look for her too. He's always had a soft spot for your mom."

"More like he always had a soft spot for her chokecherry pie."

Connor smiles. He flashes both rows of teeth, and he's charming enough to look like a movie star rather than a hyena. "It's good to see you, Providence. The circumstances are shitty with your mom, but I didn't think we'd get to see each other again."

Get to, as if our paths intersecting today is a miracle. What about all the years that passed without a letter or a phone call? I'm not sure if he's oblivious or insensitive. The bitterness rots inside me like a cavity, but I merely nod. I have the sense one slip of the tongue will sour the moment.

But the next question is one I can't resist asking. "Do you think my sisters will be at the search?"

"I'm sure they will. They've been at all the others."

"How are they? Do they look okay?"

"Grace is in my civics class this semester. She's bright. A bit of a know-it-all, but bright. I think she's planning to go to college next year, long as she stays out of trouble." He's pleased to provide me with these details, and I lap them up, a thirteen-year hunger for information about my sisters finally quelled with this scrap. It's like the first hit of nicotine. It leaves me pining for more, more, more. "And Harmony, I don't know much about her. She's living in the old apartment building in Carey Gap. Remember those ugly blue ones? Engaged to some firefighter over in Box Butte County last I heard."

The other questions I burn to ask are ones he cannot answer. Do they remember me? What I did? Have they forgiven me? Do they want to see me? What lies have my parents slandered me with? I have learned to live without my sisters the way an amputee learns to live without a limb, a once unfathomable absence turned normal. But I miss them. Harmony is now twenty-five, Grace seventeen. They have lived entire lives without me.

"And Zoe? Has she been there?" The name of my childhood sweetheart flies tactlessly off my tongue.

"Saw her at the first one, but not yesterday's. You should go see her. Her office is in Carey Gap."

"No, I don't—"

"You're not going to come all the way out here without seeing her."

"We haven't exactly kept in touch either." My tone is too sour. The veiled insult makes him wince.

There is nothing left to say. Thirteen years and this is all we can manage? We exchange another hug, this one mercifully brief, before parting ways, only to realize we are both walking the same direction. I pretend to tie my shoe so we don't have to walk together and strain to fill the empty space with small talk.

I thank the receptionist at the front desk, who is still pecking away at her keyboard as she reassures someone on the phone. *I understand your concern . . . Yes, ma'am, but . . . I understand, but . . .*

There is a piece of paper wedged beneath my windshield wipers. Another ticket—just what I need. I cringe at the notion of a deputy running my plates and cataloging the tickets I'd racked up in Kansas City over the last few years. Then I burn hot with fury, remembering the countless 911 calls placed by me, my mother, even once by Harmony. The sheriff or one of his drudges strode in with the verve of superheroes to admonish my father and urge him to cut back on his drinking. *The drink has a mean hold on your old man*, one of them said to me as he bandaged a laceration on my arm, deep and jagged from a broken bottle. *He needs your help to sober up.*

But I unfold the sheet of paper to discover it's not a ticket. It's my mother's missing poster. I didn't realize when I looked at it before, but she is smiling in the picture. She looks beautiful. She almost looks happy.

I open my glovebox. I wrap the paper around the barrel of my gun.

CHAPTER

2

August 10th

3:04 PM

INSTEAD OF FORGING further south to Carey Gap and reacquainting myself with its ghosts, I head north to the Long Grass reservation. Exhaustion seeps into my bones as I cross the South Dakota state line. I cut west through the town of Long Grass, the largest settlement on the eponymous reservation, until I reach a double-wide mobile home with the Oglala Lakota flag hoisted above it, brilliant red beating against the cloudless sky.

The dogs tell me I have the right trailer. I'm halfway across the street when they charge up to the chain-link fence, ears pinned back, teeth bared. I read once that dogs can tell if you're untrustworthy. These dogs could do with a bath and new collars, but look otherwise well cared for. No protruding ribcages. No matted fur. No sad eyes. Yet my throat still thickens with tears. I don't do well around dogs.

A car honks. I've stopped in the middle of the street. I lift a hand to apologize, but the driver swerves around me and blazes through the stop sign.

"You can come through the gate. They don't bite unless I tell 'em to."

Sara Walking Elk calls to me from beneath the trailer's awning. Her dark hair sways in the wind in a single limp sheet. Silver barbell piercings embellish her septum and the bridge of her nose. She pierces the air with a whistle. The dogs finally hide their fangs, though they still hold me hostage with their stares. I fixate my eyes on the clothesline in a neighbor's yard. Never look an angry dog in the eyes. It's the only meaningful piece of advice my father ever gave me.

"So the 'beware of dog' sign is just for show?" I ask.

Sara carries herself with a peculiar lightness, like she's tethered to the earth by the faintest force, a balloon ready to sail toward the stratosphere. She wrangles two dogs by the collar and holds the third between her knees in a game of canine Twister. "Never said they were friendly," she says.

"I can't go back to Kansas City without legs."

"Seriously, get in here." She lowers her head toward the dog beneath her, planting a kiss atop its head. "Are you going to behave, girl? You going to be good when I let you go?"

Against my better judgment, I haul my suitcase and duffel bag through the gate. She releases the dogs, and, thank Christ, none of them lunges for me. Swats on the rear send all but the biggest dog trotting toward the awning. She plants herself beside Sara with a grumble.

"The bluetick is Julius, the Rottweiler is Augustus, and this girl here is Zenobia. She's a wolfdog."

"You own a *wolf*?"

"Wolf*dog*."

I throw my hands up. "You lost me at wolf."

"Oh, she's a sweetheart." Sara kisses Zenobia's head again to prove her point, as if the dog (wolf?) not biting off her nose is praiseworthy. "She's a Czechoslovakian wolfdog. They were the national dog of Czechoslovakia, for God's sake. Besides, if

I'd mentioned I had a wolfdog, I don't think you'd have stayed here."

"I wouldn't call it a selling point."

Sara starts for a hug, but stops short and settles for an awkward pat on the arm. I'm touched she remembers my distaste for hugging. "It's good to see you, Providence Byrd. Prison khaki wasn't your color."

"Wasn't yours either."

"Bullshit. I look great in khaki."

I chuckle and follow her into the trailer. The stifling heat reminds me of my father's liquor store. He refused to run the air conditioner, even when temperatures soared into triple digits. The windows are open and the box fans are on high, but the trailer is still unbearably hot. I fight the temptation to roll up my sleeves. We dodge landmines of dog toys on our way to the dining room table, which is littered with bills both opened and unopened. Just before Sara sweeps them into her arms to deposit them on the couch, I notice at least one is stamped *PAST DUE.*

"My AC's busted, so get ready to drown in sweat until sundown." Sara wrestles with a water jug in the kitchen. The plastic warbles as she moves her hands, loosening and tightening her grip. The kitchen is ripped straight from the 1970s, all harvest yellow countertops and laminate cabinets with a pastel blue refrigerator to boot. "I know we did the whole 'Hey, let's catch up once we're both off parole' thing while we were inside, but I never thought we'd follow through."

"We sent birthday cards, at least," I say. "Better than anyone back home ever did for me."

"Well, I'm sorry our reunion isn't under better circumstances. And I'm . . ."

"What?"

"I don't know if I should say I'm sorry about your mother."

The water jug finally opens with a thin crackling noise, like a popped spine. I don't know what she should say either. I haven't made heads or tails of my own feelings yet. I first yielded to the animal instinct all daughters feel toward their mothers. As natural as it is for them to protect us, it is natural for us to protect them too. It's the least we can do to thank them for bringing us into this world. Anyone who would dare harm our mothers deserves our wrath. We would delight to watch the vultures scrape the flesh from their bones. Anything to protect our mothers. But for me, this instinct comes steeped in hypocrisy.

I have also harmed the woman who gave birth to me.

I'm miles away. I jolt into the present when Sara snaps her fingers and hands me a glass of tepid water. I only realize how thirsty I am when it touches my lips. "You should give your condolences," I say after a greedy gulp. "Even just for my sisters' sakes."

"Condolences makes it sound like she died."

"She's been missing three days and she's got the Tillman County Sheriff's Department heading the search. It's not a winning combination."

Sara leans back in her chair toward a cluttered desk and produces an ashtray shaped like California. The mere sight of it sends a jolt through me, and my fingers, stained yellow with nicotine, twitch in anticipation. I didn't smoke before prison, but after years of listening to Sara extol the wonders of the cigarette, I started craving them as if I'd had a pack a day my whole life. (I also started craving the adrenaline rush Sara described when she stole her first car, but grand theft auto was an easier temptation to resist.) My body goes lax at the first inhale. Pure bliss.

"Did you stop in Annesville on your way here? See your sisters at all?"

"I'll probably see them later at the search," I say.

"Nervous?"

"Horrifically."

"Maybe it won't be as bad as you think." Sara exhales smoke through her nose like a dragon. "Tragedy brings people together, so they say."

I've spent years thinking I was ready to reunite with my sisters, but now, with the moment only hours away, every nerve undulates with brittle energy, a million live wires without a socket. There may be tearful embraces. They may run me out of town. Other than the morsels of information Connor provided me, my sisters are strangers. Even the simplest pieces of their personality are mysteries to me.

"Blood is thicker than water," she adds.

"This is like talking to a fortune cookie."

Sara snorts as she ashes her cigarette. "I can dispense familial wisdom or I can comment on your fake tits."

"Are they that obvious?"

"They'd have kept you afloat for hours after the *Titanic* sank."

I laugh with Sara. "I've paid them off already."

"You really make that much money tattooing?" she asks.

"It's shockingly lucrative."

She releases a puff of smoke when she scoffs. "I work two days a week as a library aide, and that's a small miracle. If I didn't have my aunt and uncle helping me pay the bills, I'd probably be homeless."

We are both intimately familiar with the hand-to-mouth existence of a former felon, especially a female felon. We wash dishes in chain restaurants, weasel our ways into seedy strip clubs, or get lucky. All things considered, I'm one of the lucky ones.

Julius and Augustus lumber into the trailer and curl up on opposite ends of the couch, their tails just touching as if to remind the other of their presence. Zenobia does not move from her watch beside Sara. As terrifying as I find her bayonet-sharp teeth, I also admire her loyalty. I get the impression she'd run headlong into a burning building if Sara needed rescuing.

Ash accumulates on the end of my cigarette in a gray append-age, like a limb deprived of blood flow. I want to see how long it can grow before disintegrating. "Is your brother going to be at the search later?"

She crinkles her nose and nods. "He's none too pleased you're here."

"Did you tell him I'm on the straight and narrow?"

"Nothing is straight or narrow enough for Daniel. Ever since he made tribal police chief, he's insufferable. I swear to God, I drive one mile above the speed limit and the vein in his head starts throbbing like the Hulk."

I hope my laughter masks my envy. Sara had an endless stream of family who visited her in prison, from ne'er-do-well second cousins to her cop brother to her mother dying from a cirrhotic liver. There was a parade of loved ones wait-ing for her on the other side, and, as I gathered from our spotty correspondence over the years, the ones who haven't died have all stuck around. She has people who love her. She has family. A pang of loneliness slides between my ribs like a splinter.

Observant as ever, mindful of the landmine we are near, Sara guides our conversation back to the matter at hand. "Search doesn't start until five. It's too hot to go out before then. You can unpack, maybe take a nap."

I nod, extinguish my cigarette, and follow her to the room off the kitchen. It's clearly a storage room with an air mattress thrown onto the floor, but after five years of sleeping on a metal prison bunk, I can sleep anywhere. Unmarked cardboard boxes flank the bed like two nightstands. She's laid out a toothbrush, shampoo, and conditioner for me atop the scuffed bookshelf. As I unzip my suitcase, my muscles slackening at the imminent relief of a nap, Sara gasps like she's taken a bullet to the chest. "What the hell, Providence?"

"What?"

She seizes the bottle of vodka from the depths of my suit-case. "You knew better."

"I wasn't thinking. I won't drink it here."

It's not enough. She storms into the kitchen with the bottle lifted high, the gentleness of her gait replaced by a single-minded ire. Before I can muster an apology, she dumps the vodka down the kitchen sink. "Long Grass is a dry reservation," she says. "You don't get to flout the rules just because you don't live here."

"Sara, I—"

"You bring another bottle into my house and I'll throw your ass out on the street before you can *Sara* me again." Her eyes are flinty, cold, appalled at my carelessness but not surprised by it. She taps the bottleneck against the drain to coax out the last drops.

"It won't happen again. I'm sorry."

"We don't need another Byrd ruining Long Grass with liquor."

Another Byrd. Now I'm the one who has been shot in the chest. It is bone-chilling to be compared to my father, my exis-tence a colorless echo of his own. His liquor store, just miles away from the reservation, poisoning her people. For Sara, this is her eye for an eye. I violate her cardinal rule and ignore her tribal law, and in turn, she presses on my oldest, deepest bruise.

We don't say anything more. I retreat to the bedroom and Sara to the backyard with a crateful of dog toys, her menagerie trailing close behind her. I crave a drink, a stiff shot of my vodka, but even more, I crave biting myself.

I peel off my shirt and study the mosaic of scars on my arms. They spangle my skin from the base of my wrists to just beneath my shoulders. Counting them is like counting stars, an endeavor equal parts infinite and foolish. Dozens of them. Maybe hun-dreds. I lost track years ago. Some are perfect crescent moons, each individual tooth distinguishable from the next, and others are ragged and violent, more animal than human. A thousand tiny screams carved forever into my flesh.

The tattoos, just like the fake breasts and the Botox and the lip plumper, give me the power to direct people's eyes away from my scars. I've peppered my arms with dozens of girlish, sticker-sized tattoos—things like my Taurus zodiac sign, a set of vampire fangs, a fig sliced open at the center to reveal its sensually shaped innards, an evil eye, a set of angel numbers—and adorned the rest of my body with larger, more intricate pieces of artwork. There is the snake slithering up between my breasts, the moth on my thigh, the mandala on my neck, the sun on my left hand and the moon on my right. If I tuck my hair behind my ear, there is even one on my face, a delicate orchid flowering along my hairline.

I trace the length of my forearm until I find the bitemark I'm looking for. The gruesomeness of a fresh wound is gone, replaced by an arête of white scar tissue. Except where my incisors cut too deeply, it's perfectly round and smooth.

It's the first scar. It's the one from the day I ran over my mother.

* * *

From the moment I considered it to the moment I stopped the car, the act lasted ten seconds. Sunday morning, early March, unseasonably warm without a trace of snow on the ground. I was seventeen and finally had my license. My mother agreed to let me drive our family to church that morning, a whole quarter mile down the road, probably because she and my father were already several beers deep. I was the first one in the car. It was the only time I had ever been eager to attend church.

My mother came out of the house next. She fetched the newspaper from the end of the driveway and stood there to read the front page. I still remember it. *BUCKSKIN DINER, LONG-TIME STAPLE IN CAREY GAP, BURNT TO THE GROUND.* (This would be blasé compared to the following day's headline: *ANNESVILLE TEEN ATTEMPTS MATRICIDE.*)

My father lurched down the driveway with a bottle in his hand. He always drank beer from bottles, never cans, because canned beer was for trailer trash and the Byrds were a good, respectable family, and anything said about us to the contrary was a vicious lie. When he lifted the bottle, I thought it was to take one last swig before church. But he raised it high, swung his shoulder back, and cracked the bottle over my mother's head. She drove an elbow into his chest without missing a beat. It was hardly the first time I'd seen them hit each other.

An agonizing heat permeated my body, like someone had poured boiling water into the space between my bones and my skin. A series of ugly images clicked through my brain: my mother's dark hair tangled with blood and glass, my father's yellowing teeth fuzzy from beer, my sisters' gaunt, tear-streaked faces pressed against the living room window. But the thought I snagged on was that of my father dead beneath the wheel of his car, his viscera unspooling from his belly in bloody knots.

I was no stranger to violent thoughts. I had fantasized about repaying my parents' neglect and cruelty untold times before, but never acted on it beyond kicking their shins beneath the dining room table or leaving a steak knife wrong side up in the dishwasher to cut their hands. But this was different. This feeling could not live inside of me. If I didn't discharge this evil, I would explode.

And so I threw the car in reverse.

It was my father in the rearview mirror. It was my father I wanted to kill. But it was my mother who pushed him out of the way at the last moment, my mother who howled when the car struck her, and it was that otherworldly sound which first make me seek comfort in the taste of my own blood.

I was arrested within the hour. No one corroborated my story. Not even my mother. She chose him over me. She swore there was no beer bottle, no altercation, no violence from which I was trying to protect her. Her oldest daughter had always been a troubled girl, she told the police, and, really, she couldn't say she was surprised that I'd made her the target of my wrath. The initial charge was attempted murder.

In exchange for a guilty plea, the prosecution reduced the charge to assault with a deadly weapon. The judge took pity on me, white, baby-faced, and seventeen years old, and handed down a seven-year sentence, possibility for parole after five. My mother came to my first parole hearing and voiced no objection to my release. Considering that, a satisfactory display of contrition, and my relatively clean inmate record, the board granted my release. My parole officer agreed to let me move to a halfway house in Grand Island, a town five hours south where I wasn't a local villain. I lucked into a job cleaning offices at night until my parole ended, and then I was free to get the hell out of Nebraska.

Most days I can forget it happened. Sometimes weeks, even months pass without sparing a thought for my crime, until the tiniest trigger brings it to the forefront of my mind. A mother holding her daughter's hand. A car reversing in a crowded parking lot. No matter how many years separate me from that day, there is no new beginning. Nothing changes. Absolution is a myth. Some sins you must pay for again and again and again, as long as you live.

I don't nap. I stare at the ceiling and map the constellations of water stains. It distracts me from the ticking clock in my chest.

One more minute that my mother is missing.

Another. Another.

Tick. Tick. Tick.

3

August 10th

5:44 PM

SARA STEERS HER car down the dirt path to Sungila Lake. The path is long and helical like a vine, nauseating by the fourth curve. The dreamcatcher hanging from her rearview mirror, a craft made by her niece, tangles around itself hopelessly. We come to a clearing where the other searchers have parked. The number of cars surprises me. I expected a dozen or so do-gooders to show, but judging by the makeshift parking lot and the crowd congregating at the shoreline, there must be over a hundred searchers. A hundred people who think my mother is worth looking for. For the first time since arriving in Annesville, I have a reason to be hopeful, even if all I expect to find is a pile of sun-bleached bones.

The familiar faces overwhelm me. Eileen Capito, a miserable old crone nearing eighty, petting a search dog whose orange vest clearly warns against touching them. Connor lingering at the back of the crowd with Coach Romanoff, both wearing

August 10th

Cornhusker baseball caps. The four Nelson boys, rifles slung over their backs, eyeing everyone from a distance, ready to spring into vigilante action at the first sign of distress. Mitesh Jadhav, owner of another Annesville liquor store, limping along the path to the shoreline on the arm of his teenage daughter, Karishma. Scar tissue mottles his neck. Tallying the attendees in my head, I note four conspicuous absences: my father, my sisters, and the Tillman County sheriff.

I start to ask Sara if the sheriff is expected to show, but she is no longer at my side. She embraces a tall, sinewy tribal police officer manning a table of search equipment. I surmise it's her brother, Daniel. I offer a wave but keep my distance. I'm not keen on standing too close to the water anyway. I can't swim. Anything deeper than a bathtub makes me nervous.

People stare and whisper. They recognize me. I've always been trouble, and now, spangled with dozens of tattoos, one of which reaches all the way up my throat like a turtleneck, I look like it too. My smiles are met with uncomfortable nods and averted eyes.

As I turn back toward the car, deciding to wait there until the search commences to save myself further discomfort, I see her. Zoe Markham.

To me, she is not the promising young congresswoman the politicos fawn about, profiling her in digital think pieces with headlines like *Is This Nebraska Congresswoman the Future of the GOP?* and *Meet Zoe Markham, Republican Rising Star.* As she descends the slope down to the waterfront, her arms out-stretched like a gymnast crossing a balance beam, I see us, seventeen years old, entangled in a passionate embrace in the back seat of her car. I remember everything about her in breathtaking detail: her peach blonde hair and how she always smelled of vanilla, and the mole beneath her breast, and, loveliest of all, her one green eye and one blue eye, two separate pools to drown in. She is painfully vivacious, like staring straight into the sun.

My pulse thrums in my ears as she draws closer, her name caught in my throat.

She recognizes me and graciously rescues me from the embarrassment of calling her name. She casts a glance over her shoulder as she approaches, her glossed lips curling into a cautious smile. "Providence."

"Zoe."

You always imagine it will be a policeman on your doorstep to deliver the catastrophic news of a missing loved one. For me, it was a stilted phone call from a girl I used to love. Zoe had sputtered through thirty seconds of pleasantries before the words burst out of her: "Your mom is missing, Providence. I didn't want you to see it on the news."

She mistakes my silence for despair as I drink her in. "We're going to find her. I'd bet you anything. Everyone in the county wants to bring her home safe."

"I wish I was that hopeful."

"Look at all these people," she says. "When's the last time you saw Annesville band together like this for anything?"

Her optimism scrambles my brain. No one with a lick of common sense expects to find my mother alive. I can't tell if she's blinded by hope or if she's trying to comfort me. I change the subject. "How's Congress? I always figured you'd be a teacher, something like that."

"Beats my old law practice." She shrugs. "Civil litigation got old fast. One more landlord-tenant dispute and I would have begged to be disbarred."

In the distance, two figures snatch my attention. I'm not sure how I know it's my sisters, but I do. Harmony and Grace walk shoulder to shoulder, their heads lowered in conspiratorial conversation. My father is nowhere in sight. If there is any moment to chase after them, it's now.

But Zoe's honeyed voice, scarcely above a whisper, draws me back in. "You look beautiful. Your hair especially. I always thought you should grow it out." She reaches for my hair, but instantly thinks better of it. Her face flushes so deeply it's visible beneath her makeup. "I should get a flyer," she says. "Maybe check in with Mrs. Capito. She's been asking me about opening a VA medical office in Carey Gap for the last year. Her husband passed away in April—did you hear?"

"Is this really the time to catch up on local gossip?"

Zoe brings a palm to her forehead. "Some things never change. I always put my foot in my mouth."

"Maybe you could make it up to me with lunch or—or coffee."

The wheels in her head spin as she evaluates the political considerations. "I'm not sure if it's a good idea."

"Because of me or because of us?"

"What happened with your mom, that's between you and God. But our history is a minefield."

The religious invocation turns my stomach. "No one knows, Zoe."

"Connor Crawford knows."

"He doesn't care. There's nothing taboo about girls loving other girls anymore." I pause. "Is this about your family?"

Quick as a bolt of lightning, she hardens. "Why do you think I'm a politician, Providence? Jehovah's Witnesses can't even vote. I was disfellowshipped."

"I . . ."

"It destroyed my relationship with my family, whatever happened between us," she says. "It can't destroy my career too."

Whatever happened between us, so insignificant it doesn't deserve a name. How can it be meaningless for her? Does she not think of it at all? But she must, because if not, she could have defended herself and, cunning and charismatic as she was, saved herself from being disfellowshipped. I understand little about Jehovah's Witnesses, but I remember Zoe telling me that with enough contrition for your sin, you can avoid being disfellowshipped. Her brother narrowly escaped exile for shoplifting a pouch of beef jerky. All I can manage is a listless "I'm sorry."

"It's . . ." She squeezes her eyes shut, then shakes her head. When she opens them again, she has slipped into her politician's skin. "We'll bump into each other again before you go home, I'm sure."

"I can pretend like I don't know you, if that's what you're getting at. I don't want to ruin you."

"No, no. We can be civil. It—"

"It's not you, it's me, right?"

"Sweet Christmas, don't tell me you haven't moved on. I'm sure I'm not the only person you've loved."

I've had other relationships, pretty girls all across Kansas City, and a few of them I even loved. But I've never carried a torch for anyone like I do for Zoe. "You don't like knowing that you're special to me?"

Despite herself, she smiles. She squeezes my shoulder as a goodbye before joining the masses, where an older couple ensnares her in a heated conversation. I'd take offense to them using my mother's search as an excuse to corner their congress-woman for a screed about potholes or mail delivery, but really, I'm no better. While I groveled at Zoe's feet, my sisters slipped through my fingers like running water. I look all around, but they've disappeared.

Daniel begins dividing the searchers into groups with arbi-trary chops of his hands. One lackey distributes my mother's flyers while another lectures us on search party protocol, his words drowned out by the murmurs. I join Sara's group so I don't have to be alone.

* * *

Our group is assigned to the nearby meadow. We march for-ward in a straight line, a dozen abreast. We are told to deviate from our path only if there is a tree or other impassable obstacle blocking our way. The deputy leading our group with an over-eager search dog has forged so far ahead that we can no longer see him.

After half an hour of searching, one of the Nelson boys calls out for us. "Hold up, guys! I found a bone!" We converge upon the bare patch of earth he squats over. My heartbeat is deafening.

Mitesh Jadhav pinches the object between his thumb and forefinger. He holds it up to the setting sun for examination before throwing it back at the Nelson boy.

"It's a chicken foot, you idiot."

*   *   *

The search produces nothing of value. We return to the rallying point sweaty, exhausted, overheated, and a little less hopeful than we were a couple hours ago. I drink half a bottle of water in one swallow before dumping the rest over my head to cool off.

"It's Providence, isn't it?"

Up close, Daniel looks straight out of central casting for a handsome but jaded police chief, late thirties, his jaw square and his eyes cold. A bald patch, skin cloudy from scar tissue, cuts along his five o'clock shadow. He has eyelashes long enough to make women jealous. I make sure to shake his hand firmly.

I don't care if you're a girl, my father's voice booms in my head. *You shake hands like a man.*

"It's nice to put a name to the face," he says, though his biting tone makes it clear the last word he would use to describe our introduction is *nice*. He winces at the large moth tattoo on my thigh. "I've heard about you for years. Sara told me they called you Teeth in prison."

"They sure did."

"Why?"

I repay his brusqueness with a lie. "I used to have ugly teeth. I looked like a goblin. We were too poor for the orthodontist."

He pours his own bottle of water over his head. If I'm hot in shorts and a long-sleeved shirt, he's flirting with heatstroke in his starchy, all-black uniform. "She wanted me to give you an update myself. I can't speak for Sheriff Eastman and Tillman County, but as for the reservation, I can tell you we're going to send divers into the lake tomorrow, see if they find anything."

"You're looking for a body."

"I don't want to be grim."

I lower myself onto a cool patch of grass. Ants tickle my hands. "Grim is fine, as long as it's honest."

"Again, I can't speak for Tillman County, but . . . yeah, our focus is on recovering her remains. We have a couple patrols on the roads just in case, but I think it's better to be realistic."

"Do you think her body is on the reservation?"

"Where better to dump a body?" he asks. "Too much land and not enough cops. We're six times the size of Tillman County."

I appease him with a nod. "Did you talk to my sisters?"

"I don't know them. I'm talking to you as a favor to Sara."

Behind him, people head for their cars. An older woman I don't recognize balls up my mother's poster and drops it on the ground. "She didn't tell me how charming you were," I quip.

"I don't like you staying with her," he says. "I'd rather she leaves prison behind completely."

"You don't have to like it. She's my friend."

"And she's my sister."

I raise my hands in surrender. This is a tussle I can save for another day. "I'm here to find out what happened to my mother. Sara was kind enough to make sure I didn't have to sleep in my car while I look for her. She's a good friend."

"Maybe a little too good." He offers me his hand as I stand up, but I pretend not to see it. How magnanimous of him, being chivalrous to a felon. He shakes his head at my petty rejection and smirks. "Don't act like you wouldn't feel the same way if the shoe was on the other foot. I'm looking out for my family. You'd do the same."

"If that's what you think, you don't know the first thing about me. Family is just a word."

CHAPTER

4

August 10th

11:11 PM

I T'S THE FIRST Sunday in recent memory I haven't been tattooing. I should do something novel with my freedom, but there's
no entertainment to be found in this slice of the country. Everything closes by sundown. All I can do is putter on my laptop and
wait to feel drowsy, which probably won't be for several hours. I
scroll through Zoe's campaign website. *Zoe Markham—Fighting
for the True Nebraska.* The home page showcases a photo of her
standing in front of a green pasture, her cornsilk hair radiant in
the sunlight. She wears a pink button-up and a pair of jeans so
tight they look painted on. The blurb beneath the photo extols
her roots in the Nebraska sandhills and her devout Christian
upbringing, a clever spin on being raised Jehovah's Witness and
hating every moment of it. Her photos are all absent of a husband, her left hand absent of a ring.

I feign interest in her policy positions. They're ludicrously
libertarian. She supports marijuana legalization and opposes

driver's licenses, which, considering she knows someone who used a car as a weapon, puzzles me. There's no mention of her position on same-sex marriage. I can't tell if it's by design or by accident.

As I read an op-ed detailing Zoe's vociferous opposition to routing the Keystone XL pipeline through the sandhills, my phone buzzes. I let the unknown number go to voicemail, but it rings again. It's probably one of the new artists at work who can't find the barrier gel. No one else calls at midnight.

"Hello?"

"Providence?" The voice is too young to be one of the girls at the shop. She sounds nervous, almost apologetic.

"Who's this?"

"It's Grace."

"Grace."

"I'm sorry—I know this is, like, really weird, and out of the blue, but . . ." She trails off.

I clutch the phone so tightly it might snap in two, like the slightest movement might cause my sister to hang up. "No, no, it's fine. How did you get my number?"

"Can you help me? I'm—well, I'm in a bit of a pickle, one might say."

"What kind of pickle?"

"Dill," she snorts. "No, sorry, I'm being stupid. I promise I can explain when you get here. I'm at the sheriff's office."

"Give me an hour."

"Oh, thank you, thank you! I'll explain everything, I promise." Grace appeals to me like I'm her mother, not her older sister. Part of me expects it. I'm thirty and she's only seventeen. To her, I'm a senior citizen. "I'll tell him you'll be here soon. Thank you, Providence."

Adrenaline courses through my body and pools hot in my stomach like a shot of whiskey. I'm counting on it to get me through my encounter with the sheriff. I slip on my shoes, scribble a note to Sara, and run out to the car.

* * *

The sheriff's office in Carey Gap shares a parking lot with a church, an accidental expression of its views on the separation of church and state. The two brick buildings are indistinguishable from one another but for their flags. Both hoist American flags into the sky, but the sheriff's station pairs theirs with the rich blue Nebraska state flag, the church with a Christian flag.

Inside, the office is deserted, only a few empty desks and filing cabinets to fill the cavernous room. This isn't because it's midnight. Tillman County operates a shoestring police force, forever vacillating between six and seven officers—six if one of the fossils retired, seven if some poor kid from Tyre just graduated from the training program. The floorboards in the entryway announce my steps. Even though the sheriff is expecting me, it seems like trespassing to be here so late. I'm halfway across the room when he emerges from the back office, drawing the door to a close behind him.

"Miss Byrd." His voice is hoarse and dry like he swallows razorblades.

"Sheriff Eastman."

Josiah Eastman is a bear of a man in his late fifties, tall and broad with a lumberjack beard. He carries himself with a John Wayne swagger, though he is for once without his trademark cowboy hat to cover his shock of graying hair. His teeth are brown from chewing dip. "I'm glad you came to look for your mother." He coats *mother* in venom. We are both remembering the morning he hauled me into this office in handcuffs. "It's never too late to do the right thing."

I resent his fatherly tone. "Doing the right thing? Pretty rich coming from you."

"I always tried to do right by you and your sisters," he says. "I wasn't perfect, Lord knows. I've got a lot of regrets, but I always did the best I could."

My hand comes to my cheekbone, reconstructed with plates and screws. All the times Josiah responded to a 911 call at our house and never once did he offer me anything more useful than a bandage or a prayer. Old Tom Byrd put the fear of God into everyone, including the sheriff. They knew each other from boyhood. My father is the reason Josiah has a crooked nose, a dead dog, and, depending on who you believe, at least one child of dubious parentage. "I want to see Grace."

"You'll have to wait," he says. "Still got some paperwork to finish up."

"What did she do? Run someone over with a car?"

My joke lands with the grace of a fish flailing on dry land. To prove his "paperwork" is not an invented excuse, he seats himself at a nearby desk and opens a manila folder. "Joyriding."

"That's it?"

"It's a class-three misdemeanor. Hardly a case of *that's it*."

If he's trying to rile me up, it's working. I glance at the closed office door. Is it a crime to rush in and spirit her away? Is she technically being held? Charged with a crime? My stomach churns at the thought of Grace being burdened with a criminal record at seventeen. She's too young to realize how damning it will be. "What exactly happened?"

"She and a friend borrowed her father's car without permission. Mitesh Jadhav's daughter."

"Is Karishma here too?"

He nods, continues thumbing through the manila folder. When he rolls up the sleeves of his flannel shirt, he reveals a Bible verse tattooed across his forearm, the lettering too faded for me to decipher. Something from Philippians. Evidently he skipped Leviticus.

"They're kids, sheriff," I say. "They're bored kids who live in a shitty town with shitty people."

"I know all about what bored kids in that shitty town get up to."

"Have you called my father?"

"No. Haven't called Mitesh neither." He spits into a nearby trash can.

"Let me take them home," I say. "We can pretend this never happened."

"It don't work that way."

I feel like an enraged cartoon character with steam pouring out of my ears. "'Whosoever shall smite thee on thy right cheek, turn him to the other also.' Just let them leave, please. Nothing good can come of calling my father down here. For them or for you."

Josiah looks at the door, then back at me. "Grace is a human hurricane," he says, "and a bad influence on Karishma to boot. I've dealt with shoplifting from Grace, truancy too, but now she's fooling with folks' cars and dragging her friend into it. Karishma's a good kid."

"Grace is a human hurricane who's lost her mother."

"Karishma lost her mother last year. Don't remember her stealing a car to cope with it."

"Grief is a funny thing," I say. "Some people are good with it and the rest of us go mad trying to put our lives back together."

"So the law doesn't apply to folks who are going through a tough time?"

"Normal people don't break laws without a good reason."

"What does that make you?"

"Sheriff, I'm not a normal person, but it's no reflection on my sister. She's a troubled girl. That in itself isn't a sin." I can't tell if I'm getting through to him. It feels like throwing stones into a pond but never seeing a splash. "If I remember right, Josiah means *God heals*. Neither of those girls will heal or have a normal life if you slap them with a criminal record while they're still in high school. They don't deserve to wind up like me."

He bows his head. "Fine. You can take them home. But if Grace ends up in here again, it's done. I'm out of second chances to give."

Josiah vanishes into the back room and returns a minute later with Grace and Karishma in tow. Karishma looks sheepish. Grace raises her chin in defiance as Josiah looms over them, hands on his hips, reveling in his petty display of power.

"Next time you're in here, Grace, you're not leaving until you post bail."

"Of course, sheriff." As soon as Josiah turns his back, she gives him a mock salute.

It unsettles me to see how alike we look, brown hair so dark it looks black and big Barbra Streisand noses and tawny eyes. My poor mother. She disowned her oldest daughter only to watch her youngest turn into her spitting image. Grace does not notice our similarities, but Karishma does. Her eyes dart between us.

With Josiah's permission, I escort the girls back to the car. We're halfway to Annesville when someone finally speaks. "My dad is going to kill me," says Karishma to neither of us in particular.

"So don't tell him," Grace says.

"He has to come pick up the car at the sheriff's office."

"Oh. You won't . . . ?"

Karishma draws her knees to her chest. Every time she blinks, she disturbs the overgrown fringe of bangs covering her forehead. I can't tell where her hair ends and her eyelashes begin. "I won't tell him you were there."

"It's just—like, you know I don't want you to take all the blame. But your dad is more reasonable than mine."

"No, really?" Karishma rolls her eyes. "You mean the sociopath who shot my dad in the neck isn't a reasonable man?"

I wish I could say the revelation shocks me. My father makes a habit of threatening people with his Springfield; it's more surprising it's taken him this long to pull the trigger on one of them. "He shot your dad in the neck?" I ask Karishma.

"Yeah. Last year."

"What the f—what happened?"

"Something about the liquor stores," Karishma says.

"Jesus, I'm so sorry."

"I wish sorry paid his medical bills."

Karishma does not speak again until I pull up to the Jadhavs' house on Willow Street. The yellow bungalow is dark but for a flickering porch light. They too have a *ZOE MARKHAM FOR CONGRESS* sign in the window. "Thanks for . . . everything," Karishma says, her face brightening but falling short of a smile.

Grace squeezes Karishma's wrist as she steps out of the car. They share a doleful look. "What she means to say is, Harmony would have let us sit there all night long, listening to Sheriff Eastman chew on his tobacco like a horse chewing its bit. So thank you for having a soul."

Karishma climbs into the bungalow through an open window. Her clumsiness tells me it's her first time sneaking out after curfew. I fiddle with the air conditioning for a few moments, hoping Grace will take the passenger seat without me having to ask. Our relationship is so fragile that something as simple as declining an offer to sit next to me will send me spiraling. I drive toward my father's house at a snail's pace.

"The car smells like an ashtray," Grace says.

"Sorry. I usually don't have other people in here."

She tosses her head back when she laughs, baring a gap-toothed smile. Imperfect teeth run in the family. We never had enough money for dental work as kids. It's only because of the thousands I shelled out on aligners that my bottom teeth no longer look like tilting tombstones. "I'm trying to tell you I want a cigarette," Grace says.

"It's bad for you."

"Yeah, well, oxy is bad for Mom, but it doesn't stop her from eating it like candy."

She started taking Percocet to ease the pain of her broken bones and dislocated joints after I hit her with the car, but that was a lifetime ago. "She's still taking it?"

"Give me a cigarette and I'll give you the gory details," she says.

"I don't want you to start smoking."

Grace rolls her eyes. "Oh, my God, spare me. I already have a vape. The only difference is cigarettes look cooler. I think it's very Marilyn Monroe."

I park beneath a chokecherry tree at the edge of what I think is a vacant lot, but if I squint hard enough, I can see a charred, collapsing house in the darkness. Someone has graffitied 666 in hot pink paint across the siding. Grace finally gets into the passenger seat. When she takes the first drag of her cigarette, I see myself in her again, how she closes her eyes and surrenders to the swell of dopamine.

"She's been taking the oxy as long as I can remember." Grace coughs into the crook of her elbow. It's the only indication she isn't as seasoned a smoker as she pretends to be. "She gets clean for a few months here and there, but she always falls off the wagon. Always finds some doctor to write her a new prescription."

I draw from my cigarette to distract myself from the guilt, sharp like an icepick. *I did this to her. I did this to her. I did this to her.* "She's always been that way, Grace. She's an addict. Before you were born, it was gin. Now it's oxy. It's a—"

"A disease? You sound like Harmony. Don't tell me you believe it too." Grace scoffs. "She's only addicted to oxy because of what you did to her."

"I did a bad thing, Grace. I already know that."

"Harmony hates you for what you did to Mom."

Her cold nonchalance strikes me as an attempt to poison the well against Harmony rather than true statement of fact. I let the question hang in the air for a few moments. "Don't you hate me too?" I ask.

"I don't know."

"I think you do."

"Like, I know I should hate you," she says, "but in a way, it's like I can't because I've never known Mom any other way. It doesn't feel like you took anything from me. She's always been too skinny and she's always slept a lot. I don't even remember what happened that day. I was too young. By the time I was old enough to ask, no one wanted to talk about it. Well, no one but Harmony, and she's . . ."

"Difficult?"

"A bitch. Always trying to win points with Dad, even if it means throwing me under the bus. Like, I had a boyfriend for a little while, and she ratted me out to Dad just so she could look like the *good* daughter and I could look like a little slut."

She wants me to chime in with my own anti-Harmony slander, but I can't bring myself to do it. I still think of Harmony as a headstrong preteen desperate to discover who she is and carve out her place in the world. I shift in my seat to keep the leather from adhering to my bare legs. "Do you want to ask me about what I did?"

"Why Mom and not Dad?"

Mom. Dad. The warm names sicken me. "It was supposed to be Dad. Just didn't happen that way."

I wait for Grace to press for details, but she stares out the window, past the chokecherry tree and the burnt house. Her curtailed curiosity feels like a rebuff, punishment for a wrong answer I had no choice but to give. The end of her cigarette glows orange as she inhales.

"I miss her," Grace says.

"Do you think she'll come home?"

She scolds my naïvete with an eye roll. "I listen to true crime podcasts all the time, and they say if someone goes missing and isn't found within three days, they're dead." She mimes dragging a blade across her throat, lolling out her tongue like a dehydrated animal, but even the comic charade cannot mask the sadness in her eyes. "Today is day three."

"The turnout was good at both searches. Maybe that's a reason to be hopeful."

"They don't really want to find her. Everyone thinks of it as a fun little story they get to be part of—ooh, a local mystery, how exciting!" She bleeds sarcasm. "No one really cares what happened to her except me and Harmony."

"I care."

Grace takes another drag. "I don't think you're very different from anyone else who showed up."

"She's my mother too."

"Yeah, but you tried to kill her. I mean, you wanted her to die. What difference does it make to you if she's gone forever?"

Every response I come up with is robed in hypocrisy. *I've changed.* I don't know if I have. *I regret it.* I don't know if I do. *It does make a difference.* I don't know if it does. "I didn't have to disrupt my entire life to come out here, Grace. She hasn't talked to me in almost ten years. Last time she saw me, she told me she wouldn't care if I dropped dead. I never loved her, and I don't think she ever loved me, but I don't want her story to end this way. It matters to me that we find out what happened to her."

I can't tell her my suspicion about our father. That motive makes me a reptile. I will live up to every diabolical assumption she has about me and I will never come back from it. She will write me off as a would-be killer, exactly the evil creature she was warned about.

"Closure is a lie," she says.

Spoken like a teenager. "One day you'll need it too."

She rests her head against the window and gazes at the chokecherry tree. Its branches dip from the weight of their fruit.

Our mother would be harvesting them for her famous pie if she was here.

Cigarette still in her mouth, Grace smiles at me. I choose to see it as an assurance she still does not hate me. "Will you take me home now? I'm tired."

We stub out our cigarettes and I take her back to Cedar Street. Every light is out, a lucky peculiarity given my father's erratic sleep schedule. The stillness of the house relieves Grace, who cannot help but sigh at the stroke of good fortune. I want to ask if he still prowls around the house in the middle of the night, if our bedrooms still have no doors, if the floorboard outside my old room is still silent beneath his step, but I'm afraid she'll say yes.

Her hand is on the door. "Before you go, Grace—how did you get my number?"

"Mom gave it to me a few weeks ago," she says. "In case of emergency."

5

August 11ᵗʰ

9:46 AM

T HE NEXT MORNING, I wake to the smell of coffee and bacon. Sara's hospitality is not for me, however. It's for Daniel, who sits at the dining room table in his policeman's uniform, playing tug-of-war with Augustus. The gun on his hip reminds me of my own, which I now have stored in the glove compartment of my car instead of my purse. The last thing I want is for someone to find my gun in Sara's trailer. If I get caught with it, I don't want to take her down with me.

"Glad you finally decided to join us, Sleeping Beauty." Sara stands an arm's length away from the sizzling bacon. She flinches each time she flips a slice, as if she's cutting wires to defuse a bomb. The other two dogs sit raptly beside her. "Daniel, my guest of honor has arrived."

"We met yesterday." Daniel gives me an appraising look, unable to hide his distaste for me still being in my pajamas. I think his antipathy is reserved for me, but when he glances to his sister, his churlish expression remains unchanged. He is a cut above us both.

He talks as I help myself to a scalding cup of coffee. It's only ten and the trailer is already miserably hot, but I crave caffeine nearly as much as I do a cigarette. "I wanted to stop by on my way to the station," he says. "The divers searched the lake, but it was too murky to see more than the hand in front of their faces."

"Will they try again another day?"

He shakes his head. "Visibility won't improve. Just how that lake is. You couldn't see the Loch Ness Monster down there."

"Maybe it'd be better to drag it."

From the stove, Sara grunts. Her shoulders are tense, the crease between her eyebrows deepening. "It's sacred to our people. No one's dragging Sungila Lake."

Daniel begins to respond but thinks better of it. "We have patrols at the main roads leading in and out of the reservation. If she's still in her vehicle, we'll find her."

"But it's unlikely," I say.

"It's unlikely."

"I saw my sister last night. She—"

Sara heaps the bacon, crispy enough to shatter, onto a plate. "Whoa, whoa, whoa! Which sister?"

"Grace."

"And Grace is the . . . ?" asks Daniel.

"The younger one," I say. "She got in some trouble and—well, she called me. She said our mother gave her my number a few weeks ago so she could call me in case of an emergency."

For a few moments, no one speaks. Sara rations out the bacon across three plates and seats herself at the head of the table. She reaches for her ashtray, but a sharp look from her brother stops her.

"You'll have to enlighten me on your family dynamics, Providence," Daniel says.

"My mother wouldn't have wanted them to contact me. When she came to my parole hearing, she asked me never to contact my sisters, told me she'd forbid them from speaking my name, cut me out of the family pictures . . . run of the mill stuff when you're disowned."

Sara breaks a piece into thirds and tosses one to each dog. It induces a piranha-like feeding frenzy. "Pretty reasonable response considering you ran the woman over with her own car."

"It was my father's car," I correct. The two of them look at me perplexed, but the detail always felt important to me. She never owned a house or a car, never had her own credit card. Everything in my mother's life belonged to her husband. "What I'm trying to say is, my mother wouldn't have given Grace my phone number for the hell of it. She had to know something bad was going to happen."

"That," says Daniel, spreading his hands apart in a contemplative gesture, "or maybe she was planning to run away."

"From what Grace told me, my mother probably wouldn't go more than half an hour away from the doctors filling her oxy prescriptions for the last thirteen years."

His eyebrows shoot up. "I'm sorry—your mother has been taking oxycodone for *thirteen years*?"

I swallow the pebble of guilt in my throat. "Ever since I hit her with the car, apparently."

"Would anyone outside your family know about it?"

"Everyone knows my parents are drunks. I don't see why they wouldn't know this either," I say.

"We don't have any medical records for Elissa." Daniel leans back in his chair, his fingers interlocked behind his head. "Sheriff Eastman wouldn't share them."

"He's protecting my father," I say.

"What's your dad got on him?"

"It's never been a matter of what my father has on people. It's always about what he'll do to people. Kill your dog. Fire a bullet through your window. Shoot you in the neck. He beat the shit out of Sheriff Eastman once, before he was a cop. He thought Josiah hustled him at a pool game. Supposedly he fucked his wife too, years later. That one's probably just an urban legend."

"Okay, let's try this," he says, unamused by my tangent. "Any idea who your mother's doctor was?"

"We're estranged. What do you think?"

Daniel scrawls notes on a small pad, tears the sheet off, and crams it into his shirt pocket without folding it. He snaps a piece of bacon in two and puts both halves in his mouth. "I'll work on this," he says. "It might be a new angle."

"Covering up an accidental overdose, maybe?" asks Sara. "Some shitbird who doesn't want to lose his medical license?"

"At this point, I'd bring in a psychic if it got us a new lead."

"You need to check out my father," I add before Daniel leaves. I don't want them to lose focus on the man who should be the prime suspect. "Josiah won't. They say it's always the husband."

"All due respect, I can do my job without your interference."

I take a sip of coffee so I don't tell him to go fuck himself. "Forgive me if I don't believe you. I've never met a competent cop before and I'm not expecting you to be the first."

Sara edges her chair closer to me. She's taking my side on this one. "My brother is a sour bastard, but he's good at his job. He'll look into your dad as much as he can."

"I'm not going on a wild goose chase based on your hunch, but if you find something, something *compelling*, bring it to me and I'll see what I can do." It's the closest he'll come to an apology. He smirks at Sara as he heads for the door. "Good at my job, right?"

Augustus follows Daniel out of the trailer, and with her brother gone, Sara visibly relaxes. She heaps a spoonful of sugar into her coffee. "I'm sorry about him. He's a walking ray of sunshine."

"Does he despise my father as much as you do?"

"Other than you, no one despises Tom Byrd more than me," she says, lighting a cigarette. "It's not enough we're impoverished and unemployed and sick and shit on by the government. We have that asshole pouring thousands of gallons of liquor onto our reservation—a *dry* reservation—every year. Everyone has an alcoholic in the family. It's liquid genocide."

"It's bullshit," I agree. It is not my place to add more.

"I wish you'd run over your dad instead of your mom." She fidgets with her bridge piercing. "We'd all be better off for it."

"I tried," I say. Sara is not the only person who's heard the true story of what happened that March morning, but she's the only one who's ever believed it.

Sara rattles her lips with a long breath, as if she hadn't considered this. "If he—" She accidentally ashes her cigarette into her coffee, then pounds a fist against the table. Coffee spills over the brim of her mug. "Goddamn it!"

I leap at the opportunity to make myself useful and prove I'm nothing like the man she so viciously hates. I grab a wad of paper towels to sop up the mess, but as I wipe the table, I make the mistake of rolling up my sleeves. I don't even bother to yank them down. There's no point. Sara has already seen my bite marks.

"You're still doing it?" Sara's voice is heavy with disappointment.

"I don't want to talk about it."

"You said you stopped years ago."

"You're surprised a criminal is a liar too?" I ask.

"I worry about you, you idiot. God, that time you did it after shakedown? I thought you were going to bleed out."

I was nineteen. I hadn't bitten myself since the day they transported me to the prison in York. I had a good sense for how deep I could bite without serious injury, but that shakedown was uniquely violating in ways I still can't talk about. Sara had to use her own jumpsuit as a tourniquet to stop the bleeding. The next day, with my fresh bite mark on display, another inmate started calling me Teeth. She meant it as an insult, but eventually I turned it on its head and used it to scare new inmates. No one wanted to trifle with a girl whose nickname was Teeth.

I abandon the clot of wet paper towels and focus on fixing her a fresh cup of coffee. I can't bear to face her. Throughout my life, I've disappointed countless people, but the only person I've ever felt bad about letting down is Sara. All she wants is for me to be healthy and happy, and I can't even manage that.

"I take my meds. I'm in therapy. I'm doing my best."

"I know."

I pull down my sleeves.

* * *

Sara goes to work at the library in the afternoon, giving me a few precious hours of solitude. I settle into an uneasy truce with the dogs and sit at the dining room table with a pencil and a sheet of paper. Drawing tattoo designs by hand is an antiquated practice, but I like doing it from time to time. It feels like a love letter to the art.

I begin sketching the outline: a female hand, her nails long and elegant, a cigarette cradled between two curled fingers. Tendrils of smoke unwind from the cigarette even though it's lit from the wrong end. I already know which scars I will place it between. As I fill in the woman's nails, regret nips at my ribs. If I'd brought my tattooing supplies, I could have fresh ink by sundown.

My phone buzzes from beside me, the screen lighting up with a FaceTime from my boss, Kiera. I stand my phone up against the vase of faux roses at the center of the table just as her beaming face fills my screen. She has a Miss America smile that even the best veneers can't buy.

"Hey, sweetheart. Just calling to check in."

Kiera Geraghty is the only person on earth who can call me sweetheart without making me bristle. She did it the first time we met. She shook my hand in the middle of her tattoo shop and said, "Hi, sweetheart. I looked at your work. You're one hell of an artist."

"I won't pass a background check," I blurted. It was the fourth shop I'd interviewed at by then, the previous three balking at my aggravated assault charge. My scarlet letter. My mark of Cain. If she was going to turn me down, I wanted her to do it now, before I could get my hopes up.

"That's okay," she said with a wink. "Neither would I."

I started working for her two days later.

"I'm surviving," I say. "Barely. There's no AC at my friend's place."

"But you made it okay?"

"Yeah, no issues. And I know I was vague about how long I'd be gone, but—"

Kiera waves her hand dismissively, her blonde topknot toppling to one side with the gesture. The cat trees in the background tell me she's at home. She's the proud mother to an army of cats, half a dozen of them, all named after healing crystals. She has a son too, a human one, but I've always been more fond of animals than kids. "It's your mother, Providence. Don't worry about anything else. Your job's not going anywhere."

"Thank you."

"Have we ever had a conversation that didn't include you uttering those words?"

But Kiera deserves those words every time they cross my lips. Without her, I'd be homeless at best, back in prison at worst. She seeks out people who learned to tattoo in prison and gives us the space we need to evolve into real artists—and best of all, she never pries into our pasts. Her philosophy is simple: as long as we didn't harm an animal or a child, she has a place for us. I know Kiera did time, but I've never asked what for. I've never even Googled it. When the other artists gossip about it, I put in my earbuds and crank my music as loud as possible. All I know is whenever the news runs a story on gun violence, Kiera scurries out of the room. I don't need any of the gory details.

I do need a cigarette. As I slide one between my lips, Kiera groans. "I thought you were trying to quit."

"I said I was trying, not that I would succeed."

"How are you going to pay your medical bills when you get lung cancer?"

"I don't like to think that far ahead."

She carries me into her kitchen and places her phone on the windowsill. She holds up a dirty pan to the camera as if to prove she's doing something productive with her day off. "You seen your dad?" Her voice turns hard as anthracite.

"I saw Grace, my sister. I've told you about her a few times. She wasn't even in kindergarten when I went away."

"Is she a good kid?"

For a fraction of a second, I consider asking Kiera if we'll need a new receptionist in a year's time. Maybe I could arrange a job for Grace, give her a way to leave Annesville. I banish the thought before it can take root. There's nothing I can give her that would atone for being an absentee sister all her life. "Better than either of us were at seventeen," I say as I light the cigarette.

"Jesus, don't put it like that. You couldn't lower the bar more if you tried."

I steer the conversation away from our pasts. "Can you make sure Margot is watering my plants? I don't want my peace lilies to die. I gave her the key to my apartment before I left."

"Sure."

"And the guy I did the palm tattoo for before I left—will you call him to reschedule for a few weeks out?"

"Of course."

"You're an angel, Kiera."

She rolls her eyes as she scrubs a greasy dinner plate. Her arms are turning red from an eczema flareup. "And you're a flatterer. Anyway, I've got to run, Providence. You come back to us safe, sweetheart, you understand me?"

"Sir yes sir."

"I mean it."

"So do I."

The call ends and the loneliness returns, but I tell myself it's a good thing. I'm lonely because I have people I miss. I'm lonely because I'm away from the people who love me.

People love me. I am lovable. Positive self-talk. Affirmations of my worth. My therapist taught me to do it every time I feel undeserving of care or affection, which is more often than I care to admit. Empathy for myself is in short supply.

Aloud this time:

"People love me. I am lovable."

CHAPTER

6

August 11th

12:57 PM

THE ANNESVILLE CHURCH is quiet. Always is on Mondays. I am alone except for a pair of landscapers trimming the hedges.

The church makes me think of my mother. She is a splinter lodged in the grooves of my brain. I drive up to the dingy portable classrooms situated at the edge of the grounds and try to imagine her trudging home after Bible study. Church was the only place my mother was allowed to go alone. Unless there was a blizzard, she walked there. She liked to take the long way, even in heels. If you walk half a mile onto the prairie beyond our house, you'll find a neglected service road for a long-defunct water tower. Follow it far enough and the road bends to the east, where it eventually runs parallel to the church. As the service road reaches its terminus, you'll pass three white crosses fixed atop a manmade hill: Gestas, Dismas, Jesus.

As I approach the portables, I see my mother's poster taped to the doors, surrounded by colorful notes reading *COME*

HOME ELISSA! and *WE MISS YOU MRS. BYRD!* My first reaction is gratitude, to be floored by the outpouring of well wishes for my mother's safety, just as it had been when I saw yesterday's search party turnout. Now Daniel's words poison the feeling.

I still have a child's quixotic notion of what it means to run away. I cling to the fantasies that inspired me to run away time and time again as a teenager. Once I escaped Annesville, I could cast off my chains and begin my life anew. I kept a list of places I would decamp to, the usual suspects like Los Angeles and San Francisco and New York. At one point, I had diligently mapped out the trains I would need to reach my destination. I would pack clothes, books, and food into a duffel bag before sliding out the window and fleeing down the street, a phantom into the night. I never made it further than Tyre before a deputy or a well-meaning neighbor returned me to my parents, never pausing to question why I was so clearly undernourished or why I flinched whenever they touched me.

I entertain a fantasy of my mother doing what I once did, only she makes it beyond Tyre. She sails out of Tillman County, on to Scottsbluff, further west to Cheyenne, Salt Lake City, Reno, then finally reaching the promised land of California. Or perhaps she heads east in pursuit of anonymity in New York City, the way troubled women do in the movies. Maybe she even sneaks into Canada somehow, despite not having a passport. When she wasn't neck deep in the bottle, my mother could bullshit with the best of them. It brings a smile to my lips to imagine her in a new city with a new name. The only hope my mother ever had at happiness was a clean break.

Just as easily, my mind gravitates toward darker alternatives, the countless grisly fates that can befall a missing woman. I find no thrill in imagining my mother suffering such an end, but the irony of this is not lost on me.

I am admiring the artwork in my mother's honor when the door to the other portable classroom groans. Karishma chokes the drawstrings of a bulging trash bag, redness creeping up her neck to her cheeks when she recognizes me. "This is my punishment," she says hurriedly. "Dad told the church ladies to put me to work, so I'm cleaning up the portables."

How different my life would be if my father's version of punishment had been taking out the trash at church instead of a palm to the face or denying me food for days on end. I wish I could say it relieved me to know at least one father in Annesville is decent, but it only stokes the jealousy living low in my belly. "They have janitors come every week," I say, but the pause has already dragged on too long. Karishma meets my smile with one of her own, taut with nervousness. I peek over my shoulder to see if anyone is watching, maybe monitoring Karishma to make sure she isn't slacking off, but it's still only us and the landscapers, who are eating lunch on the bench overlooking the graveyard. When I smile at her again, I realize. She doesn't want to be alone with me.

"I'm not a homicidal maniac." The remark only intensifies Karishma's horror, as if the mere reference to violence confirms my thirst for it. "Just like you and Grace aren't car thieves. It's a thing that happened. It's not who you are."

"It was joyriding, not grand theft auto."

"You see the point I'm trying to make."

Karishma sets the trash bag down. A clump of tissues rolls out. We both see it but don't move to pick it up. "It's, like . . . I like your mom. She's so nice. She didn't deserve what you did to her."

She waits for me to agree, but I won't give her the satisfaction. Who does she think she is? Who made her the arbiter of right and wrong? She didn't live in my house. She didn't see the things I saw. She didn't live the horrors I lived. Yet here she is, in her infinite teenage wisdom, to chastise me.

"She used to give me rides home from school with Grace," she continues, oblivious to my agitation. "She would bring pie."

"Chokecherry pie." The flaky crust glistening with butter, the tart bite of the chokecherries. My mother would pick me up before Harmony and allow me to sneak a slice without my sister's knowledge. *Our little secret*, she would assure me with a wink. As I bask in the warmth of the memory, one of precious few pleasant moments I cherish from childhood, a twinge of sadness surfaces behind my ribs. If my mother was baking pies and picking me up from school, she was sober. It was as rare as it was blissful, more infrequent as the years wore on. Eventually she would stop bringing pies and stop picking me up from school, instead withdrawing to the darkened bedroom with her bottles.

The wind blows across the prairie and stirs up dust. It draws my attention to the shelf clouds looming at the edge of the sky. It's August, for Christ's sake. Tornado season should be over by now. "When's the last time my mother drove you home?"

Karishma furrows her overplucked eyebrows. "You and Harmony both do that."

"Do what? What are you talking about?"

"Say *mother* instead of *mom*. It's weird."

"When's the last time, Karishma?"

"I don't know," she says. "Maybe a few weeks ago."

So she's been sober recently. She was sober, maybe even clean, and compelled to give my phone number to Grace at around the same time. The new information frustrates me. I am trying to put a puzzle together with all the corner pieces missing. My mother is a stranger to me. Karishma knows her better than I do.

Karishma hooks the trash bag on the crook of her arm. "I need to finish up before this storm comes in."

"You'll be swept up into a tornado like Dorothy if you stay in the portable." The reference is lost on Karishma, who cocks her head and squints at me like I'm speaking Latin. I don't bother to elaborate. "Hey, before you go—do you see Harmony much?"

She scoffs. "Sometimes, when she's not off in the mental hospital."

"The what now?"

"You were in jail," she says. "Same difference."

"Jesus Christ."

"Grace doesn't like to talk about it much, okay? Harmony is . . . well, I think the exact phrase Grace once used was *cuckoo for Cocoa Puffs*."

"Is—?"

Karishma is midway to the other portable, shrugging with her gloved hands. A gust of wind scatters her bangs and exposes two swollen pimples on her forehead, staring at me like a second pair of eyes. "She's a nutcase. You're probably better off leaving her alone."

I thank her for the heads-up, but I don't mean it and the wind drowns me out anyway. Karishma thinks I'm a nutcase too. Harmony and I can bond over that, share a few sisterly drinks at the pool hall and wax poetic about how the ghosts of our youth still haunt us all these years later, how we have become defined by the very epithets our father once hurled at us.

Somehow, I doubt it.

* * *

I decide to ride out the storm at the Tyre pool hall. The patrons inside are enraptured by a nail-biter Rockies game, unaware of Mother Nature's approaching apoplexy. Billiard balls, abandoned midgame, are rainbowed across the green felt tables. The men at the tables swap baseball observations over beers in cans, beers in bottles, beers in glasses. I slink to the furthest corner of the bar and take the barstool beside the brick wall decorated with the tires of Tyre. Anyone who gets a flat tire in Tillman County is expected to donate the casualty to the pool hall. Your generosity is rewarded with a beer and a game of pool on the house.

I watch the game despite myself. Baseball makes me think of my father. I tagged along on a double date to a Royals game once, and the whole time I heard his voice in my head like gunfire, rebuking the commissioner who bastardized his favorite sport with the universal designated hitter. *Pussies.*

The bartender scarcely looks old enough to be serving me the stout in his hand. He can't keep himself from peeking at my chest. "From the gentleman down there," he says, pointing his thumb toward the only other person seated at the bar.

"Coach Romanoff? Are you—?" I stop myself from berating the bartender, instead dismissing him with a pinched smile. I refuse to look at Coach Romanoff again. Another look will be construed as an invitation. "Tell him I said thanks and I said piss off, in those exact words."

"I don't—"

"My old softball coach shouldn't be buying me drinks."

"No, I mean he—"

"I think Chuck and Jimmy could use another beer, kid." Coach Romanoff claims the peeling vinyl stool beside me and shoos the bartender with a flick of his hand. "Miss Byrd, you looked a little lonely sitting here by yourself."

The boys always got the first name treatment from Coach Romanoff. The girls were addressed by last name only, a habit he defended as chivalry, but I saw only as an affirmation that I belonged to my father. I wasn't allowed to be Providence; I was only allowed to be Tom Byrd's daughter. "I like being alone," I say.

"That's not how I remember it. You were always a social butterfly when you were on my team." He drains the last sip from his beer and licks the foam along his upper lip. "You were a firecracker too. No one got thrown out of more games than you, least not until Harmony came along."

"You coached her? Did you sit next to her in the dugout too?" I scoop a handful of almonds from a bowl on the counter and pop them into my mouth one at a time like Tic Tacs.

The bar erupts with cheers as the Rockies batter slices the ball under the first baseman's glove. Bottom of the ninth, Rockies down two, one out, runners on the corners. "I put her at shortstop, just like you, but—well, but not as good, frankly. She didn't move like you. If I had a quarter for every time she bobbled a routine grounder, I'd be on the Forbes List. And that swing? She reminded me of my four-year-old playing tee-ball."

His knee brushes against mine, and the hairs on the back of my neck stand up. I am sixteen again, alone with Coach Romanoff in his office, pretending not to notice he's sitting a little too close to me. "Who do I remind you of?"

"Oh, you're one of a kind, Miss Byrd."

When his knee grazes mine again, this time longer and with intention, a bilious lump forms in my throat. "If you want to fuck me, you can say it. I'm sure you've been jacking off to the thought of me since I tried out for you in those tight softball pants."

"Hey now, I—" He sputters.

"Or am I too old for you now? I am thirty, after all. I'm technically past my prime."

He fails to disarm me with a blush and a smile. "I think we've misunderstood each other."

"No, I don't think we have."

"I'm going to step outside for a moment to make a call," he says, "and when I come back, maybe we can try this conversation again, hmm?"

Coach Romanoff stalls for a moment, waiting for my acknowledgement, but I glue my gaze to the Rockies game and continue popping almonds into my mouth. I swallow a couple without chewing. Just as I begin to relax, the bartender reappears with another stout in his hands, his shoulders slumped forward in apology, ready for me to explode.

"Tell that washed up asshole I don't even like stout."

"It's not from him," he says quickly. "It's from the gentleman back there."

He points toward a half dozen men congregated around the furthest pool table. They prop themselves up on their cues like exhausted hikers steadying themselves on trees along the trail. "You'll have to be more specific."

"In the Tulowitzki jersey."

I see my father then, one foot lifted onto the chair, stretching forward to ease the strain of his bad right knee. His belly sags low. His ugly Richard Nixon nose is even bigger than I remember, stretched by the hands of Father Time himself. He is nearing sixty now, suffering the indignities time eventually visits upon us all: his once dark hair streaked with silver, his once athletic frame hidden beneath too many beers. His face is worn like a catcher's mitt, dappled with sunspots and scored with crow's feet, his fishlike lips curled into the cruel frown I still see in my nightmares. He lifts his own foamy glass of stout toward me in a mock salute. I'm so mortified by the gesture that I salute him right back.

I've attracted the attention of a hollow-cheeked brunette skulking around the restrooms. My first instinct is gratitude. She too recognizes the girl code women adhere to in bars and clubs. If another woman is in distress, even one you don't know, you rescue her from the situation and whisk her to safety.

"Well, well, well," the brunette says, grasping the bottleneck of her beer between two fingers, "it's about time you showed your face here, you stupid bitch."

Too late, I realize it's Harmony. She approaches me deliberately, one gunslinger challenging another to a duel. Harmony is a diluted version of me and Grace—brown hair where ours is nearly black, brown eyes where ours are amber, a little paler, a lot thinner. She's all veins and bones. Her sunflower yellow dress swallows up her frame and drags along the floor. She's pretty in a sad, strange way, like Sally from *The Nightmare Before Christmas*.

She pokes the bottleneck into my chest. If her lumbering gait hadn't already given away her drunkenness, her slurred words do now. Each syllable collides with the next like crashing cars. "I have waited thirteen years to call you that, you know? You're a stupid bitch."

"Say it again. Maybe it'll make you feel better."

"You don't speak to me." She digs the bottleneck deeper between my breasts. "You will never say a word to me. I am only—" She burps in my face. "I only talked to you so I could tell you to drop dead. I wish you were dead. Dead or rotting away in a prison cell, where you belong."

The rest of the pool hall ceases to exist, the world melting away so we can share this pernicious moment. The symphony of cheers that ensues when the game-winning home run sails over the left field fence come from another dimension.

I ready myself for more of Harmony's animosity. I promise to absorb every insult she has been saving for me. But she makes good on her promise to ignore me. No sooner than the words have left her lips, she has gone to our father. He pretends to be engaged in another conversation, but he's been watching. His cruel frown has become a cruel smile as he delights in my wounded expression.

Harmony pecks his stubbled cheek to earn money for another drink. He makes a show of opening his wallet and placing the bill in her opened palm, a king bestowing a gift to a servant girl. Benevolent. Chivalrous. It is only because I remember the beats of this quid pro quo that it nauseates me. When we were kids, something as simple as asking him for lunch money required a lavish display of affection.

Harmony turns the money into two shots of whiskey. She downs them in rapid succession, her beer the chaser. There is no pleasure in her drinking. These shots are the means to an end.

The first shot glass whizzes by me and shatters against the wall. The second collides with my ribs like a shotgun slug before she heads out without another word.

My father's posse roars with laughter, like Harmony and I are acting out an elaborate skit for their entertainment. One of them says, "She's always been piss and vinegar, girl. Don't take her so serious."

"Providence has never been able to take a joke," my father says. He labors over the three cumbersome syllables of my name the way people do when they first meet me. My parents' first act of cruelty against me was my name. They burdened me with a name from which no nicknames could be wrung, then denied me a middle name to use as an alternative.

"I can when they're funny," I snap.

"I wasn't talking to you, I'm talking about you. Mind your business."

I throw a ten on the counter and storm out of the bar, determined to catch Harmony, but she has vanished into the ether. The rain lashes my face. My sister lives in Carey Gap. It's not far. I can drive there and confront her, let her know I'm not going to let her abuse me for kicks. If she wants to read me the riot act, fine, I can take it, but I'll make her use her words instead of throwing a drunken tantrum.

I'm barely in the car when my phone vibrates.

"What?" I shout into the receiver.

"Providence?"

I beat my head against the top of the steering wheel. I double-check the phone number, but I don't recognize it, nor do I recognize the male voice on the other end of the line. "Who the hell is this?"

"It's Connor."

"Connor, I'm in the middle of something."

"Can whatever you're in the middle of be paused? It's about your sister."

"My sister is precisely what I'm in the middle of." I start to turn the key in the ignition but stop quickly. It's fruitless. My entire body is shaking. I can't drive like this. "Harmony is so drunk she threw a shot glass at me."

"Harmony? No, I'm talking about Grace." He interprets my pause as permission to elaborate. "How fast can you be at the high school?"

"Ten minutes if I floor it."

"If you floor it in this weather, you'll be getting here in a body bag."

"Well, I'm assuming she's in trouble."

"We can talk about it when you get here," he says.

On the horizon, a sliver of white sunshine promises respite from the storm. I resent the position I've been thrust into. I am wearing a costume tailored for someone else, designed for a role which I am unqualified to play. In the last ten minutes, I have depleted what few reserves of sisterly love remained after so many dormant years.

I drive twenty over the limit until I'm in the parking lot, where the final students trickling out greet me with pinched smiles and wary glances. I can't tell if it's the tattoos making them nervous or my manic energy.

*   *   *

I expect Grace to be charged with a minor infraction. Dress code violation. Plagiarizing an essay. I can handle that. Anything more serious requires maternal skills I lack.

After crisscrossing the campus in search of Connor's classroom (a group of boys dressed for football practice took pity on me and pointed me to Mr. Keaton's old room), I am out of breath, agitated, and shivering in my wet clothes. I'll get in and out, quick as possible. I'm less interested in Grace's misbehavior than I am in the opportunity for us to talk on the car ride home, which she'll certainly need with the bus long gone. We can stop for pumpkin ice cream at the fifties-themed parlor back in Tyre. We can talk. Really talk.

That modest fantasy is my carrot on a stick. I ease the classroom door open and feel my heart plummet into my stomach when Connor is the only person in the room. Am I too late? Is it worse than I imagined? What if they called the police? What if she had a weapon? What if—?

Connor writes furiously on the whiteboard. His words are so illegible, he may as well be writing in hieroglyphics. I glance around the room and try to get my bearings. The walls are decorated with framed copies of infamous American news headlines. *OAHU BOMBED BY JAPANESE PLANES. DEWEY DEFEATS TRUMAN. FORD TO CITY: DROP DEAD.* A life-size cardboard cutout of Barack Obama waves at me from behind the rows of desks. George Bush peeks out from the storage closet.

Connor's voice tears my attention away from the former presidents. "Remember when I asked you not to speed on the way here?"

"Where's my sister? How bad is it?"

"Let me finish—"

"Damn it, Connor, just tell me what's going on!"

He underlines a word that looks vaguely like *justice* before turning around. He winces at the mere sight of me. I must look more feral than I feel. "I don't know how to sugarcoat this, so I'll come straight out with it: she punched another girl in the face. Probably broke her nose, from the looks of it. They're in the principal's office now."

"What'd the other girl do to deserve it?"

"Jesus, Providence."

"She's not a delinquent. She's not going to punch someone in the face unprovoked," I insist. My defense of my sister is as impassioned as it is disingenuous, because everything I've learned about Grace suggests that she is, in fact, a delinquent, a bad seed, damaged irreparably, stealing cars and throwing punches and God knows what else. *Human hurricane.* But I remember being denigrated with the same labels at her age, and I remember most clearly the pitiless sting of silence when no one came to my defense.

He riffles through a desk drawer for a pill bottle. He swallows the giant tablet with no water. "This whole ordeal is giving me a migraine," he says by way of explanation. "Come on, let's walk and talk. They're waiting in the principal's office."

Our cross-campus trek winds around dingy portable classrooms and through the withered courtyard grass, where a troupe of theater students are woodenly reciting lines that sound vaguely Shakespearean. Connor fills me in on the details as we walk: his students were turning in an assignment at the front of the classroom when another student grabbed Grace's shoulder from behind. Whether it was a deliberate provocation or a clumsy way to ask Grace to move is unclear and, frankly, ceased to be relevant the moment she introduced her fist to the girl's nose. To anyone else, it's a violent overreaction. To me and my sisters, it's an act of self-defense. Nothing good ever happens when someone grabs us like that.

I reach for my face. My fingertips rest along my reconstructed cheekbone in a loose constellation. I had been making a grilled cheese, slathering both sides of the bread with mayonnaise like Gil taught me. My father seized my shoulders. I swung around and hit him. He cracked me across the face with his pistol.

The principal awaits us behind a massive mahogany desk. She looks more like an aging Hollywood starlet than an education professional, bedecked with ornate jewelry on her fingers, wrists, and ears. Her silver hair is wrapped into a chignon, her mouth a slash of peachy lipstick. Disgust flickers across her face as she assesses my appearance. As she recites a school board-approved spiel about violence on school grounds, she crunches her nose every time our eyes meet.

Four chairs sit before the desk, two to the left and two to the right. Judge, prosecution, defense. Grace's victim, bloody tissues hanging out of both nostrils, and a middle-aged woman I assume to be her mother, occupy one set of chairs, while Grace sits on the other side with the empty chair reserved for me. Connor slips into the background, shoulders against the wall, far from the fray.

Grace mouths *I'm sorry* as I take my seat. She wears a red Rosie the Riveter style scarf around her head, fastened at the top with a bow. It used to be mine. In a box deep in the attic, where the few Byrd family photos are preserved, there is a picture of me, then a reedy thirteen-year-old, with my hair wrapped in the same scarf as I rock baby Grace in my arms. You cannot tell I'm holding a baby. Grace was only hours out of the NICU in Scottsbluff and still impossibly tiny, despite the exhaustive medical intervention which made her existence possible. I'm not smiling at her. Instead, I'm scowling into the setting sun, cursing the heavens for forcing me to open my life to another sister who, once my mother's tenuous sobriety buckled, would become my responsibility.

"For Christ's sake," my mother said as she tinkered with the camera, "at least pretend like you're happy to meet your new sister."

"Let's take her back to the hospital. Please, Mom. I'll never ask you for anything again if you take her back."

The principal's monologue has yet to stop. ". . . and frankly, I think it's shameful that this incident occurred at all, much less in a classroom, much less in front of your teacher and your peers. When we look at our code of conduct, we—"

"What does the code of conduct say about punching innocent people in the face?" cries the girl with the tissues.

"You grabbed me from behind!" Grace counters.

"Oh my God, I *touched* your shoulder! Like—like—" The girl taps her mother's shoulder for effect. "Just like that, like a normal fucking person!"

The girl's mother swats her on the knee. "Katy, watch your mouth."

"I have to watch my mouth, but she gets to punch me in the *fucking face?*"

"I'm sure Grace is sorry," I pipe to Katy and her mother. It's a useless thing to say, but saying nothing at all seems unforgivably spineless. "We all know how hard it is to be a teenage girl."

"Sorry isn't going to fix my daughter's nose."

"Well, I don't—"

"And to be quite frank with you, I shouldn't have expected anything different from one of Tom Byrd's girls. You're all barnyard animals."

I put a knuckle between my teeth and clamp down. I want to bite straight through my finger like a baby carrot. I know Grace wants me to retaliate. She perches on the edge of her chair as she waits for me to lob the first salvo of a verbal firefight. All I have is the nuclear option. I can tell this woman what she already knows: that my father is a beast in human skin, that he beat his daughters, neglected us, did things to us we cannot even reveal in the privacy of our psychiatrist's office. And for what? For the fleeting satisfaction of humiliating this woman and accepting her insincere condolences? To become the object of yet another person's pity? There's nothing worse than pity. Grace isn't old enough to realize it yet.

I meet the woman's contempt with a smile. When I look at Grace, she turns her entire body away from me to stare at the wall.

"She should be expelled," the woman says without a trace of irony. She's the type to condemn petty thieves to the electric chair.

"We can all agree that punishment is necessary," the principal says, "but I hardly think depriving Grace of a high school diploma is necessary."

At this, Connor chimes in. I'd almost forgotten he was here. "Grace is a smart girl. She shows a lot of promise."

"So does Katy," the woman retorts. Her daughter nods in agreement, which dislodges her tissues. Crusted blood rims both her nostrils.

"She absolutely does, ma'am. Both these girls have bright futures ahead of them. That's why, whatever punishment we agree on, I don't want it to affect Grace's education. In-school suspension, maybe. She could transfer into Mr. Garcia's class so Katy can have the distance she needs."

Connor, always the diplomat, smooth as silk. He had the principal nodding along before he even finished talking. He's good at playing the hero too: an in-school suspension means Grace doesn't have to be home alone with our father. The same way Gil looked out for me, Connor is looking out for Grace. This seems like the natural order of the universe: the Crawford men protecting the Byrd sisters. I hope no one catches the grateful look I give him.

Once they've negotiated the particulars of Grace's punishment, Katy and her mother start to leave. They're halfway to the door when Katy turns to us again. "I'm sorry, Grace. About your mom. I really hope she comes home soon."

Silence. Grace folds her arms across her chest and remains fixated on the wall. "Thank you, Katy," I say before her mother can insult us again. She accepts my olive branch with a clipped nod before cupping her daughter's shoulders and steering her out of the office.

The principal says goodbye to Grace and Connor, but not to me. She doesn't even glance up from her computer when I offer to shake her hand. It dawns on me then that it's not the tattoos or the plastic surgery or the stench of cigarette smoke that makes me repugnant to her: it's who I am. Providence Byrd, would-be murderer. Who wants to shake hands with a woman who tried to spill her own mother's blood?

As the three of us cross the empty locker hall, I chase the rejection away with my affirmations. *People love me. I am lovable.* But the sentiment rings hollow when my own sister won't even glance at me. I have failed her somehow, on a level I can't understand.

"Can you take me home now?" she asks, staring dead ahead.

"I need to talk to Con—I mean, Mr. Crawford alone for a minute, okay?"

She rolls her eyes. "I'm not a child. You can talk in front of me."

"Grace, just head outside for a minute. I won't be long. It's—"

She unleashes a guttural wretch and tosses her hands in the air. She revels in the opportunity to inflict her histrionics on someone without authority to punish her. "You're useless, Providence!"

She tears off down the hall, throwing the double doors open with enough force to fling them off the hinges. Alone with Connor, my first instinct is to apologize—for Grace's behavior, for my own incompetence, and for the cosmic forces conspiring to embrangle us in this awkward encounter.

I rest my head against the cool metal of a locker. "I'm so sorry, Connor. I don't—"

"You have nothing to apologize for."

"Why did you call me? I barely know Grace. I'm not . . . well, Grace said it best. I'm useless."

"It was you or your dad," he says. "The less he knows, the better, right? That's what you always said when we were kids— keep him the dark." He presses his hands against the side of his head, a telltale sign that he's losing his battle against a migraine.

"I broke protocol to call you. He's the primary emergency contact."

"And I'm guessing my mother's the secondary contact, and that left you with no one to call but me."

"No. You're the secondary contact."

"That doesn't make any sense." I feel the color drain from my face, as if escaping through a tiny hole punctured in my jaw. I slump down to the floor and Connor follows, and only for a moment, it's like we're teenagers again. He's quizzing me on the constitutional amendments while I'm inhaling the extra bologna sandwich he brought me for lunch. He's keeping an extra flannel shirt in his locker for me to borrow when I have bruises to conceal. "I mean it, Connor. There's no universe where I should be my estranged sister's emergency contact."

He lifts a palm. "Scout's honor."

"Who made me her contact? When?"

"That's above my pay grade," he says.

"Then whose pay grade is it and where can I find them?"

"Providence, what's going on?"

"Before my mother disappeared, she gave Grace my phone number," I tell him. "If she made me her emergency contact . . . shit. She had to know something was going to happen to her."

"Making arrangements."

"She didn't have brothers or sisters, or friends, or anyone she could turn to if she was in trouble. I'm it."

"What about Harmony?" he asks.

"She's always been a wild card." I can't imagine Harmony upending her day for Grace the way I just did. Pure fiction.

"Right," he says, skepticism elongating his syllable, "but just from a practical perspective, it would make more sense for her to pick Harmony as Grace's emergency contact. You live two states away."

I consider this and shake the thought from my head. "My mother must have known I'd come looking for her. A chance to right all my wrongs."

Connor massages his knuckles against the side of his skull. There is a desperation to the tiny circular motion, a frantic attempt to stimulate blood flow and revitalize his peaked expression. "That's a good thing though, isn't it? If she left of her own volition, then it's more likely she's not in danger."

"But the thing I can't wrap my head around is—why now? Why leave now, after thirty years and three children?"

"God willing," he says, "she'll be able to tell you why herself."

*   *   *

We drive past the pool hall. My father's car is gone. He'll be home, waiting for us.

Grace surprises me by insisting on pumpkin ice cream. We claim the last available picnic table outside the ice cream parlor to bask in the sunshine and watch the storm clouds drift eastward.

"You let Katy's mom walk all over you." Grace nibbles the corner of her chocolate-dipped waffle cone like a rabbit. I encouraged her to create the most extravagant ice cream imaginable so she would like me more. I envisioned sprinkles and whipped cream; instead, Grace has constructed the Mount Everest of ice cream, topped with cookie crumbles, fudge, peanut butter cups, gummy bears, and more decadent toppings I suspect she added not because she liked the taste, but to make the treat more expensive. Just looking at it would put a diabetic in a coma. "Like . . . you let her call us animals. That's so fucked up."

"Don't say *fuck.*"

"Oh, now you care about what I do?"

The ice cream tastes like autumn. It's sweet enough to make my molars ache. "What did you want me to say to her, Grace?"

"I don't know! Literally anything at all would have been better than sitting there and taking it like you did, stupid smile on your face." She corrals a chocolate chip into her mouth with the tip of her tongue, guiding it through the gap between her front teeth.

"Nothing I said was going to make her think any different of us. Some people are only ever going to think of us as Tom Byrd's daughters. They're going to think we're trash, no matter what we say. You don't reason with people like her. You let them be wrong."

"But they're not wrong," she mumbles.

"Is that what you think of yourself? That you're trash?"

"Is there a better word for us?" She engrosses herself in scooping her monstrosity into the extra bowl the cashier provided us. *You'll be needing this*, he said upon witnessing Grace's creation. She breaks the cone into fragments with her plastic spoon. "We're a poor, dumb, backwater family full of drunks and addicts."

"It doesn't define *you*. You're not the sum of your family."

She points her spoon at me. "But you're contradicting what you just said. It doesn't matter who we are individually. All roads lead to him."

"That's not true," I say. "Not everywhere. I made my own life."

Grace appraises the tattoos on the tops of my hands, the dueling sun and moon. I wait for her to compliment them, but her face is slack with disinterest. "Is it a good life?"

"Good enough. I finally made enough money last year to move into an apartment all by myself."

"Was it, like . . . hard to find roommates? Because of what you did?"

It takes otherworldly strength to keep from wincing. Her vagueness stings. "All the girls I work with are troubled. Lots of us have been roommates with each other."

Her eyebrows shoot up. "Troubled how?"

"Prison. We all took up tattooing while we were inside. My boss, Kiera—she did ten years. She couldn't get a quote-unquote 'real' job when she came out, but she was a brilliant artist. When she started her own shop, she made it a point to hire other people who'd done time. That's how I started."

"There wasn't another skill you could learn?" She points with her spoon to my hand tattoos. "It's so permanent. Like, what happens when you're fifty?"

"Then I'm fifty with beautiful artwork on my body."

"I don't really like it."

"You sound like Mom." The word tastes wrong, *Mom* instead of *mother*. She would hate what I've done with my body. "Do you want to talk about her?"

"Why?"

"Maybe you need someone to talk about her with."

Her eyes narrow. "Got to be honest, you're not high on my list of people to talk about Mom with."

"I can probably tell you stories you haven't heard before."

"Like what?"

She watches me fumble for a happy recollection that does not exist, her smirk growing wider the longer I flail. "She came to one of my softball games. Just one. But it was the one where I broke the school record for stolen bases. Coach Romanoff dumped Gatorade on me and everything. I was soaked and sticky and gross, but she still hugged me and told me she was proud of me."

"And what about Dad?" she asks.

"We're not talking about him."

"But I'm asking you."

"He was there, sure," I say.

"And did he say he was proud of you?"

"Of course he did."

I leave out the part about him berating me on the drive home. "You could have stolen third in the seventh," he said. "You weren't paying attention. I was embarrassed for you."

I also omit what happened after our mother fell asleep in the back seat, how my father made me atone for my incompetence—at least, I thought she had fallen asleep. She was awake the whole time and she knew. She was just grateful it was me in the passenger seat for once, not her.

I want to tell Grace about the suspicion that brought me back to Annesville, about the throbbing pain in my chest telling me that my father is a murderer, but I keep it inside for now. She'll know soon enough. It's only a matter of time before my mother's body is found, and then she will reach the same conclusion I have: our father must die.

*   *   *

The screen door to the house is open. Each gust of wind beats it against the clapboard exterior like a twenty-one gun salute. There's no use trying to rush Grace out of the car. He heard us pull up. We have enough time to exchange a solemn look, apologizing to one another for things we lack the vocabulary to verbalize. I wonder if it's a shared personality trait, innate to both of us, or if it's a consequence of our upbringing. Nature or nurture. The lines have always been hopelessly blurred to me.

Our father lumbers onto the front porch, armed with a beer and a book, careful to avoid the pitfall of rotting wood beyond the welcome mat. I've forgotten reading is one of his hobbies. As often as baseball games provide entertainment in his drunken stupors, so too do books, usually chronicles about ancient Rome or Greece thick enough to double as doorstops. It's an intellectual pursuit I cannot associate with such a brutish man. I've also forgotten he wears reading glasses, and it satisfies me, petty as it is, that my vision is impeccable. Anything to one-up him. Anything to affirm I have become better than him, even in the most insignificant of ways. His face softens as his eyes rove over me. I don't fall for it.

Grace slingshots out of the car but stops short of approaching him. Her hastily removed lipstick has left a faint pink stain around her lips. "I'm so sorry I'm late, Dad. I—I missed the bus, and . . ." She lowers her head in contrition.

"Why did she miss the bus, butterfly?"

"Math tutoring." The lie rolls from my tongue with ease. It's a defensive instinct, natural as the hiss of a rattlesnake or a gazelle stotting into the air.

"Bullshit. It's Gracie's best subject."

While the nickname makes Grace wince, I burn with jealousy. Grace was Gracie, Harmony was Harmonica, and I was butterfly, most infantilized of all. "Precalculus is hard," my sister whines.

He doesn't acknowledge Grace. "Are you telling me the truth, Providence?"

"Yes."

My father slides a bookmark into his paperback and runs his tongue over the front of his crooked teeth. I worry I've only made things worse for Grace by lying and forcing her to participate in the charade. I consider, briefly, pulling her back into the car and speeding away, and then, even more briefly, speeding away without her.

The porch rasps with relief as he descends the steps. "You call me if you need to get a ride home," he says to Grace. "Don't call her. Not now, not ever. You understand me?"

"I understand."

"Good girl. Get in the house."

She glides into the house without a glance back at me, and I can't help but feel betrayed to have been left alone with this man. He takes the final swig from his beer and casts the bottle into the street. When he leans in through the car window, his beer-soaked breath nearly makes me retch. "Fancy seeing you twice in one day, butterfly."

"I was hoping you'd be passed out on the floor of the pool hall."

"And I'm hoping this thing's in park," he says, drumming his palm against the roof of my car. "You're not great with cars."

"You're a barrel of laughs."

"Where are you running off to?"

"None of your business."

"Couple folks saw someone with Missouri plates headed up to the reservation yesterday," he says. "Indians got an extra tee-pee for you?"

"It wouldn't kill you to read less about ancient Rome and more about Wounded Knee." Rather than striking me for back talk, he manages a tepid laugh, and I relish having the upper hand once again. He can't hit me anymore. I have the power, and naturally, I let it go straight to my head.

"Am I free to go now, officer?"

"Depends. Am I going to see you at the search tomorrow morning?"

Tomorrow's search will chip away at the swath of prairie between Annesville and Chadron. Nothing out there but cemeteries, abandoned nineteenth-century military outposts, and enough open sky to make you nauseous.

"I'll be there with bells on."

"As long those bells are loud enough to get your mother out of whatever foxhole she's hiding in."

"You can't tell me you think she's just hiding somewhere for fun."

My father rakes his fingers through his salt-and-pepper hair. Whether it's anxiety or agitation, I can't quite tell. "Your mother's always had a flair for the dramatic, just like you."

He reaches into the car. Reaches for the sleeves of my shirt. Before I can yank my arm away, he hooks his index finger around my sleeve and tugs down. In the midafternoon light, my scars are milky white. Grotesque. Once you see them, you don't see the tattoos anymore. He may as well cleave open my chest and expose my insides to the world.

"Make sure you keep those covered up. They'll scare people—and I don't mean the tattoos."

CHAPTER

7

August 12th

12:32 AM

MIDNIGHT. I DRIVE through the reservation, careening down remote, lightless roads with no destination in mind. I acquired the habit on parole when I was tethered to my halfway house by an invisible fifty-mile leash. Aimlessly driving country roads became my preferred hobby. The streets of Kansas City offer a less bucolic diversion, but occasionally I still find myself navigating the rural stretches east of the city, hugging the banks of the Missouri River and dreaming about following the water all the way to St. Louis.

Missouri. Miserable place. It's my punishment for near-matricide: living out the rest of my days in Missouri.

My mother's body is probably on a road just like this, but there is no earthly trace of her to be found. She has disappeared. She has wandered into one of the world's dark corners, fallen into one of its holes, and she disintegrates more with each passing day, not quite dead but not quite alive. A ghost who cannot be properly mourned. What sweet sorrow it must be to slip into the next life without even a sound.

It can't end like this. What I did to my mother has defined my entire life to this point, and, perhaps as it should, it will define the rest of my life too. It shapes me into who I am, for better and mostly for worse, entwining me with my mother like conjoined twins who share organs and spines and brains. It's a twisted form of codependency. Without my mother, I don't know who I am. If I never ran her over, who would I be? Would that person be even vaguely recognizable to the woman I am now?

As my mother yawped beneath the car, her bones crushed, her tendons torn, not even the intended target of my wrath, I did not feel remorse. I could recognize the other emotions. Disgust. Shock. Horror. Even guilt. But guilt is not the same as remorse. Guilt touches you on the surface, but remorse echoes through your marrow. I always fall just short of it, eluding me like the end of a rainbow. I am always chasing it, desperate to prove I can feel the one emotion that would absolve me of my greatest fear. Remorse separates humans from animals. We are not the only species that kills for sport, but we are the only one that feels remorse when we do—and if I cannot feel remorse for what I have done, then am I even human at all?

An oncoming truck blinds me with its brights. Before my retinas can be further scorched, I peel off onto another side road, which runs out after half a mile. When I come to a stop, it takes me several moments to realize the vast, treeless expanse unfolding before me is not the prairie, but a lake.

The water is black and sedate like an oil spill. A single light on the opposite shore illuminates a boatless dock. I take the gun from my glove compartment before approaching the water. I'm less worried about a serial killer snatching me from the bushes than I am about becoming the midnight snack of perturbed wildlife. A murderer I can handle; a bear or a cougar would, frankly, make me shit myself. There's a reason I explore the countryside in a car instead of on foot.

I leave my sandals on the craggy strip of sand separating the water from the grass and wade into the lake. The water kisses my knees. I wish I could swim or at least that I was brave enough to throw caution to the wind and plunge beneath the water. But I'm scared. Of drowning. Of the quiet. People muse about the silence underwater, like it's something sacrosanct and beautiful, stealing precious moments away from the noise of the universe. I think the universe isn't noisy enough. Even now, with the chirring crickets and sighing wind to remind me I am not alone, the quiet closes in on me like the jaws of an invisible beast.

I'm anxious. Short of breath. The gun is foreign and unwieldy in my hand. I have no more business handling it than a toddler who has broken into their parents' gun box. I chuckle as I unlatch the safety.

I fire at the dock light and imagine it as my father's face. It's a series of sensory throttles: the muzzle flash, the gun recoiling into my shoulder, the acrid smell of gunpowder, the ear-splitting crack like the peals of a thousand church bells. My breaths are deafening in the ensuing silence. I wait for something to happen. I wait for police sirens to come screaming down the dirt road, or for an irascible creature to pounce at me from the shadows, or for something, anything other than this noiseless purgatory. It feels like I've detonated a nuclear bomb, only for there to be no mushroom cloud, no blinding pulse of light.

I raise the gun to fire it again, but my arm is trembling. My cheeks are wet, my breathing ragged.

CHAPTER

8

August 12th

8:22 AM

THE NEXT MORNING, I have just enough time to visit Gil before the search begins. The longer I loiter without visiting him, the more cowardly I am. It's not until I'm following the nurse down the hallway that I realize I'm dressed completely in black, come to pay my respects to the enervated remnants of the man I once loved like a father.

"You picked the perfect time to come in." The nurse has a peculiar smile, one side of her mouth lifting as the other droops ever so slightly, like a stroke patient. It's the same cute, pocket-sized girl who brought me to Gil's room the other day. She still looks familiar. She smells familiar too, like freshly baked pastries, sugary and buttery. "He's just finished his morning coffee."

"He's like me," I say. "Neither of us are human until we have our coffee."

She walks one pace in front of me. Her cocoa-brown ponytail is fastened impossibly high on her head and swishes with every step she takes. "He talks about you sometimes. He likes to tell us about how he taught you to drive."

"How do you—?"

The nurse flattens herself against the wall so a wheelchair can pass. "Softball. You were shortstop; I was first base."

"Jesus Christ, Penny Eastman?"

Now the other side of her mouth lifts too, imbued with enough joy to complete her smile. She is happier to see me than she should be: her father, after all, is the sheriff. I was never able to disassociate the softhearted, bubbly girl I knew Penny to be from the man I hated almost as much as I did my father.

"I wasn't sure if it was my place to go *hey, remember me?* when you brought Gil in a couple days ago," she says. "But . . . it's so good you're here, looking for your mom. I know you were . . . troubled, growing up. It seems like you're in a better place."

"I live in Missouri and my apartment has mice. I think you're being generous."

Despite her deer in the headlights look, Penny musters up a laugh. She waits for me to remedy her discomfort by brushing off the remark as a joke—*ha-ha, no, I'm happily married with two kids and working at a Fortune 500 company*—but I can't bring myself to do it. It's unfair of me to punish her for Josiah's misdeeds, but I cannot unlink them in my mind. Any act of kindness I show to her becomes an act of kindness toward him, and that requires a level of magnanimity of which I am incapable. I nurture that ancient grudge like the precious first spark of a fire.

"While you're in town, I'd love to have a drink together." We arrive at Gil's room. He is hunched over a small table, laboring over a puzzle designed for children. The pieces are comically large. "It's been too long since we've talked," Penny says. "I'd really love to chat while you're here."

"Sure," I say. I don't mean it, and I'm puzzled as to why she's keen on catching up with me like a long-lost best friend. I chalk it up to a morbid fascination—with me, with my family. People used to say we were cursed. One of our forebearers was a graverobber.

Penny insists on exchanging phone numbers, then scuttles down the hallway with her ponytail bobbing along behind her, back and forth like a hypnotist's pocket watch. I knock for Gil's attention even though the door is open. "Hi, Mr. Crawford. Is it okay if I come in?"

He grins at me. "Sure, Elissa. Come on in."

All my muscles constrict, my body attempting to collapse in on itself. *Elissa.* He thinks I'm my mother. Every time I think the universe has exhausted its supply of cruel jokes to play on me, it cooks up another.

"Mr. Crawford, I—"

Gil waves his hand as if swatting away a gnat. "Call me Gil. You've known me nigh on twenty years now. Help me with this puzzle, will you? Got to get that last corner. Wish I could find my damn chessboard instead."

Considering his declining mental faculties, the puzzle has been pieced together with skill, its border complete but for the pesky final corner. He was always good at puzzles. It was his hobby of choice, that and chess. I set my purse on the floor and take the seat across from him. We sift through the box. Gil holds each piece up to the light for scrutiny like a surgeon checking to see if his scalpel is still sharp before making the next cut.

"These corners." He discards an examined piece back into the same box he plucked it from. No wonder he can't complete the last corner: he has made assembling the puzzle a Sisyphean effort. "Useless until we find all the corners."

"Why don't we make another pile for the pieces we've already checked?"

"Hmm?"

I place the puzzle box lid on the windowsill. Just outside, two hummingbirds hover beside a feeder filled with red nectar.

Gil's room overlooks a small courtyard with overgrown shrub-bery and a water fountain tinged green with algae. "After you look at a piece," I say, "drop it into the new box here, like this."

"Good idea." He proceeds to drop the next piece in the wrong box. "How's Marjorie? She's been so busy, haven't seen her lately."

I feel like I'm hurtling through whitewater rapids, flailing my arms to catch hold of a rock or a tree root, anything to keep from drowning. I resent Penny for leaving me here without instructions. What do you do when a person you love thinks you're someone else? What do you do when they ask about their dead wife? Gil's eyes are eager and hopeful. I have to lie, like I did about Coach Romanoff. I have to crawl inside his world.

"We're getting to the end of the month," I say. "That's when they get busy in her office. She'll come around soon, I promise."

"Next time you're in Carey Gap, you should go to lunch together. Marjorie's always been fond of you."

"I've always been fond of her too." This much, at least, is true. His late wife was a sweet woman.

"Remember the song she likes to play on the piano? The old Civil War ballad?"

"'Lorena.' It was a beautiful piece of music," I say. "I like when she sings it too."

We lapse into an uncomfortable rhythm. Gil drops pieces into the wrong box and I fish them out. The corner continues to elude us. Across the hallway, another resident watches *Wheel of Fortune* at sonar blast volume. We can hear contestants buying vowels and going bankrupt.

"You shouldn't be hanging around Mitch Perkins."

Mitch Perkins? Who the hell is that?

"I don't know what the two of you get up to—and frankly, it isn't my business—but Tom is . . . well, Tom is Tom." Gil crinkles his nose. "Not exactly slow to anger, is he?"

"That's from Proverbs, isn't it?"

"James," he says. "Let every person be quick to hear, slow to speak, slow to anger."

It's my turn to be slow to speak as I turn the name over in my head. *Mitch Perkins.* Most last names around here ring a bell to me, a person I went to school with or a family with a reputation for handing out princely portions of Halloween candy, but Perkins comes up empty. I file the name away to give Daniel later. It's that or poking around the Tyre pool hall and asking too many questions, drawing too much attention.

"You should go to church more," I say after a moment. It strikes me as something my mother would say. "It'd encourage Providence to go, I bet."

An emotion I can't quite recognize flickers on his face, like my name unlocked a vault of memories previously inaccessible. He balances a puzzle piece between his thumb and index finger, the tip of his tongue peeking out between his lips in concentration. "Go easy on her. She's a good kid."

"I don't know about that," I say.

"I think she'll surprise you."

"How so?"

This gives him pause. "She could be an astronaut."

"I don't think she wants—"

"Not a real astronaut, no." His laugh is still hearty and warm. It's the laugh of a man who gives each character a unique voice when he reads storybooks to his son, a man who dresses up as Santa every Christmas. "But she'll leave Annesville and go to college, and that's even more impressive than going to the moon in my book. You should be proud of her, Elissa."

I am not an astronaut, nothing even close, but in the distorted slice of reality Gil and I currently share, I can be. No one dreams of somebody they love tattooing for a living, even if it's good, honest work that pays for the silicone in my chest and the veneers in my mouth. They want doctors, nurses, entrepreneurs, firefighters, teachers, lawyers. Astronauts. In another life, under a different set of circumstances, I like to think I could have been one of those things. I wish someone else cared about me enough to rue my lost potential.

"Of course I am." I clasp my fingers together in my lap. "But I worry one day she'll do something horrible and . . . she'll ruin her life, and maybe the life of someone close to her."

"Parents have had that worry for eons. Somehow the kids survive their own stupidity and somehow we still love them in spite of it."

"Blood is thicker than water."

Triumph at last. Gil holds up the corner piece. "That's not how the saying goes. The real expression is the opposite. *The blood of the covenant is thicker than the water of the womb.*"

CHAPTER

9

August 12th

10:03 AM

THE PRAIRIE OUT here is endless like the ocean, nothing but knee-high brown grass as far as the eye can see. Perfect place to dump a body.

I'd expected a lower turnout for this search, the locals' interest in my mother flagging with each passing hour, but the people of Annesville have proven me wrong yet again. Half the town is here on this scalding summer morning, and they've brought an uncharacteristically neighborly spirit with them. The Nelson boys distribute water bottles from the coolers in their trucks while Eileen Capito hands out umbrellas (who has this many umbrellas?) to the women to shield us from the sun. Davy Hernandez, owner of the barbershop, leads us in prayer before the deputies unleash us on the desiccated prairie. I might not be the praying type, but I'm still moved by the gesture. When his voice cracks on my mother's name, *Elissa*, a lump gathers in my throat.

And that lump turns to stone when familiar baritone belts across the prairie. "You're a good man, Davy Hernandez. God bless you."

"Your whole family is in our prayers, Tom."

My father is a raincloud blotting out the sun, the ocean receding from the shore to portend a tsunami. Always a harbinger of doom. He is without my sisters, Grace presumably in school and Harmony presumably three sheets to the wind at the pool hall. In the sunlight, his crow's feet run deeper and the wattle of his liver-spotted neck hangs looser. He parts the crowd like Moses at the Red Sea, gesturing for us to form a circle around him.

We do. He thanks us profusely for showing up to the search, then thanks God for giving him such generous, selfless neighbors. His eyes never once meet mine.

Credit where it's due: he's delivering the performance of a lifetime. To the unsuspecting observer, the tears in his eyes might seem genuine. You might be tricked into thinking that this man—flawed though he may be, despite all the nasty rumors that eddy around him like horseflies swarming roadkill— misses his wife and just wants her to come home to him safely. Deep down, Tom Byrd is a good man, or at least, he wants to be.

He's trying, can't you tell? And isn't it the trying that matters?

Every time he says my mother's name, the taste of gin blights my mouth, memories of the drunken good-night kisses she left on my forehead when she thought I was asleep.

Beside me, Zoe materializes from thin air. She stands close enough for our forearms to brush. Her blonde hair is coiled into milkmaid braids that should make her look matronly, but because she's Zoe and even the sun seems to dim in her presence, she is undeniably radiant. The sleeves of her pink flannel shirt are cuffed at the elbows, exposing the tender white flesh of the forearms I once kissed.

The lustful memories stir to life unexpectedly, and the frothing sensation between my legs is as delicious as it is traitorous.

I am here for my mother. I play my chastisement on a loop in my mind. *I am here for my mother. I will not be distracted by a pretty girl.*

". . . and I'm sure some of you have noticed that my eldest daughter is here with us today." Finally, I become the focus of my father's attention. He feigns a hitch in his voice when next he speaks. "And I'll tell you something, it means the damn world to me to have Providence here. She's put the past in the past. We all have. What really matters is all of us showing up for Elissa, right here, right now."

The stares of old neighbors scourge my cheeks. A few of them gawk now that my father has pointed me out, having been unable to recognize me beneath the layers of plastic surgery and tattoos. I will doubtless be the subject of dinner table gossip this evening. Lips like a blowfish. Fakest tits I've ever seen. And, my God, was that a tattoo on her *face*?

My father approaches me. Opens his arms. Hugs me. A play in three sinister acts. His stubble scrapes my reconstructed cheek as he clenches me against his chest, so tight that I cannot see the sky above me or smell anything but the vinegary odor of his body. His hand cups the back of my head tightly enough to puncture holes in my skull.

How long does it last? A second? A minute? A day? A lifetime?

When he finally releases me, the world spins like a record. As the deputy begins dividing us into groups, I stammer out an excuse about leaving something in my car, promise I'll be right back, and then I hurry to the flattened brush where everyone has parked, even though it feels like the earth is crumbling beneath my feet with every step, feels like my skin has calcified into an exoskeleton too small for my body. I am unclean. No, worse—dirty. My father has held my body against his and left behind hideous stains only I can see.

I grab the hand sanitizer from my car and start rubbing it on my hands, my wrists, my neck, any strip of flesh that might have grazed his own. I'm dabbing it behind my ears like perfume when Zoe approaches. The silver necklace she's worn since we were in middle school bounces against her collarbone with each step, the *Z* pendant sparkling iridescent in the sunlight.

"Are you okay, Providence?"

"Peachy keen." I make a show of tossing the hand sanitizer back in my car.

"You've always been a bad liar," she says.

"I like to think I've gotten better in the last thirteen years."

I read different emotions in her mismatched eyes. Blue: caution, unease, pity. Green: warmth, softness, empathy. I can't tell if she's going to touch me or turn away. I don't know which would hurt less.

Fifty yards away, the deputy divides searchers into groups of four or five. My father joins Davy Hernandez, two of the Nelson boys, and Desdemona Thompson, an old teacher of mine. When she caught any of us daydreaming, she struck our hands with rulers. I left class with purple, swollen fingers many days, but I didn't mind much. It hurt less than what happened to me at home. The deputy catches me looking and beckons me over, hand curling into a *come hither* motion like I'm a yappy dog that needs to get inside.

I am here for my mother. I take the first step back toward the searchers, but Zoe blocks my path.

"Just wait." Zoe's voice is unexpectedly sweet, like biting into a hard candy only to find it soft and fudgy in the center. She brings her hand to my diaphragm. "Give them a head start. That way, when we go back, we can search together."

She pauses. Then she says, "You shouldn't have to be out there with him. Not even in a group."

*   *   *

Our tardiness irritates the deputy, but Zoe's plan works. He assigns the two of us a small search quadrant, hands us a walkie-talkie and two frozen water bottles, and tells us to be back at the rallying point no later than one o'clock, hell or high water. As soon as the deputy turns around, I tuck the water bottle between my breasts to stay cool. Into the high grass we go.

"Watch out for snakes!" the deputy hollers just before we're out of earshot.

We walk an arm's length apart, eyes trained on the ground. Every step I take with only the prairie grass beneath me gives me a jolt of relief. Even though I don't expect to find my mother here, I can't banish the thought of stepping on her decaying remains. Carrion. The heel of my boot accidentally tearing flesh from bone.

After half an hour of marching through the prairie, we stop for a water break. I tilt my head back to pour half-thawed ice water down my throat. The sky stretches infinitely overhead, not a whisper of a cloud to be seen. Just blue, blue, blue.

"I still think we're going to find her alive," Zoe says, running her hands lazily over the top of the grass. Her face is dewy with sweat. "I'm not just blowing smoke."

"Hope springs eternal," I deadpan.

"I can tell you mean that as an insult, but I'm choosing to interpret it as optimism."

"If someone hasn't killed her by now, I'm sure the withdrawals have."

"Your mom is resourceful. She'll keep herself alive," she says.

"How would you know?"

She gazes across the horizon, where everyone's cars are now just colorful specks in the distance. "I talked with her after church sometimes." She says it sheepishly, turning what should be a source of reassurance for me—my mother had someone who cared about her, even just a little bit—into an admission of guilt.

My resentment is hypocritical. I understand this immediately. That's why I swallow it down, rotten as it tastes, and try to smile instead. "I'm sure she'd be happy you're here. Are your parents going to come out and help the searches?"

"They—" She clears her throat, stands up straighter. "They moved a long time ago. They're all in New York now."

"That sounds a little worldly for them."

"They're five miles down the road from World Headquarters. They love it."

Zoe's family are barely even silhouettes in my memory anymore. Her father was almost always at work, her mother was an unsmiling blonde who wore Mary Janes everywhere (even her own house when they had guests), and her brother was a freckled boy with a stutter that years of speech therapy could not treat.

I do, however, remember their head-scratching religious practices. No birthdays. No holidays. No dances. No extracurricular activities. No saying *good luck*, but saying *if it is Jehovah's will* instead. No saying *bless you*. Muting TV commercials with demonic content. Burning objects with demonic spirits attached to them. Zoe could not call me her friend, only her acquaintance, because I was not a Witness. Under another set of circumstances, I don't think I would have been invited into Zoe's home at all, but they were the only Witnesses in Annesville, and since I was a regular churchgoer—still a Christian, albeit an astray one—they were willing to tolerate my presence.

Zoe gestures toward the sprawl of the prairie, the expanse of our quadrant we've yet to search. "We should probably keep moving. I don't—"

"Was it me? Was that why you were disfellowshipped?"

Her pained laugh slices the air between us. "What else could it have been?"

We thought we were alone. We couldn't hear those Mary Janes clip-clopping on the stairs over the rushing blood in our ears. Her mother screamed so loud you would have thought I was murdering her daughter instead of kissing her.

"Why didn't you—?"

"Fight it? I was already going to college," she says quietly. "They would have disfellowshipped me over that too. There was no point in subjecting myself to the elder board for . . . what we did, not if I was going to end up back there in a few months anyway."

What we did. There it is again, the agonizing euphemism. "Do they—?"

She claps her hands together, squeezing tight enough to drain the color from her fingers. "Providence, please. I don't want to talk about this. We're here for your mom, okay? We shouldn't lose focus on that."

She takes off in long, loping strides that make it clear she isn't going to wait for me if I fall behind. I have no choice but to follow.

*   *   *

Whatever compassion Zoe had for me earlier has long dried up by the time the search concludes. Like the first, this search unearths no trace of my mother's whereabouts, and everyone is sunburned, exhausted, and grumpy when they disperse to their cars. She bids me a hasty goodbye before climbing into her truck. She's the first one back on the road.

I'm aiming to be the second one out of the makeshift parking lot when my father knocks his knuckles against my window. I only roll down the window a few inches.

"What? Your windows don't work?"

"The air's on," I lie. "I don't want to let the cold out."

My father spits onto the dirt, then wipes the viscous remnants from his lips. Beads of sweat roll down his giant nose, steady like the drip of a leaky faucet. He huffs and puffs for a moment before speaking. "What you got going on this evening?"

"Why?"

"I'm having your sisters over for dinner. I'd like you there too. Been too long since I've had all three of my girls under my roof, and . . . to tell you the truth, Providence, it'd make your mother happy to know you tried to be part of the family again."

I open my mouth to reject this moronic, horrifying, insulting request, but stop myself. This is my chance to prove to Grace that I'm not useless. Suffering through one evening as a buffer between her and our father, her and Harmony, choking down the foul plateful of tuna noodle casserole our father will invariably serve—it's the least I can do to atone for my many misdeeds.

It'll just be a few hours. I can handle it.

He reads my mind. "See you at six, butterfly."

10

August 12th

4:55 PM

A s emotionally unprepared as I am for my impending dinnertime rendezvous, I am also physically unprepared. The nicest clothing I brought from home is a blue button-down shirt I wear to gay bars to show women I'm not a straight girl who made a wrong turn. I can't wear it. My father will say I look like a lesbian. If I dressed too conservatively as a teenager, he called me a lesbian; too scantily, he called me a slut. I beg Sara for something to borrow and she obliges me with a dandelion yellow dress that hides my cleavage and flares from the waist. I look like a sweaty Easter egg.

"I think you should cancel," Sara calls from the dining room. She hunches over her checkbook while I sit cross-legged in front of the mirrored closet door to finish my makeup. As I feather blush across my cheeks, I notice my smile lines are a touch more pronounced than they should be for a thirty-year-old, and rather than vowing to give up the vice causing my premature aging (cig-arettes), I make a mental note to look into stronger dermal fillers when I go home. With the tattoos, I alter my body as a canvas, but with the cosmetic enhancements, I remake myself. Nature does not dictate my appearance: I do. The more I change about my appearance, the less I resemble the frightened seventeen-year-old in my mugshot, the easier it becomes to convince myself that my pain happened to someone else. Piece by piece, I chip away at who I once was. Lift my eyebrows. File my jawline. Freeze my forehead. Enhance my lips. Enlarge my breasts. The most recognizable feature I've kept intact is my enormous nose. I've made half a dozen consultations with plastic surgeons, but I can never bring myself to pull the trigger. I tell myself it's because the surgeon must break my nose to fix it and the thought makes me queasy. Really, it's because I don't know if I'm ready to be completely unrecognizable to myself just yet.

"If you have arsenic you want me to sprinkle on my father's plate, I'm happy to oblige."

"I'm serious, Providence."

Zenobia wanders into the bedroom and stretches out across the air mattress, her tail drumming against my pillow. I can't decide if she's fond of me or if I've accidentally stolen her favorite sleeping spot. I surmise the answer when she ignores my outstretched hand.

"Hello?"

"I'm listening," I say.

"I don't think you are. It's a—I mean, you're in therapy. I don't know what your therapist is like, but mine says it's important to avoid triggers. For me it's graveyards. Makes me think of my dead family. But for you, spending time with your dad is probably the trigger to end all triggers."

She's right, of course. As the hour draws nearer, the moment I will have to ring the doorbell of my childhood home creeping close, I am unspooling from anxiety—but admitting it would be a failure. I'm supposed to be stronger now, the way steel must be forged in fire before it can become a sword.

"Do you want me to do the thing they do in movies?" Sara rests her shoulder against the doorframe. She extends a cigarette toward me, but I shake my head. "I call you half an hour into dinner, fake an emergency, you have to begrudgingly abandon your long-lost family to rescue a friend in need . . ."

"We're friends?"

She smirks. "Screw you. I'm following girl code."

"It's going to be a miserable experience," I say as I pry open an eyeshadow palette, "but at least my sisters won't think I'm completely worthless."

"What do you care what they think?"

"I want them to like me."

"One dinner won't make them like you."

I pretend to be engrossed in selecting an eyeshadow to hide how deep the words cut. One dinner won't make them like me, but sometimes loyalty demands self-sacrifice. My sisters need to know I haven't forgotten what it means to be Tom Byrd's daughter. They need to know I'm one of them too, not the turncoat they've imagined. Their horrors are my horrors.

I dip my brush into the beige powder and dust it into the crease of my eyelid. "I know that," I say after a moment.

"Family is overrated anyway."

"At least you have them. At least if you died, you'd have more than just the priest show up at your funeral."

Sara laughs, and I smile along with her, even though it wasn't a joke. "I can think of three people who might show," she says. "Me, that Kiera girl you're always gushing about, and whoever you ran off to meet this morning."

"Gil Crawford? He needs an act of God to make it to Christmas."

"The guy who brought you the books, right? What's wrong with him?"

"Alzheimer's," I say.

"My *kunsi* had it. It's like watching someone die in slow motion." She shares a dolorous look with the dog, who mauls a rawhide bone dangerously close to my pillow. Ropes of slobber dangle from her jaws.

"No one deserves to get Alzheimer's, of course, but Gil . . . he's the only adult in my life who ever really loved me. It's not fair for it to be him instead of my father, or Josiah Eastman, someone like that." The shift in Sara's mood is subtle enough to slip past the untrained eye, but after hundreds of hours locked in the same prison cell, I have her emotional tells memorized. "If you have something to say, go ahead and say it."

"Gil knew about your dad."

"Everyone did, Sara. It wasn't a secret that my sisters and I were mistreated." Immediately I regret using the word *mistreated*, but the euphemisms make it easier to talk about. I can either minimize my suffering, or I can never talk about it at all.

"It's nice he fed you dinner and helped you with homework and bought you presents at Christmas, but he's no hero. He still let you go home every day."

"He did what he could."

"He knew you were being abused." Sara lowers herself onto the air mattress beside me. It seems like a gesture from an older sister, the type of bonding moment I could have shared with Harmony or Grace if my life had taken a different turn. "I know you love him, but he could have done more for you."

"I could say the same about a lot of people."

We ease into silence. Sara rests her head in the curve between my neck and my collarbone, her hand clasping mine. I have spent years starved for simple affection like this. My friends back home will send me a text to make sure I've gotten home safe after a night out and bring me groceries while I recover from surgery, but I've never been able to melt fully into their arms the way I can with Sara. She sees me. She knows me. She loves me.

"It's not your fault," Sara says. "None of it is."

"I know."

"I'm sure you do. I just don't think you've ever heard some-one else say it."

*　*　*

I don't recognize the house when I step inside. It's like looking through a funhouse mirror and trusting that, improbable as it may seem, this is the same place I spent the first seventeen years of my life.

The only familiar thing is the treacly scent wafting from the kitchen. Grace is baking chokecherry pie, the recipe passed to her from our mother, to our mother from our grandmother, and so on up the maternal line. I never learned the recipe myself. Like our mother, Grace turns the kitchen into a war zone as she cooks, utensils strewn across the black laminated countertop and soiled dishes wedged into the sink like Tetris blocks, cabinet doors left open in her wake. A peek into the refrigerator confirms my fear I will have to suffer through tuna noodle casserole for dinner.

"Where is everyone?" I ask, sweeping the toast crumbs from the counter into the sink. I need to feel useful. Anything to distract myself from the knot in my stomach, tighter than a noose. Outside the window above the sink, the rusty windchimes tinkle. Air conditioning is a luxury not offered in the Byrd house. Unless there's a tornado warning, every window stays open all summer long.

Grace snaps on a pair of yellow rubber gloves and bumps me out of the way with her hip. She scrubs the dishes at world record speed. Our father hates coming home to a dirty kitchen. "Harmony will be late to her own funeral. And Dad . . ." She glances at the microwave clock. "Liquor store is still open for another ten minutes. He's closing early just for this."

"Can I help?"

She drops a fork into the dishwasher with a clang. "There's a water dish for the cat out by the shed. It probably needs to be refilled."

"He lets you have a cat?"

"Just a stray I feed."

The sharpness of her tone dismisses me. I seize the opportunity to tour the rest of the downstairs. There is a new leather sofa in the living room, right beside the lumpy, tattered recliner my father installs himself in to watch Rockies games in the summer, Broncos games in the winter, and Nuggets games in the spring. Above all else, the living room is a shrine to his hometown teams. The sole Rockies pennant hangs above the entertainment center, flanked by metal signs shaped like home plate and emblazoned with the team logo. Elsewhere there are bobbleheads, throw blankets, photographs of Coors Field, baseball and basketball jerseys, and even a coat hanger personalized with my father's name and Broncos insignia. The only decoration in the room unrelated to sports is the small urn of his mother's ashes on the mantle. Byrd men are buried in the family plot; Byrd women are cremated and left to gather dust. There's a beer on the end table, still half full. I move it off the coaster to spite him.

I hold my breath through the cloud of mildew in the laundry room and don't breathe again until I'm in the backyard. I find the water bowl in a sliver of shade beside the toolshed, where, my better judgment notwithstanding, I linger too long. Nestled against the fence is a stone with *ANNIE* painted on it in childish scrawl. It's a memorial for my childhood dog. We couldn't bury her, and my father was sorry for that, but he wanted me to have a place I could mourn. *Make something for Annie. Make something pretty.*

I hope he doesn't shoot the cat. Please, God. If the universe is a merciful one, he will leave the cat alone.

I smoke a cigarette to calm my nerves and pulverize it beneath the heel of my shoe when I'm done. My relief is short-lived. Back in the kitchen, the scent of the chokecherry pie now mingles with tuna noodle casserole to create a smell I can only describe as ghastly. A bundle of nerves clogs my throat. Grace is still at the sink, enveloped in a plume of steam. "Did you see the cat?" she asks without looking up. "Big orange furball?"

"No sign of him, but he'll have fresh water when he comes around."

"Still feeding that stray?" Harmony's voice is like a stone thrown through a window. She kicks off her grubby sandals in the entryway and traipses into the kitchen. For Grace, she gives a kiss on the cheek. For me, nothing. "What's his name again?"

"Bucket," Grace says sheepishly.

Harmony helps herself to a cold beer. She flicks the cap off with a steak knife. "Like something out of a cartoon."

"I found him sleeping in a bucket. I thought it was a good name for a stray."

"I think it's a great name." I pluck the beer cap off the floor and toss it into the trash can. As I sit beside Harmony at the table, the same cherrywood one Gil Crawford built for us when I was young, she unfolds the newspaper for the sole purpose of blocking me from her view. I should be irritated by how little she's changed in the years since we last saw each other, the pitifulness of a twentysomething with the emotional maturity of a preteen, but it stokes a protective fire within me that, before now, I'd only felt toward Grace.

Grace crams the last bowl into the dishwasher. Her forehead glistens with sweat. "You can help yourself to the beers too, Providence. Dad won't mind."

"He always minds when it comes to beer."

"He said it's a special occasion."

All three of us glance at the clock at the same time. It's already seven. He's locking up the liquor store right now.

"Tuna noodle casserole, right?" Harmony asks.

Grace nods and takes the empty seat between us. She crosses her legs once at the thighs, then again at the ankles, an unnatural contortion better suited to a yoga class than a dinner table. "It's the only thing he can make," she says. "That and scrambled eggs."

"He always made a ham at Christmas," I add.

Harmony scoffs but does not elaborate.

"He still makes the Christmas ham." Grace smiles at us both, but the corners of her lips falter when she fails to break the tension. I give her my undivided attention. Let Harmony be the one to look insolent. "He bought new lights for the house last year too. Mom thought he was going to fall off the ladder and kill himself putting them up."

"God willing," Harmony snorts.

Grace sighs. "Harmony, stop."

"Come on, don't act like it wouldn't be the best thing that ever happened to us if the old man kicked the bucket tomorrow. It's too bad Providence tried to murder the wrong parent."

I steer the conversation back to normalcy. "We always had good Christmases. The decorations, the ham, chokecherry pie . . ."

"They took Grace and I to Carey Gap to look at lights every year," Harmony says, emphasizing *Grace and I* to underscore my exclusion.

"They took you and me too before Grace was born."

She ignores me again.

"I'm surprised I didn't see you at the search this morning," I quip to Harmony.

"I had other business to attend to."

"More important than finding our mother?"

She laughs too hard. "That's rich coming from you. You don't really give a shit if Mom comes back or not. When this is all said and done, you'll just go back to wherever you came from and pretend none of this ever happened. You don't have to live with the consequences of what happens here. You get to go along your merry way, and we get to clean up the wreckage. Same as it's always been."

Outside, the porch steps creak. Our reactions are lightning quick, like we've been digging through our parents' sock drawer for spare change and need to hide the evidence before they come upstairs. Beers on coasters. Newspaper folded up. The last suds in the sink washed down the drain. Grace meets him in the entryway, beer in hand. I taught Harmony how to welcome him home. She must have taught Grace too.

Our father stalls in the doorway to soak in the scene before him, his face alight with a placid smile. I try to imagine this moment as innocent. I try to think of it as any man, finally home after a long day's work, eager to spend an evening with his children.

"My three girls. I've been waiting years for this." Youngest to oldest, Grace then Harmony then me, he plants a kiss atop our heads, a ceremony he performs with the grandeur of a priest blessing his sinners. "Gracie, open this beer for me."

"Sorry, Dad."

"Serve up the casserole while you're up. I'm starving."

Grace buzzes around the kitchen with the measured efficiency of a waitress. She divvies up the utensils alone, more like the help than part of the family. "Let me make myself useful," I offer.

But when I stand, my father takes me by the wrist. His touch is more tender than it was this morning, and it throws me off balance.

"She can do it herself, butterfly."

"I don't mind—"

"All under control," Grace chirps as she distributes the napkins. My father gets his first.

Harmony angles toward our father as he takes the head of the table—right next to me. "How did the search go?"

"Useless again. Fucking sheriff's department couldn't find treasure if you gave them a map with *X* marking the spot. I'm planning to go down there tomorrow and give Sheriff Eastman a piece of my mind. Whole thing has been a travesty so far. How hard is it to find some old man's wife after she's run off?" His Adam's apple pulses grotesquely as he swills his beer. He sets the bottle down with a satisfied *ahhh*.

"Was work any better?" Harmony asks.

"Busy morning, slow afternoon. Accident on the road up to the reservation."

The two-lane highway linking Annesville to Long Grass is a magnet for drunk drivers. Head-on collisions and cars coiled around utility poles routinely bottleneck traffic to one lane or shut the road down entirely. Our father regales us with the colorful account of a man who tried to shoplift a handle of whiskey by shoving it down his pants. He doesn't pause to thank Grace when she sets his plate before him. Her shoulders deflate as she fetches the other plates. She is going above and beyond to fill the gaps left by our mother, but to our father, she is merely doing what is expected of her. He doesn't care which woman opens his beer and dishes up his dinner. We exist to serve him.

At last, the four of us are seated at the table. The tuna noodle casserole is heaped on the center of my plate in an amorphous gray mound, its surface cratered with peas and cubed mushrooms. I'm reaching for my fork when my father takes my hand. I hunch my shoulders and squeeze my arms against myself until I am as small as I can possibly be.

"I'd like you to say grace," my father says to me.

"I'm out of practice." I look to Grace for help, but she is absently picking the peas out of her food and corralling them to the edge of the plate.

His crows' feet deepen when he smiles. He gives my hand a gentle squeeze. "It's like swimming. You never forget."

"I don't know how to swim."

"Come on now. Don't be difficult."

He takes Grace's hand, and, begrudgingly, Harmony takes mine. I am surprised by the ease with which I recall the grace prayer and how steady my words are, even as my thoughts dissolve into indistinct panic. "Gracious God, we have sinned against Thee, and are unworthy of Thy mercy. Pardon our sins and bless these mercies for our use, and help us eat and drink to Thy glory for Christ's sake. Amen."

My father lowers my hand into my lap. He holds it a moment too long before letting go. His knuckle brushes against my thigh. Beneath the table, I rub my palm against my knee again and again, until the traces of his clammy, calloused touch are only a memory. But now his touch is other places too, the small of my back and the curve of my knee and the nape of my neck. I don't realize how much I am sweating until a breeze rolls through the window and feels like winter against my damp skin. Every part of me is slick with sweat. I am sweating into this borrowed dress. I am sweating beneath my veneer of makeup. I am sweating behind my ears. I am sweating between my thighs.

"Providence? You're turning gray." Grace's archless eyebrows lift in alarm. "I can get you a cold washcloth."

I shake my head. "Hot, that's all."

My father hooks a finger beneath the sleeve of my denim jacket. There it is again. His touch, light against my inner wrist, rough like the scales of a crocodile. "It's this goddamn jacket. You'll get heatstroke if you don't take this thing off."

"I'll be fine."

"What have you got to hide, butterfly?"

I throw myself out of my chair and fly up the stairs two at a time. The bedrooms still have no doors and the floor still creaks, creaks, creaks until the dead spot outside of my old room. I lock myself in the bathroom. Fragments of downstairs conversation float up to me and I cannot understand any of it. Suddenly they are speaking another language. I claw at the denim, try to escape from it, but it is a straitjacket. I fight for every breath. My heart-beat throbs in my ears so furiously I expect my eardrums to burst and torrents of blood to gush down my neck.

I need the release. I need it right now. I hike up the sleeve of the jacket as far as it will go, a few measly inches above my wrist, and I bite deep and I bite long, and when the salty tang of blood hits my tongue, I inhale through my teeth. I swear I can see bone when I suck the blood away, but the bite still doesn't feel deep enough. I want to rend my flesh from my bones. I want to free myself from the body in which I am imprisoned, the body that forces me to remember even when my mind tries to forget.

I don't know how long I have been sitting on the bathroom floor with toilet paper pressed against my wound when someone knocks. I throw the bloodied tissue away and hide the bite beneath my sleeve, as if the intruder might be able to sense it through the door if I don't cover it up.

"Your food is getting cold and I have to pee."

"Go use the other bathroom, Harmony."

"I can tell you're not on the toilet. Open up."

I do.

She is slumped against the wall with her neck lolled to one side. Whether she's just tipsy or already roaring drunk, I can't tell. "I have a bone to pick with you."

"Do I look like I'm in the mood?"

"You look like shit. You're sweating like you're giving birth."

I try to slip past her, but she blocks me by extending each of her spindly limbs toward a different corner of the doorframe, a spider upon its web. "Just a girl, standing in front of another girl, asking that girl to leave Grace the fuck alone."

"*Notting Hill*? How drunk are you?"

"I mean it, Providence." She hisses the last syllable of my name. "Leave Grace alone."

"She's my sister too."

"And you will ruin her! She thinks you are a godsend. She thinks you are the sister she's been waiting for all these years. Me, she already knows I'm a disappointment. But you? I've had to listen to her talk about how *oh, Providence actually seems nice* and *oh, Providence came to help me when I got in trouble at school.* Mom is gone, you come galloping in to save the day, and when you piss off back to wherever you came from, you will leave her alone, and hurt, and miserable. We all have the same parents, but you are not her sister. I am her sister. I am the one who's always been there, through everything. I am not perfect, but I try, God damn it. You are using her to fill some miserable void in your life, and you don't care that it will destroy her when you leave." She blinks back tears. Her nose crinkles and her mouth twists into a frown. "Please. I have never asked you for anything, but I'm asking you for this. It's the least you can do for me."

She's right. About all of it. There are the two of them, connected in ways I scarcely understand, and then there is me. I yearn for sisterhood; they already have it. They don't need me. The same crush of loneliness I felt when Sara embraced me descends upon me once again. However the search for my mother ends, if it ever ends, I will eventually leave Annesville and I will have the luxury of trying to forget. For Harmony and Grace, their lives will steep in this calamity for years to come.

I dig my fingernails into my palms, channeling my anger into my skin instead of my voice. The only advantage I have in an argument with Harmony is my ability to stay calm. She'll have me on the back foot if I get emotional. "If Grace wants me to leave her alone, fine. If she asks, I'll do it. No questions asked. She has a right to keep me out of her life. But I'm not doing it for you."

Harmony feigns interest in the notches hewn into the doorframe, where our mother measured us on every birthday. Most birthdays, anyway. We each have a few years missing. It was a maternal ritual she undertook only when she was sober. As Harmony's arms fall to her sides, I catch sight of the engagement ring on her left hand. "You don't have one decent bone in your body. You're rotten right to your core," she says. "You're a killer. Least get the right parent this time. Do us all a fucking favor."

"If you want him to die that much, do it yourself."

"I have Grace to think about. Who do you have?"

*   *   *

Through dinner, the bite mark throbs. I slide my fingers along the avulsion and trace the shape of each individual tooth. By now I know exactly what shape each one makes, how the canines on my left side differentiate from the right and how perfectly spaced the dental work has made my front teeth. I return to the bite mark every time my father speaks; I bit myself exactly where he touched me.

My father allows me to help Grace with the dishes. He is three beers deep by the time he and Harmony retreat to the living room for the Rockies game, and I can tell by his bearish growl they are losing. He then says something else to make Harmony laugh.

When he excused himself for the game, she hopped up, grabbed two cold beers, and volunteered to join him. Peering over my shoulder, I see she's not even sitting at the farthest edge of the couch, cowering away from his recliner like I would be. The only thing between them is the end table on which both of their beers rest. Harmony's legs drape over the arm of the couch. She is within fatherly range. This is her defense mechanism: while Grace and I would move heaven and earth to stay away from him, she wins his favor by pretending to like him. If she doesn't put up a fight, she's not a tantalizing target. He likes it when we fight back.

"I should have played softball." The running water overpowers Grace's voice. The chokecherry pie, burnt on the top, cools on a wire rack beside us.

"For him?"

"It disappointed him when I wasn't interested in it."

"It wouldn't change anything. He'd still be . . ." I trail off.

"He'd like me more."

I let the words hang. I'm about to change the subject when I think of what Sara said earlier. *I know you loved him, but he could have done more for you.* "Is he nice to you?" The euphemism is worse than not asking at all, but the words wilt on my tongue when I try to be more direct.

"Yeah."

"You can tell me the truth."

She hands me a plate to load into the dishwasher. "Why would I lie about that?"

"I'm not saying—"

"Why can't we talk about something normal? Like, why can't you ask me about school, or about my friends, or if I have a boyfriend? I want to be normal for, like, five minutes. I don't want to talk about this serious shit."

"Don't say *shit*."

"I'm almost eighteen," Grace says. "You can stop treating me like a kid."

"You're right. I'm sorry."

It earns me a smile. The more I see the gap between her front teeth, the more it charms me.

We don't speak again until Grace starts cutting the pie. "Do you ever . . . like, you'll just be doing something normal, like folding laundry, and you start thinking about it? Things he's done? And you can't get it out of your head? It gets stuck there and I—I want to reach inside my skull and take out my brain so it stops."

"For me it's usually nightmares."

"All the time?" she asks.

"Not always. I have a lot of sleeping problems."

"Like what?"

"Someone so much as takes the first step up to my apartment and I'm wide awake. I sleep with a white noise machine to drown sounds out."

"What's your apartment like?" The dreamy look in her eyes tells me she isn't asking to be polite, but to open a portal to a world outside Annesville. Grace's universe is a tragically small one, existing almost entirely within the saltbox house on Cedar Street and under our father's watchful eye.

"It's small, just one bedroom, but it's cozy. I filled it with plants so it would be bright and cheery—peace lilies, mostly. They're my favorite. It has a fireplace too, but it doesn't work, so I bought lots of candles to stick in there instead. But my favorite thing is the view from my bedroom. If I look hard enough, I can see the Missouri River, just barely."

Her smile is small and sad. "I want to see a big river like that, not just the dribbling little creeks around here."

"Maybe I'll be able to show you someday."

I envision it with painful clarity. As summer steals into fall and the trees turn the color of marmalade, we'll drive out to the limestone bluffs halfway between Kansas City and St. Louis and have a picnic lunch on the banks of the river. I'll bring a bottle of champagne for us to share because that seems like something a big sister should do, sneak her little sister her first sips of alcohol. Maybe we'll talk, or maybe we'll just pass the hours in blissful, easy silence, swathed in the warmth of each other's company.

"Where would I sleep if there's only one bedroom?"

"You'd take the bedroom and I'd sleep on the couch." I look toward the stairs. My throat tightens. "It has a door, Grace."

Grace shoos a moth away from the pie, but says nothing. In the living room, the television screen bathes Harmony and my father in harsh white light, the two of them engaged in seemingly lighthearted conversation. The camaraderie is a betrayal.

"What about Harmony? I bet she'd let you stay with her."

Grace shakes her head furiously, like a swimmer trying to get water out of her ears. "I don't want to live with Harmony."

"Did she do something to you, Grace?"

"No, just . . . everything with Mom and Dad. She refuses to talk about it. I'm not even sure she talks about it in therapy."

"At least she goes."

"It doesn't do her any good. If you're going to therapy and you still try to kill yourself, what's the point?" She clenches her eyes to wish away her last words. "I'm sorry. That wasn't my secret to tell."

"Mum's the word."

Grace hands me the plate with the largest slice of pie, clearly intended for our father, in a gesture of gratitude. From the living room, he bellows, "Come on, girls. Come be part of the family."

It is there, in the living room—forks chiming against plates, baseball announcers prattling on about ERA and WHIP, my father chewing pie with his mouth open—that I really notice my mother's absence. When I close my eyes, I picture her curled up in the rocking chair with her favorite shawl wound around her shoulders, a specterlike presence too drunk or too sad to make conversation. But she was always there.

"If I'd had sons," my father says through a belch, "they'd be out there on Coors Field right now. I'd have raised three Tulowitzkis all by myself."

"Three shortstops on the same team?" Grace asks.

He points at me with his beer. "We thought Providence was going to be a boy. She would have been Thomas Byrd Jr." He mutes the television as a commercial comes on. "I still remember when the doctor handed you to me and I saw the pink blanket. I thought they'd made a mistake."

"My mot—Mom had an ultrasound. You knew I was going to be a girl."

He shakes his head. "No, butterfly. I think you're remembering wrong."

I am not. My mother showed me the ultrasound when I was a teenager, with the words *baby #1 is a girl!* jotted along the top of the picture. I chew on a bite of pie until it liquefies and trickles down my throat like sludge. Even when my mouth is empty, I keep chewing. I can't stop moving. If I'm not chewing, I am tapping a foot. If I'm not tapping a foot, I am quivering. I'm fighting against primal instincts. My brain triggers the fight-or-flight response over and over again, and the longer I remain planted on this couch, the more unbearable the adrenaline becomes.

He laughs to himself, like he's come up with a brilliant punchline for a joke he has wanted to tell all evening. "But listen, I've got to ask . . . Grace, Harmony, what do we all think about the fake tits?"

"Dad!" Grace chokes on her pie. "Don't say that."

"Sorry, sorry. Just—it's the elephant in the room, you know?"

Harmony can't help herself. "Elephants, plural."

"How'd you get the money for those, butterfly?"

My gaze falls to my chest. I see them for the first time the way other people do, as silicone cries for attention, instead of the first and only way I have ever been able to dictate the terms of my own sexuality. "None of your business."

"Guessing you didn't marry a rich man."

"No."

"Ah, nothing wrong with that. Your mom didn't marry me because I was the richest man in Annesville, that's for damn sure." She married him because she was sixteen and pregnant with me. He only proposed because he was twenty-seven and thought, erroneously, he was staring down a statutory rape charge if they didn't tie the knot. He told the story to prove my mother was a slut. Sixteen-year-olds shouldn't be so easy, after all.

"Do you miss her?" Harmony asks.

"I miss her like hell," he says, "but I know she'll walk through that door any minute now. I'll never get rid of her. Like a bad penny."

"Someone must have kidnapped her."

"Harmony, stop," Grace pleads.

"Use your brain, Grace." Harmony taps an index finger against her temple. "You're always talking about those stupid podcasts you listen to. You can't tell me you think she's enjoying a vacation in Yellowstone."

"I know nothing good happened to her, okay? I don't like thinking about Mom being kidnapped. It makes me sick."

"All I'm saying is someone probably took her, tied her up—"

"Enough!" Our father clouts the side of his recliner. "Quit it. You're scaring her. That's enough from all of you."

"It's not that I'm, like, naïve about it." Grace looks at her plate while she talks. The last shard of crust crumbles when she stabs it with her fork. "I try to have a little hope is all."

"Hope is dangerous," Harmony says. "You give someone a shred of hope and they cling to it for the rest of their life."

I cringe at my father's roar before I even hear it. We violated his cardinal rule: when he asks for something, he only asks once. "Not another goddamn word about your mother. Not one more goddamn word."

The game is back on. He dials up the volume loud enough to catch the attention of a passing jet airplane. Only Harmony is unaffected by his pivot from jovial to cross. She stretches languorously across the couch and shakes her beer to coax out the dregs. I notice the severe dip from her ribcage to her stomach, how her hipbones strain against her skin. I examine her for scars, but Harmony doesn't even have moles or birthmarks, never mind mutilation as extreme as my own. No trace of how she tried to end her life. I want to ask her the same questions Grace asked me. What is it like for her? Is she haunted too?

"I'm going outside for a cigarette," I say when the Rockies pull their starting pitcher. The manager, a toad of a man, waddles out to the mound with his hands stacked on his hips.

"Grab me another beer while you're up."

I get in the car and floor it.

11

August 12th

8:14 PM

THE DRIVE TO Long Grass takes me twice as long tonight. First it is because I convince myself to drive under the speed limit, a safety measure against my mental state and drunk drivers alike. Then it is because I put on my hazards, pull over, and use every trick in my therapeutic arsenal to bring me back from the brink. Focus on your five senses, exactly what is in front of you, nothing more.

Sight: the black, starless sky.

Sound: the rumble of my engine.

Smell: the cigarette I just ashed against the window.

Taste: cigarettes and chokecherry pie.

Touch: my clammy skin adhering to my fake leather seats.

I chain-smoke four cigarettes, smoking each one down further than the last. My father never smokes his all the way down to the filter. Suddenly I'm back at the dining room table, only now I'm a knock-kneed fifteen-year-old and the cigarette in my hand is the first one I've ever smoked. He watches me take drag after drag until it burns just past the halfway point, and then he plucks it from my lips.

"Never smoke further than this, butterfly," he said, pinching the filter to a pulp between his ragged nails. "This is where the cancer is."

As I light my fifth cigarette with the cherry of my fourth, a car pulls up behind me. The driver is illuminated by the cabin light, and even though his face is lowered, I know exactly who it is. I'd recognize that stupid cowboy hat anywhere.

"You stick out like a sore thumb with those Missouri plates." Josiah stoops beside my window to meet me at eye level. Shadows obscure his face, only the whites of his eyes and the brown of his teeth visible. Together, we exhale a single noxious cloud of nicotine. My cigarette commingles with his chewing tobacco.

"There's nothing illegal about pulling over to smoke a cigarette."

"Technically? Shoulder's closed here," he says.

"Short on your ticket quota this week?"

"Believe it or not, Providence, I pulled over to make sure you were okay."

"I don't believe it." I imagine him watching me. Staking out my father's house. Biding his time. Following me into the inky darkness. My eyes drift toward the barren prairie surrounding us. We're the only living souls for miles around.

A terrible thought emerges. "How did you know where I was?" I ask.

"Out on patrol, and like I said, those Missouri plates."

"Or maybe my father told you I'd be in town tonight."

Josiah chuckles. "See, that's how I can tell you're a city dweller now. In small towns, not everyone is out to get you."

But Annesville is not like every other small town. This is my own personal haunted house with monsters lurking in every corner, distorted by every shadow.

"If I can be honest, I'm only interested in talking to you if you know something about my mother."

"As soon as we find her, you'll be my first call. You've got my word."

I'm seduced by the thought of being the first person to know my mother's fate—so seduced by it, I nearly divulge my conversation with Gil about Mitch Perkins, but I swallow the words before they take shape.

He sweeps his tongue over his bottom teeth, lower lip protruding from the disturbance. "Honest to God, I believe we'll bring your mother home safe. I know the odds and the statistics, but I also know to trust my intuition when it feels this strong. She's still alive."

Grace and her podcasts. She'd have a sharp comeback for Josiah, but all I can manage is a half-hearted nod. Her words from yesterday rattle through my mind—*you're useless, Providence*—but I drown them out before I can start to believe them. If I was useless, I wouldn't have faced Tom Byrd at dinner.

"Mind if I take a look at your registration? I promise I'll be out of your hair after that."

I nod and reach for the glove box. When I open it, my gun stares back at me.

Fuck fuck fuck—

I grab my registration and slam the glove box shut. I can only pray I've moved fast enough for the gun to slip past Josiah's well-trained eye.

I haven't.

"What was that in your glove box?"

"Probably just my cigarettes."

He takes a cursory glance at my registration. This is no longer of interest to him. "Very funny, Miss Byrd. Why don't you open it up for me again?"

"No." So much power in a single word. I lift my chin high and pretend like I'm not deafened by the blood rushing through my ears.

"I'd hate to search it myself."

"You need a warrant."

"I only need probable cause."

"All I've done tonight is have dinner with my family." I strain to keep my voice even. If I talk too loudly, he'll think I'm defensive. If I talk too quietly, he'll think I'm scared. He doesn't need to know that right now I'm both. "I'm not stupid enough to do anything that would send me back to York."

As he gnaws his tobacco, his face taut like a bungee cord stretched too far, I envision everything I've built turning to dust. My chair in the tattoo shop, my apartment, my peace lilies—all of it, gone in a single instant. I did my research before I got the gun: unlawful possession of a firearm is a three-year mandatory minimum, but with my history, I'd be facing a much longer sentence.

My powerlessness in this moment is suffocating. I am a snake with no fangs, a lion with no claws. I force myself to meet Josiah's eyes. They say the left eye is the window to the soul, and I will him to see through my hardened exterior to the little girl still living inside of me.

He stretches his arm across the top of my window. "Where are you headed off to?"

"Long Grass. I'm staying with a friend there."

"She's a good friend?" he asks.

"The very best."

"One who wouldn't let you do something stupid?"

"Never."

Josiah looks off into the distance, the flat landscape faintly illuminated by my headlights. He raps once on the top of the car. "Then you best get going before it gets much later. The drunks will be out soon."

I don't breathe until he pulls away.

*   *   *

I lied. I don't go to Sara's. I go to Daniel's instead, and I check my rearview mirror all the way there to be sure I'm not being followed.

If Daniel is perplexed by me asking to see him so late, or if he can sense the distress percolating inside me, he is polite enough not to say anything. He sits on the front porch of his trailer, shrouded by a mosquito net pocked with gaps and tears, his feet elevated in a plastic lawn chair. His coffee mug reads *WORLD'S BEST DAD* in girlish pastels suggesting a daughter. "I think that's my sister's dress," he says once I'm within earshot, maneuvering my way around the dismembered cars on his lawn.

"She let me borrow it."

"She'll probably let you keep it if you ask nice enough. Our mom always made her wear it to family dinners. Once she died, Sara was relieved she'd never have to put it on again." Even during the only personal anecdote he's shared with me, Daniel remains aloof. "You said you needed to talk about your mom?"

It was a weak excuse, but the only plausible one that could explain me arriving at his doorstep at this hour. The truth is, I'm still reeling from my brush with Josiah, and if he's tailing me or planning to send a legion of deputies with a search warrant, I want to be around another cop when he does. Daniel won't stand for Tillman County encroaching on his jurisdiction, and I'd like to think he'll defend me, even if it's mostly out of loyalty to his sister.

"Mitch Perkins," I blurt. "She hung around someone named Mitch Perkins. He sounded like a pretty bad guy."

Daniel moves his feet so I can sit down. "Been in prison since last summer. Fifteen years for arson. It was a hate crime to boot. Sounds like a real charming guy."

Fifteen years is probably what I'll be facing if the sheriff finds my gun. I'm stupid for leaving it in the glove box. I should have slid it under the seat, put it in the trunk, done anything with it except leave it in a compromised hiding place. "So he didn't have anything to do with her disappearance."

"Is that really why you called me this late? To ask about Mitch Perkins?"

"I spent the last couple hours with my father and my sisters. They talked about my mother, and now I can't get her out of my mind. I know it could have waited until tomorrow, so I'm—" I cut myself off before I can apologize. All evening long I've felt sorry for existing. "Everything is so far out of my control and telling you about Mitch Perkins was the one thing I could control right now."

Daniel sips his coffee the same deliberate way I take a pull from a cigarette, savoring every moment of the pedestrian pleasure. He sets the mug down beside his badge and his pistol. As much as he's just a man enjoying a cup of coffee on a warm summer evening, he's also an off-duty police officer surveilling his street at odd hours for mischief. "I understand. I appreciate you coming to me. I'm sure you don't trust cops."

"I went to prison."

"And I think," he begins, "I'm about to wipe away what little goodwill you have for me."

"What?"

"They're not interested in pursuing leads about your father."

How convenient to have no interest in pursuing the one person who once wrapped his hands around my mother's neck hard enough to leave palmprint-shaped bruises behind, who once crushed the bones of her feet beneath his steel-toed boot. Hell hath no fury like Tom Byrd. "They're not even going to question him?"

"His alibi checked out," he says. "He was at the liquor store."

"I've seen Jell-O more solid than that alibi."

"Eyewitnesses back him up," he says.

"Because no one in the history of any criminal investigation has ever intimidated a witness, right?"

"Good God, you do not let up, do you?"

The purr of an engine jolts me to attention, but it's only a lifted pickup truck barreling past the trailer. The neighborhood dogs bark and howl. "I'm sorry, I should have offered you a cup of coffee," Daniel says as the dogs begin to quiet. "Can I get you one?"

Somewhere between my brain and my mouth, the *no thank you* I start to say transforms into "Yes, that would be nice." I want to press pause for ten minutes and catch my breath. The trailer releases an air-conditioned sigh as he opens the door and goes inside. I comb the night sky for the few constellations I can recognize—Orion and his bow, Ursa Minor (or is it Ursa Major?), Scorpius and how its stars fray into a cat-o'-nine-tails. I reach my arms out in a dramatic stretch, Jesus on the cross, and when I lower them, I accidentally touch Daniel's gun. He's left it out here with me. I decide to see it as an act of trust rather than carelessness. Sheriff Eastman would never do it.

He emerges with my coffee, also in a *WORLD'S BEST DAD* mug, this one devoid of feminine design. "I can get cream and sugar," he offers.

I insist I like my coffee black even though this tastes like burnt firewood. Each sip intensifies my need for a cigarette. Caffeine is the poor man's nicotine.

He notices me looking at the stars and asks about constellations, not because he is eager for an astronomy lesson but because he wants to be polite and we aren't familiar enough to ask personal questions. He shares the Lakota name for Orion's Belt, *Tayamnicankhu*. He talks fondly about Sara, and the depth of his love for her makes me dislike him a little less. At least we have that in common.

He excuses himself to get a sweatshirt from the trailer, once again leaving his gun behind. I'm so distracted by it that I reach for the wrong cup of coffee and gag when an unexpected flavor hits my tongue. Cutting through the coffee is the unmistakably smoky, nutty taste of bourbon.

A well-mannered girl would keep her mouth shut and put her head back in the sand where it belongs. But I've never been a well-mannered girl, and I can't pretend to be one now. All that time waxing poetic about his sister and he can't be bothered to uphold her deepest conviction, his own tribal law: no alcohol. When Daniel comes back onto the porch, I toast him with his own mug.

"You're holding out on me," I coo. "Maybe I wanted a splash of bourbon too."

He looks at the mug. He doesn't lie or invent an excuse. All he says is, "Please don't tell my sister."

* * *

Back at the trailer, Sara is curled up on the couch like a shrimp. A bowl of cornflakes teeters on her chest and threatens to spill when she waves at me. "You made it back alive," she says, muting the TV. It's a reality dating show, women in string bikinis and chiseled men frolicking around a beach house, not a care in the world beyond maximizing their camera time.

"I'm a cockroach. I'm unkillable."

She points to the empty couch cushion with her foot. "Do you want to talk about it?"

I sit. "It was exactly what I expected. Triggers on triggers on triggers."

"How were your sisters?"

"Damaged."

"How could they not be?"

On the TV, a freckled girl sobs into the camera. Her eyes are swollen shut from the violence of her tears. The primal grief of first heartbreak.

"I think I was the nail in their coffin," I say. "Maybe if I hadn't done what I did—"

Sara's rebuttal is lightning quick. "It's not your fault." She takes a bite of cereal.

"I certainly didn't help."

"Your sisters . . . I know this is bleak, but there was nothing you could do, good or bad, that was going to make them happy or well-adjusted. You grew up in that house. You understand what they're up against. It's like all that 'pull yourself up by your bootstraps' shit they preached to us in prison, remember? It's bullshit. You can try and try and try, but in the end, you can't brute-force your way into a normal life."

"I'm not used to you being that fatalistic."

"Some of us have longer odds than others," she says. "You. Me. Your sisters."

"What about someone like your brother?"

I haven't forgotten about the bourbon. The taste lingers heavy in the back of my throat like a half-swallowed pill.

"Ah, yes," she says, "because nothing says well-adjusted like becoming a cop. You know he used to drink too? My aunt and I took out loans to send him to rehab in Rapid City a few years ago."

Of course it can't be as straightforward as him simply being a hypocrite chafing against their restrictive tribal laws. "I had no idea."

"I prefer not to think about it. I didn't talk to him for almost a year after it happened." She refocuses on the TV, where the teary girl with freckles has been replaced by a teary girl with a lip ring. This girl is much prettier when she cries, face less red, eyes less swollen. Her tears shine like diamonds as they blaze salty trails through her blush.

"But you still love him," I say.

"He's my brother. I could have done worse in the sibling department."

Our conversation peters out to silence, the perfect opening to tell her about Daniel's bourbon. But my voice stalls. Were it any other vice, I would keep my nose out of it—but it's alcohol. It's the very thing Sara despises most in this world.

I know the toll alcoholism has taken on her family: the bottle stole both her parents and indirectly stole her sister, T-boned by a drunk driver and crushed like tinfoil at nineteen years old. Right now it gnaws away at aunts, uncles, cousins, and friends, and it has returned to gnaw away at her brother once again. I don't know if she can forgive a second betrayal from him. Sara does not bend for people. And if she can't forgive him, if she lapses into the same acrimonious relationship I have with Harmony, then who does she have?

She has no idea how calamitous it would be to lose the last piece of her family. As much as I like to tell myself family is just a word, the truth is that it is an essential piece of the human experience. There are found families, families you choose, families born out of unimaginable circumstances with bonds stronger than steel, but blood is different. Blood is innate. Blood is animal.

I've yet to find something that can replace it.

I choose to see my silence as an act of mercy, not an act of cowardice. I ask Sara to turn the volume back on and lie down on the opposite end of the couch. The trailer has finally cooled enough for a blanket, and she tosses an afghan the size of a parachute over us. We tuck our feet beneath each other's bodies and watch the pretty girls cry on their white sand beach.

I think of my mother then. How she has probably died without ever seeing the ocean.

CHAPTER

12

I HAVE A SIXTH sense for tragedy, finely honed by palms to my face and the squeak of my bedsprings at unholy hours of the night. I feel it deep in my bones, the way animals sense earthquakes and old women sense rain on the wind. My chest throbs when I wake up that morning. My heartbeat feels like a backhand strike against my ribcage. Something is coming. All I can do is brace for impact.

Focus on what is in front of you.

Sight: the water stains on the ceiling bleeding into one another.

Sound: my own breath, lungs emptying and filling, emptying and filling.

Smell: something inexplicably sour, like roadkill.

Taste: my tongue fuzzy and metallic from sleep.

Touch: numbness tingling between my joints, creeping around my bones like kudzu vines.

Tiny knocks at the door. Sara cracks it open, white sunlight slashing across the room. It should feel warm, but it doesn't. It can't cut through the numbness. My friend hesitates at the threshold. She chokes on her words. She crosses her arms over her chest, each hand reaching for its opposite shoulder, and looks down at the carpet.

And I know what's wrong.

And I say it:

"She's dead, isn't she?"

And I'm right.

* * *

A little boy from the reservation found her. He was hiking with his father when they saw deer grazing, and the boy, no more than eight years old, tiptoed off the trail for a better view. Guided by an invisible hand or another supernatural force beyond comprehension, he noticed a human foot jutting out from a sparse blanket of leaves.

The boy and his father are still there when I arrive at the scene. The boy is crying. His strangled wail echoes through my bones. This is the thing I will always remember. Other details, such as the vulture-like mourners busily erecting a makeshift memorial in my mother's memory and the blistering heat and the white sheet over my mother's body, will be sanded away by time. But years from now, I will still hear this little boy's cries in my dreams.

I am in a daze, numb except for an ache deep in my core. My lack of emotion is anticlimactic. I am being cheated of something. To be a motherless daughter is the most primal pain of all, yet I am not mad with grief. I am lost in labyrinthine recollections of my childhood, staring blankly ahead as if I've suffered a traumatic brain injury and been rendered a vegetable. Behind a strand of yellow caution tape strung around the trees, police comb the nearby woods for evidence. Crime scene marker number one denotes the pile of foliage my mother had been buried under, and a trail of leaves lead from her resting place to the stretcher she lies on now. Her bare feet stick out from beneath the sheet. The left dangles by a single bloody tendon.

Time has turned molten. Hours feel like days.

Two people bookend me and weave their arms through mine. Connor to my left, Zoe to my right. It touches me to see them band together and come to my aid. I rest my head in the curve between Zoe's shoulder and neck.

"There are . . . there are things they need to do to her body," Connor says without looking at me. He lets me keep my fragment of intimacy with Zoe private. "You don't want to see that."

"He should have buried her," I say.

Zoe's voice strains above a whisper as the wind whips her flaxen hair into a tangle. "What?"

"Whoever killed her," I say. "He left her out here to be eaten by vultures and coyotes. He should have buried her. It's the least he could have done."

"Providence . . ." Connor begins. He stands with his back to the crime scene. He never had a stomach for gore. Just being near the carnage is making him turn green.

"She'll never get buried. The women in my family only get cremated. She'll gather dust on the mantle. He should have at least buried her."

Connor and Zoe exchange a look, but I remain fixated on the crime scene. One of the tribal police officers places a yellow marker beside a gnarled tree. A tatter of fabric? A strand of hair? There must be dozens, maybe hundreds of invisible traces of my mother scattered in these woods, all screaming *Elissa was here.*

"And her shoes," I say. "Where are her shoes?"

They steer me away from the crime scene and back up the trail. The onlookers wait for a police officer to provide an update, to emerge from the woods like Moses descending Mount Sinai with the Ten Commandments. On a distant bench, the little boy continues crying. He clings to his father's arm as Daniel kneels before them with a notepad, trying to draw information out of the shell-shocked boy. The boy sniffles, shakes his head, and asks for his mother. *I want my mom. I want my mom.*

While Connor and Zoe squabble about who should drive me back to the trailer, I approach the boy. I open my mouth to interrupt Daniel's gentle questioning, but nothing comes out, and I stand there unnoticed with my mouth ajar like a baby bird waiting for its mother to deposit worms into its maw.

Daniel acknowledges me with a curt glance. "Now isn't the best time."

I point to the boy. "Can I talk to him? I feel like—I feel like we might need each other right now."

"That okay, sir?"

The father nods. The boy shrinks further when I sit beside him on the bench. He's so young, so innocent, the last person in the world who should be drawn into this sordid ordeal. It is the smallness and senselessness of the injustice which makes it so insidious. Why couldn't it have been anyone else to find her body? Why not his father? Why not me? Why this poor child?

"Do you need a hug?" I ask the boy.

He crumples into my arms. I hold him as he cries.

*   *   *

"It was kind of you. Checking on the little boy."

Zoe does not look at me when she speaks. Her eyes remain glued to the countryside sprawling before us, miles upon miles of flat earth without so much as a tree or bush to disrupt the visual monotony. She props her arm on the armrest between us. Her palm upturns, her fingers relaxed in invitation, and I can't tell if I'm imagining it or if she truly pities me enough in this moment to indulge me with a chaste embrace of our hands.

"He wanted his mom," I say.

"You were the next best thing."

I place my hand beside hers, close enough for our pinkies to touch. Zoe senses this is all the courage I can muster and entwines her fingers with mine. A few hours ago, the gesture would have sent me soaring; now, it merely tempers the ache suffusing every inch of my body. I close my eyes and commit her touch to memory.

Zoe white-knuckles the steering wheel with her free hand. She drives at precisely the speed limit. Once a square, always a square. "It reminded me of something your mom would do."

"Don't."

"What?"

"That's not who she was. She was . . ."

"I don't think you knew her anymore."

"She was still an alcoholic. She was still letting my father abuse my sisters. She was still the same at her core," I say. "Grace told me she was hooked on oxy too."

"You always said addiction was a disease."

I ball my free hand into a fist and look out the window. Trees populate the horizon as we near the town of Long Grass, our drive approaching its end. "It doesn't mean I have to forgive her for it."

"She knew about us," she says.

"No, she didn't."

Zoe finally meets my eyes. The sidelong look distracts her from the road long enough for her truck to judder over the center rumble strip. "She came to my office a few months ago," she says once the truck is squarely back on its side of the road. "I figured she was coming to ask about the VA office in Carey Gap they've been promising for years. People either complain to me about that or about their property taxes. Anyway, she said my mom called her that night. When we . . ."

"When we kissed."

"When we kissed." Hearing her call the act by its name, even if she's only parroting me, is healing in itself. "So she knew. All these years, she knew, and she never threw the Bible at me, or made me feel guilty, or treated me any differently. She just came into my office that day and said, 'I really don't understand it, but I'm glad you made my daughter happy.'"

"I'm glad my mother could absolve you of your homosexual guilt."

Zoe frowns. "Way to miss the point."

"And what is the point, Zoe? That you got to have the heart-felt conversation with my mother I never did? That when she found out I'd been with another girl, she offered you her acceptance instead of me?" But I realize instantly that my mother used the only power she had to accept me: silence. The catastrophic kiss happened a month before I ran my mother over. If Zoe's mom really called her the night it happened, if my mother really knew all along about our tryst (and if she knew about the kiss, then who can say she didn't know about the things we did in Zoe's back seat?), she had an entire month to ruin me. Send me to the church for counseling. Ship me off to conversion therapy. Out me to my father, God forbid.

My intestines coil like a snake eating its own tail. My mother guarded my secret, and I repaid her discretion by breaking her bones.

Zoe opens her mouth to speak, but only a bewildered sigh slips out. "I thought you'd want to hear a happy memory I have of your mom."

"It's a happy memory I should have. Not you."

"Sweet Christmas, forget I said anything."

"At least it would have meant something to me," I fire back.

"Don't start."

But I have started, and now I can't stop. "Now you get to keep my mother's approval in your pocket, something to cheer you up when you feel guilty about still being in the closet."

"I'm not in the closet," Zoe insists.

"What else do you call a girl who's ashamed that she has sex with other girls?"

"We were teenagers. I was confused and lonely and . . . repressed."

"So it was just a science experiment for you?"

We stop at a red light. After almost an hour of constant motion, the stillness makes me queasy. I need more distance between me and my mother's dead body, more distance between me and the weeping boy. "We shouldn't do this right now," Zoe sighs. "You're tired. You're grieving. Now is not the time."

I am too exhausted to argue more.

The dogs tear into the front yard when we pull up to the trailer. Sara's car is gone, probably a few minutes behind us. My grief is catching up with me. I want to be asleep when we finally collide.

I start to gather my things and get out of the truck, but Zoe does not let go of my hand. She wants to kiss me. Her lips are parted. Her head is tilted. I know exactly how it will feel: the softness of her mouth, the shyness of her tongue, her fingers wreathing into my hair and drawing me closer, closer, closer, until I drape over the center console. Zoe always kissed me in a frenzy, like the only air she could breathe was that which we had shared. I close my eyes and feel her drawing closer to me, like a planet pulling an asteroid into its orbit.

But at the last moment, I turn my head. The heat between us turns to ice as her lips brush my cheek.

"I thought you wanted me to kiss you," she whispers.

"Not like this."

"I'm trying to comfort you."

My desire for Zoe is sharp, but my grief for my mother is sharper. "Don't kiss me out of pity, Zoe. I don't deserve that."

The rumble of Sara's car turning onto the driveway draws the moment to an unceremonious end. When I meet Sara on the front porch, she squeezes my shoulder affectionately. The dogs follow us inside, each carrying a toy in their mouth.

"Do you want food?" Sara is already opening the kitchen cabinets. "Maybe a cup of tea?"

"I just want to sleep."

"Oh, Providence, I'm so sorry."

"I'll be okay." My voice is fragile.

"It's never easy, losing a parent," she says. "Take it from someone who's lost both. Even if you know it's going to happen, it always feels too soon. It's like watching a bridge collapse while you're still standing on it."

I shower and wash my face. Sara leaves a cup of tea on my nightstand. I draw the curtains, turn off my phone, and collapse onto the air mattress. The sheet I cast over myself is as white as the one covering my mother's body. I think of her mangled leg when I close my eyes. Every few minutes, I reach for my ankles to make sure they have not spontaneously severed from my body. I palpate my legs and try to guess which tendon was keeping my mother's ankle attached.

Sara knocks at the door. When she opens it, Zenobia trots in.

"She's been scratching at your door," Sara says. "She can tell you're sad."

I cannot even bring myself to sit upright. I ache all over. "I'm not sad. I'm . . ."

"She'll be good company for you."

Sara closes the door before I can protest or ask her to take away the tea. Zenobia noses through the pile of dirty clothes on my suitcase, then hops onto the air mattress. She curls up beside me and presses her back against mine.

* * *

Silence suffocates the trailer, heavy and dark like widow's weeds. Sara has gone to bed. The dogs have purged themselves of their evening barks and howls. Now there's only me and my white noise machine playing ocean waves on a loop. When I dial Grace's number, it's mostly because I'm desperate to hear another human voice.

She answers in a small, muffled tone. "Hi, Providence." I picture her lost in a puddle of blankets, her hair mussed and her eyes rimmed with salt.

"Hi. I just—I thought I should call. See if you're okay."

"I feel like I'm underwater," she says. "It's like I can see the surface, but no matter how hard I swim, I can't break through. She didn't deserve this, to—to just be left like that. Like a piece of trash."

"Carrion," I say, rolling onto my back. My movement disturbs Zenobia, who makes her displeasure clear with a sidelong glare. She licks her chops sleepily before lowering her head back onto the corner of my pillow.

"What?"

"Dead flesh. It's what vultures eat."

She chastises me with a temporary silence. "You're making things worse."

I read between the lines: *if you'd had your way, she would have been carrion thirteen years ago.* My heartache will never be pure.

"Is Harmony with you?"

"She stopped by on her way to the bar." She sounds sheepish, as if Harmony's desertion is a reflection of her own character. The three of us echo through each other inescapably. "Mitesh and Karishma stayed longer when they dropped off their casserole. Everyone's bringing casseroles, like I'll forget my mom was murdered if I just shovel a few platefuls of tater tots and Velveeta into my mouth."

"It's what you do when people die," I say.

"I wouldn't care if they brought the casseroles and left, but they all try to tell me stories. Now that she's dead, they all have something nice to say about her. Like, suddenly half the town is in tears, telling me 'Oh, she was such a bright light at church' and 'I always loved her chokecherry pies.' No one ever said anything nice while she was alive."

"Do you . . . ?"

She draws a sharp breath. "Do I what?"

"I could come see you. If you don't want to be alone."

"Dad wouldn't . . ." She trails off.

"I know. I know."

Wishful thinking, like always. I should abandon the thought, but I can't. The fantasy unfurls in detail so crisp it feels like a memory instead of an invention: me and Grace on the couch together, our father nowhere to be found. She rests her head against my shoulder like a weary traveler finally offered respite, and I twine her hair into a lazy braid to busy my fingers. There's a movie on in the background, something lighthearted and funny to distract us from the maelstroms churning within us. We drink hot chocolate even though it's summertime, because— and I'm not sure how I know this, but I do, I do, I do—Grace loves hot chocolate. We don't say anything, but we don't have to. It's enough to be near each other.

Anger lashes me like a whip. Here I am, pining for the sweetness of sisterhood, while Harmony has rejected it with casual carelessness, like a restaurant patron declining a second glass of wine. *No more for me, thank you.* While she numbs herself with shots and floats around the pool hall like a ghost, Grace is trapped at the house, maybe alone but maybe with our father. He skulks from room to room, beer bottleneck grasped between his fingers, waiting for her most vulnerable moment to strike.

A sob claws at my throat, but I force it down. "Will you please call me if you need anything?"

"I will."

"Promise me."

Her voice sounds as tortured as mine. Two animals scrambling to break free from the same cage. "I promise."

13

August 16th

11:20 AM

I THINK THIS IS grief. I am not sure. It is one thing to think my mother is dead, but to know is another beast entirely. Now it's really over. Our story ends here.

My brain is on fire with *what if?* What if she had been able to forgive me? What if I had been able to forgive her? What if she had protected me from my father? What if she had managed to stay sober? What if she had never taken the oxy? What if she had still been able to love me? I follow each strand of existential yearning to the same end, back to my parole hearing eight years ago. *I don't care if they let you go. I don't care if you die tomorrow. It doesn't matter to me anymore.* After so much suffering and violence, at the end my mother only wanted to forget me—and now she is gone, and now I cannot forget her.

For two days, I scarcely leave the bedroom. Almost everyone I work with at the tattoo shop leaves a voicemail of condolence. Sara brings me food three times a day, like I'm back in prison doing another stint in solitary. This morning, she comes bearing bread and a purplish, pudding-like sauce. "It's *wojapi*," she says as she sits beside me on the air mattress, Zenobia napping between us. "Think of it like a berry sauce. Dip the frybread in it."

The *wojapi* is bittersweet like chokecherry pie. I submerge a piece of frybread. "I thought you hated cooking."

"I'm out of cereal."

I laugh for the first time in days. Zenobia is alarmed to hear me make a noise other than a sigh. I look to Sara, hoping my laughter will assure her I'm not dead from the neck up, but her eyes are stoic and glassy. My first thought is that she's discovered Daniel's drinking habit and, worse, discovered I didn't tell her as soon as I found out. "What's wrong? I'd ask if someone died, but I already know the answer."

"Don't shoot the messenger, all right?"

"What a vote of confidence."

"Daniel called a few minutes ago," she says, reaching up to pull back the curtains and blind me with daylight, "and said Sheriff Eastman is on his way here to talk to you."

"The man can't even let me grieve in peace."

"He spoke to Grace earlier and he's talking to Harmony tonight. Daniel says it's due diligence."

I push the bread into my mouth with tired fingers. I am acutely aware of how pathetic I am, spending days locked in this stuffy room, staring at the ceiling and torturing myself with recollections of my mother. Once the real memories ran dry, I created false ones. The chokecherry pie became my mother helping me pick my wedding dress.

"I think it's heartless to ask us about it so soon after they found her body. It's . . ." I trail off.

"Like I said, don't shoot the messenger."

We make the bed with fresh linens, but before I can retreat into my cocoon of grief, Sara leads me into the living room. I had forgotten how bright the rest of the trailer is. She seats me at the dining room table with the *wojapi* and frybread. "Eat, then get dressed. You'll answer the sheriff's questions, and then you can resume hibernation."

"Do you have something black I can borrow? Something you'd wear for a funeral?"

"I have plenty of those. My family drops like flies."

*   *   *

The dress is laughable. It covers every inch of my skin from the neck down, my cleavage tucked safely beneath the jewel neckline and my legs hidden in fabric puddling on the floor beneath me. I look more like the grim reaper than a daughter bereaving her mother. Despite how ridiculous it is, I am grateful my costume is such a shameless display of sorrow. I want the sheriff to see me as a woman in mourning and not as a former felon who is scared to death to be questioned by the police.

I meet Josiah at the front gate. Here I am, nothing to hide. His cruiser reads K-9 UNIT—STAY BACK, but the threat of canine intervention is an empty one with no police dog in sight. He tips his cowboy hat as he gets out of the car, pausing to survey the agglomeration of trailers surrounding us. "Jesus," he says in the direction of adolescent boys clamoring around a basketball hoop. They are laughing and smiling, happy as children should be, nothing like the boy who found my mother. "We never did right by the Indians out here."

"That's an understatement."

He gestures to the *BEWARE OF DOG* sign hanging from Sara's front gate. "May I come in?"

"The dogs won't be a problem. My friend is in another room keeping an eye on them."

Josiah frowns. "She won't be eavesdropping, I hope?"

I know better than to talk to cops alone. Without the time or money to recruit a lawyer, Sara eavesdropping from another room is the next best thing. "He has to stop when you say you want a lawyer," she'd said as she herded the dogs into her bedroom. "It doesn't matter if you're not being Mirandized. I'll come out there and tell him where he can stick it if you need me to."

"She's got pretty good ears, but that's not a crime," I tell him.

The dogs yowl as he crosses the threshold, sensing an unwelcome intruder in our midst. Josiah pays them no mind as he settles in at the head of the table. He spreads the contents of a manila folder before him, pictures and notes and typed documents I can't decipher without asking questions or getting too close. Josiah's every move is a trap until proven otherwise. As he licks his fingers and flicks through papers, I remember the first time he responded to a 911 call at our house. I was seven, too young to understand why the bedroom door was locked and why my mother was crying and saying *stop*, but old enough to know something was wrong. My father palmed my shoulders before he let the sheriff in. "The police aren't your friends, Providence. They'll punish you if you get something wrong. Think long and hard before you say anything to them."

"Smells like an ashtray in here." He thinks I don't notice him turning on a recorder.

"Just me."

Josiah's mouth quirks into a smile, then flattens into a solemn line. "Before I ask you anything, I want to offer my condolences. I really thought she was still . . . I'm sorry any of this had to happen. Honest to God, I'm so sorry."

"Me too."

"Do you remember much from the book of Matthew?" he asks.

"'Blessed are the peacemakers, for they shall be called the children of God.'"

My recitation impresses him. "The seventh beatitude. Do you remember the fifth?"

"Not off the top of my head," I say.

"'Blessed are they that mourn, for they shall be comforted.' I read it last night, and you came to mind."

"Did I?"

"I know your relationship with your mom was difficult," he says. "Hell, *difficult* ain't even the half of it. But you've still lost your mother, and you're allowed to mourn too. Your sisters don't have a monopoly on grief."

I want to dismiss the words, but the comfort I reap from them is too great. I turn to the window so he can't see the tears welling in my eyes. Where was this fatherly warmth when I needed it all those years ago? I shake away the thought. He's playing the good cop, buttering me up, coaxing me into letting my guard down. I won't fall for it. "I appreciate that, sheriff," I say.

"What I want to start with . . . it's nothing nice, I'll be frank. But I think you deserve to know exactly what happened to your mother."

He slides a sheet of paper in front of me before I can ask him to spare me the gory details. The genderless human diagram is riddled with Xs to denote my mother's injuries. The medical jargon is impossible for me to decipher—pulmonary laceration, diaphragmatic rupture?—but I don't ask him to explain for fear of looking stupid.

"Your mother's pattern of injury was consistent with being hit by a car. She suffered blunt force trauma to the head and torso." He points a nicotine-stained finger at the head of the diagram. "Might have been manslaughter, but we're learning toward homicide because her body was transported to the woods and disposed of."

I stare at the coroner's report. Josiah waits for me to speak, but my tongue has turned to stone. No matter what I say, he will manipulate my words and sand down their edges until they fit into the version of the story he has already decided on. I am more fearful now than I was at seventeen when I was handcuffed and Mirandized.

Who better to blame for hitting my mother with a car than me?

Josiah clears his throat. "How long have you been here, Miss Byrd?"

"Since last Sunday."

"And what time did you arrive here, at your friend's trailer?"

Two questions in and my stomach is already pretzeled into the Gordian knot. "Late afternoon."

"Straight here from . . . Kansas City, isn't it?"

"Right."

"You didn't stop anywhere else?" When I shake my head, he sighs. "All right. Let's go back in time a bit, shall we? Let's go back to when you tried to kill your mother."

"I didn't try to kill *her*."

"The charge was reduced to assault with a deadly weapon in the end, sure, but you don't run someone over with a car just to break a few bones."

"I served my time," I say. "What I did was horrible. Unforgivable."

"You know what I always found interesting? After your arrest, you never once said you were sorry. Not a drop of remorse."

"Why aren't you asking me more important things? Like where I was?"

"We'll get there."

"I live ten hours away. I worked every single night that week. You can call my boss, Kiera Geraghty. She knows my shifts to the minute. She'll tell you I was doing my first palm tattoo the night my mother disappeared."

But these facts are of no use to him. His sharp turn from affable to hostile leaves me reeling. "When is the last time you spoke to your mother?"

"My parole hearing."

"Are you sure?"

"I think I would remember otherwise."

"That's what I think too," he says, offering me another piece of paper. "But your mother's phone records show she placed five calls to you the day before she disappeared."

The highlighted phone number is, indeed, my own. "I didn't answer."

"Why wouldn't you answer a call from your long-estranged mother? What if she wanted to reconcile?"

The last question is the one tormenting me. I don't remember the calls because I don't remember my mother's number. I decline calls from unknown numbers as a rule. The *what if?* questions rattle in my mind like dice in a cup. What if she needed me? What if she was in danger? What if she was scared? What if the last thing she wanted to hear was my voice? What if she hadn't forgotten about me after all? With each beat of my heart comes a twinge in my chest, the muscle trying to rend itself in two.

"I didn't know it was her," I say quietly. "But she—Grace told me she gave her my phone number, in case of emergency. She made me Grace's emergency contact at school."

"How do you know this?"

I stop short of mentioning Connor's name. I want to leave as many people out of this quagmire as possible, even if I doubt he would do the same for me. "I was called to her school about a disciplinary matter."

"For an estranged sister, you seem awfully invested in getting Grace out of various, ah, *disciplinary matters*, as you put it."

My eyes drift to the recorder, now completely visible. What I want to say next requires me to bare my soul. *I need my sister to love me.* The thought of my words living forever on tape, a confession of the loneliness I have endured for my entire adult life, will hollow me out, like I must scoop out my insides and display them in a museum for the world to examine. "I'm close by," I manage. "The least I can do is help if she asks for it."

He peppers me with mundane questions then, where I live and what I do for work and where was I on the night of my mother's disappearance. My heartbeat is just beginning to slow when Josiah puts me on the back foot again. "What kind of car do you drive, Providence?"

His gravelly voice curdles my name. "I didn't notice when I pulled in," he elaborates.

"It's the blue Honda out front. Nothing fancy."

"Mind if I take a look at it on my way out?"

"Of course," I say without thinking. Sara is in the other room fuming at my stupidity.

Josiah saunters outside. He shields his eyes from the sun, even though his hat shades his face. He peers through my windows and scrutinizes my front bumper. (Thank God I took care of the damage from an old fender-bender before driving out here.)

And then he raps on the passenger window. "Unlock it for me? Just want a quick look inside."

The gun.

I've forgotten about it. He hasn't.

The dogs charge into the front yard. Sara stands tall on the metal steps to the trailer. "I don't think she will, sheriff."

"I don't believe I've had the pleasure, Miss . . . ?"

"Sara Walking Elk."

"Sara then," he says over the dogs' rancor, his eyes drawn to my glove box like a magnet. "I don't mean no harm. I only want a peek."

"If you want a peek, you can come back with a search warrant," she says.

"In my day, we called this making a mountain out of a molehill." He waits for one of us to crack. A few moments ago, I would have, but Sara has given me enough backbone to hold firm. "All right then. No harm done. I'll come back with a warrant if need be."

"This isn't your jurisdiction," she says. "You'll have to go through my brother if you want to search anything on Long Grass."

"I wouldn't dream of treading on your sovereignty."

She huffs at his sincerity. "You could start by shutting down the Annesville liquor stores. We're a dry reservation. They shouldn't be allowed to sell to us."

"Sara, not now. Please."

My protestation comes too late. She has hijacked the conversation, and it's no longer about me or my mother anymore. She fits her feet into the gaps of the chain-link fence and lifts herself higher than the sheriff. My five-feet-nothing friend turns into a giant. "When else am I going to have his ear?" She turns to Josiah. "It's blood money, sheriff. They kill us to keep the lights on."

"Your quarrel is with the state of Nebraska," Josiah says. "That's far above the authority of the local sheriff."

"We *have* taken it up with the state of Nebraska. What did they say? Wait. Wait through years of bullshit court hearings and bullshit discovery and bullshit deposition. What happens while we wait? We die, and we watch people die."

"I'm not unsympathetic to your plight."

Sara unleashes a long breath. The fence rattles as she drops back to earth. "Hundreds of years of white men telling us what to do, telling us where we can live, where we can go to school, which deities we're allowed to worship, and the first time we ask them for help, they shoo us away. Respectfully, sir? Fuck you."

"She'd be twice the politician Zoe Markham is," he muses once she hauls the dogs back into the trailer.

"Politicians have agendas," I say. "Sara doesn't. She wants people to stop dying."

"We've all seen enough death and misery for one lifetime. It makes you tired."

Josiah shakes my hand goodbye, but holds on to it for an extra beat. With his duties to his badge fulfilled, he eases back into the paternal role he has invented for himself. It is not his job to offer me comfort. I can't understand why he does, and I chalk it up to another underhanded scheme. If he does make good on his promise to return with a warrant, he wants me to remember him as a good guy at heart, someone who showed me kindness in my hour of need. It will soften me up for an interrogation down the line.

"I really am sorry about your mother. I hope you remember the verse I shared with you."

"'Blessed are they that mourn.'"

"They shall be comforted. And so will you."

*　*　*

It takes three drinks to rinse the memory of my mother's maimed foot from my mind. By sundown, I'm too drunk to spell my own name. The Tyre pool hall thrums with life, the diehard Rockies fans replaced today by diehard Nuggets fans transfixed by the NBA draft. My universe has been pared down to noisily racked ivories and vodka sodas burning my throat when I swallow, the hot tang like vomiting in reverse. I whip my head toward the door every time the bell on the handle chimes. It's only a matter of time before my father strides through the door. I'm just plastered enough to pick a fight with him.

As the bartender brings me my next vodka soda, my phone buzzes on the countertop. I keep it face down for a moment, my eyes closed, willing it to be Grace. Same as every time before, it isn't. It's a picture from Margot of my peace lilies, shriveling up and shredding their leaves. I shouldn't laugh, but I do. First my mother, now my plants.

My phone vibrates again, but I see Kiera's name on the screen before I can allow myself a morsel of hope.

"Oh, sweetheart," she says when I answer. "I just heard about your mom. I'm so, so, so sorry."

"Thank you." I hide my drunkenness by using as few words as possible.

"If you need more time, if you need anything at all—"

"Margot killed my peace lilies."

"What?"

I knock back the vodka soda, light on the vodka, in two gulps. I lift up my glass to tell the bartender I'm ready for another. "She sent me a picture. They're dead."

"You're drunk."

"And I'm sad about my plants. Will you buy me new ones?"

"You better not be driving home," Kiera warns. In the background, her son laughs and shrieks. I can feel the jealousy oozing from my pores. For Kiera—for nearly everyone else I know—life marches on unchanged. This time tomorrow, she won't be thinking of me or my mother. "Grief is no excuse to drive drunk," she says.

"I'll promise not to drive home if you promise to buy me new peace lilies."

"Okay. I'll buy you new peace lilies."

The pause between us stretches too long. Even the sounds of the bar cannot make it comfortable. By the time I'm ready to speak again, I have a fresh vodka soda. I squeeze my lemon slice with one hand and watch the juice, pulp, and seeds drip into the glass. I don't care how gross it is. At this point, I'd drink ethanol if it would numb me. "I don't miss her, you know. My mom. My mother. She's dead, and I know it's sad and permanent, but lots of people have dead moms. Is your mom dead?"

"She drank herself to death when I was a kid."

"What was her drink of choice?"

"Whiskey," Kiera says.

"My mother liked gin. Beer too, if we were out of gin. She used to get so drunk she couldn't walk to the bathroom to puke, so she had this blanket on the floor she'd vomit into. My dad always held his liquor better, but he had a blanket he'd piss on so he didn't have to get out of his recliner. The living room always smelled like piss and vomit."

Kiera is quiet for a moment. "My mom was never that bad."

"I found out she was addicted to oxy too. The painkiller?"

"I know what oxy is."

"It's my fault. I broke so many bones when I hit her with the car. She was probably in agony all the time. Suffering. I didn't want her to suffer. God, what a stupid thing to say. Fucking joke, right? *Boo-hoo, I got my mother hooked on painkillers*, okay, Providence, but you tried to kill her, so how bad can you really feel?"

"You've never grieved anyone before, have you?" Kiera asks.

It's imperative that I redirect the conversation before Kiera can plumb the depths of my grief. "Do you miss your mom?" I swallow an ice cube whole. It hurts, but the pain grounds me. I am still here. It feels like I'm disintegrating, the way oceanside cliffs do after being centuries of being battered by waves, but somehow, I'm still here.

"I didn't know her enough to miss her."

"Well, I don't miss my mother."

"I think you do," she says tenderly, "otherwise you wouldn't be drowning your sorrows like this."

"I need to go."

"I mean it, Providence. Call someone. Don't drive home."

People love me. I am lovable.

"Maybe slow down after this one, if you don't mind my saying so." The bartender arranges canned beers like a bouquet in a bucket of ice. It's the same bartender who brought me the stouts from Coach Romanoff and my father. Even while I'm dressed in funeral garb, he cannot help but steal glances at my chest.

"I mind, but only a little bit." After trying and failing half a dozen times to stow my phone in my pocket, I give up and slide it into my bra.

"Did you know her?"

"What?"

He scrambles for the right words. "I mean you're dressed like you're in mourning. For Mrs. Byrd."

I try to down half the vodka soda in one gulp, but my gag reflex betrays me mid-swallow. I manage only a tiny sip and expel the rest back into the glass, where it mixes with my spit to create a cloudy, viscous mixture. "My plants are dying."

"They . . . well, they must have been dear to you?"

"More dear to me than my parents."

He trundles out from behind the bar, beers in tow. The men at a nearby pool table whoop when he approaches them. *Perfect timing, kid!* They aren't worried about dead plants or dead mothers. Their only concerns are what beer to drink and which freakish athlete their basketball team will draft. Again I check my phone and again there is nothing from my sisters.

"So, listen . . ." The bartender's sheepish glance gives away his question before he can even ask. "I wanted to . . . well, I think you're really pretty, and—"

"Where's the bathroom? I'm about to piss myself." My words barely sound like English. They're muted by the thunderous booing as the Knicks announce their pick. I love the time-honored tradition of booing teams from New York. I join in with my own hoots of disapproval. Fuck the Knicks.

He directs me down a dank hallway. I keep my hand on the wall for balance until I'm locked inside the single-occupancy bathroom. The urinal overflows. The mirror above the sink is broken, honeycombed around the edges by missing shards of glass, cracks thin like cobwebs radiating out from the center. Someone has written profanities where the missing glass should be. *SLUT. BITCH. MOTHERFUCKER.* I grab a pen from my purse and write *CUNT* across them all.

I lower the toilet lid and sit. My knees are drawn to my chest in a self-embrace to keep me from toppling onto the grimy floor.

A few minutes ago, I was comfortably drunk, rapturously drunk, delighted to be beyond the tentacles of reality, but the longer I sit, the faster the alcohol catches up with me. That's the problem with drinking. It feels good until it doesn't.

I hold the phone to my ear. I might be too drunk to spell my own name, but I still have enough presence of mind to know that getting behind the wheel right now would be suicide. I call Sara, Zoe, Connor, but no one picks up. I am left with one uneasy ally to call, and of course, he answers on the second ring.

"I wasn't expecting to hear from you tonight."

"Hi, Daniel."

"You sound like you're in a cave."

"I am in a cave." I talk slowly to make myself a fraction more intelligible. "I'm . . . spelunking deep into a cave of abject human misery."

"Spelunking deep into the bottle sounds more like it."

"I need a ride back to Sara's."

"Where are you?"

"Tyre," I say. "The pool hall. I've been admiring the tires of Tyre."

"The what?"

I rest my chin between my knees, but it does little to alleviate the sensation of rocking back and forth like I'm on a boat. "The . . . they collect tires. Tires, from your car. Because the town is called Tyre, get it? Like the city in . . . Lebanon, I think? Somewhere in the Middle East. The birthplace of Fido."

"That was Dido, Providence."

"If you're not going to give me a ride, tell me now so I can go stand on the side of the road with my thumb out."

He allows a few seconds of silence to pass, long enough for me to wallow in embarrassment before throwing me a lifeline. "It'll take me half an hour to get there," he says over jangling keys.

"I won't move a muscle."

*   *   *

To call myself three sheets to the wind is generous. The world is swimming. It barely registers when the pool hall erupts into cheers as the Nuggets announce their pick. The stranger beside me offers a high-five, mistaking my glassy-eyed stare at the television as rapt attention; I miss and nearly break his nose with the heel of my hand. I cheer loudly and yell nonsense at the screen. I bemoan the loss of my peace lilies to everyone within earshot. By the time Daniel escorts me out of the bar, even the bartender is relieved.

In his car, I miss twice before successfully buckling my seatbelt. My words tumble out half-formed, a potter's clay not yet fired in the kiln. "You're the only person who answered my call. Isn't that pathetic?"

"It's a weeknight," he deadpans. "People work."

"*People work*, ooh, aren't you just so down to earth? I have a job, you know. A real one. I pay taxes."

"I never implied otherwise."

"And I have people. I have friends. But most of them aren't here. They're in Kansas City, and I'm here with my dead mother, and . . . I feel very lonely right now. Like I'm on a deserted island."

The road is empty. It isn't quite nine o'clock, but the sidewalks in Tyre have already rolled up. The pool hall is the only building still lit, a lighthouse at the mouth of a blackened sea. Daniel grabs a plastic bag from the back seat in case I need to vomit, which, given the frequency and depth of the potholes we rumble over, seems inevitable.

"I wish I had more people who loved me," I tell him.

"It won't always be this way," he says when we pull onto the highway. In the rearview mirror, Tyre is a ghost town. "You're still young. You'll get married. You'll have kids. You'll be part of a family."

"No one marries felons and I got my tubes removed."

"Sara said you were a lesbian."

"Are you disappointed?"

"You're not my type," he says, like he's rejecting me. As if there's between us anything to reject. "I mention it because if you don't sleep with men, why get your tubes removed?"

"So I don't become the victim of the second immaculate conception."

"Don't be glib."

I roll down my window to invite in the tepid summer night. The fresh air rolls through the car like the nausea through my body. "I got my tubes removed because I don't want kids. Simple. Don't overthink it. I'm sure I look like perfect mother material to you anyway."

"Some people would say you did this to yourself."

"*You* would say I did this to myself."

He shifts in his seat.

"I always thought at some point the world would stop punishing me for what I did to my mother, but every day it . . . I don't know. I never get to move on. You think it ends when you get out of prison, and then you think it ends when you're off parole, but then you realize you can't have the job you want and you can't live in a decent apartment, and forget going to college . . . and then your mom is dead." I say it without thinking. *Mom.* "And then your peace lilies are dying too. What's it all for? Why are we here and what's the meaning of life? There. Now I'm being glib."

"What did you want out of life when you were young?"

"I wanted to be an astronaut."

He narrows his eyes at me, unsure if I'm being a smart-ass or if I'm being genuine.

"If you knew something about my mother . . ." I trail off and whisper the word to myself, committing the movements of my mouth to memory, the way my lips constrict on the *m* and part on the *th*, how the *r* judders in the back of my throat. *Mother*. Not mom. It tastes wrong. Mom is poison. Mom is acid. Mom is a chokecherry pit. *Mother. Mother.* "If you knew something about what happened to her that I didn't, would you tell me?"

"Certain things I can't talk about."

I tense my jaw. "So you do know something."

"Anything I tell you is only half the story. The other half you'll have to get out of Sheriff Eastman."

"I haven't told Sara about the bourbon," I say. "Give me a reason to keep it that way."

He searches my face for any hint that this is my drunken idea of a joke. "Sheriff Eastman is looking into everyone who was at the church the day your mother went missing. There's a couple of landscapers who aren't too keen on talking to police."

"Do you think they know something?"

"No. My guess is they're undocumented and think they'll get deported if they talk to the police."

"And what about my father? Are they still doing a poly . . . the lie detector test?"

"Polygraph," he supplies.

"Yeah, polygraph."

"They are, but don't put too much stock in it. They aren't admissible in court."

"Did you ever find her shoes?"

"Shoes? No. We're not worried about the shoes. Probably dragged off by a coyote. The body is enough."

I retch into the plastic bag, but nothing comes up. The alcohol has coalesced into a lump like a hairball. "Did you know my mother called me? Five times the day before she disappeared."

"From your tone, I'm guessing you didn't pick up."

"Numbers I don't recognize are usually creeps I tattoo. Some of them think you're putting your hands on them for fun, not because they're paying you." I blink a few times, trying to hold on to the thread of conversation. "You have to make sure Josiah really looks into my father, Daniel. My mother—she wouldn't have—the only reason I can think for her to reach out to me is if something was wrong. I mean, really wrong."

"I haven't forgotten what you said."

"Did she feel it when the car hit her?"

"We shouldn't talk about this."

"Tell me," I insist.

But when I see his eyes darken, I don't want him to say the words. His forlorn expression tells me everything. "She didn't die on impact, no."

"What killed her then?"

"Respiratory injuries."

"So she suffocated."

"I would ask the medical examiner. She can—I'm probably getting some of the terminology wrong. The medical terms all get lost in translation."

I wonder if she screamed. I wonder if her lungs allowed her to make any noise at all. I bite my knuckle, bearing down with just enough pressure to make it hurt. "I hope she was high," I say after a long silence. "The oxy would have numbed the pain. Maybe—I know it's a fucked-up way to look at it, but maybe I helped her in that way, you know? She only took the oxy because of what I did to her. Maybe that meant her last moments weren't painful. I don't like the thought of her dying scared."

"One time, years and years ago, I went out on a call about a domestic disturbance. Asshole threatening his wife with a gun. He was quick on the draw, and he shot me in the chest." Daniel brings his hand to the right side of his chest. "I finally understood what the phrase *blinding pain* meant. It was like someone ran a hot poker between my ribs. But when I was lying there on the ground, every time I tried to lift my head, I wanted to put it back down and close my eyes. The pain stopped eventually, and all I wanted to do was sleep."

"But you lived."

"In the end. They rushed me to the hospital, put a tube in my chest, and fished out the bullet. But for a while, lying there, I thought it was over. I would die in that asshole's driveway. Most Lakota people don't think of it as dying. Usually we call it *walking on*, beginning the next part of your journey, and when you think of it that way, it makes death a hell of a lot less scary for most people. It still scared me though. At least it did back then. So when I was lying there with a bullet in my chest, I thought I would die scared. I was at first. But by the time it was really the end—or at least, I thought it was the end, started drifting in and out of consciousness—I wasn't scared at all. Time was slow and the world was quiet. I just wanted to sleep."

"What were you thinking of?"

"My daughter Scarlett's birthday was that weekend," he says. "She was five, finally old enough to have a real birthday party. She had begged me for an ice cream cake. I was hoping her mom would remember to pick it up if I wasn't there to remind her."

"You didn't have your life flash before your eyes, like in the movies?"

"No."

"I hope my mother didn't either," I say quietly. "I hope she drifted away. She was born with nothing and she died with nothing. Her father hit her and her mother, and she grew up to marry a man who hit her and her daughters. The only things she ever liked to do were drink and take pills. I don't think anything in her life ever brought her joy or made her proud."

"You'd be surprised. It's little memories parents cherish most. Everyone has those."

The chokecherry pie. I can see her smiling in the front seat of the car as she passes me the saran-wrapped slice, red berries and filling oozing everywhere, and it is then I can finally feel the absence her death leaves with me. The word *mother* is meaningless to me. Mother is someone I hated. I cannot grieve for my mother, but I can grieve for the woman who brought me pie. That woman, so rarely and ephemerally part of my life, gone just as quickly as she appeared, loved me, and I loved her too.

I do not realize I have tears until they streak down my cheeks. I cry silently until my chest aches from suppressing my sobs. Then I begin to wail.

CHAPTER

14

August 18th

10:55 AM

A**T THE NURSING** home two days later, I am reduced to a teenager once again. Gil beams when I appear in his doorway. He is stationed at his window-side table with the same puzzle and a flaccid tuna fish sandwich. He has plucked out the onions and piled them on a nearby napkin. "Providence! Shouldn't you be in school today?"

"Not today, Mr. Crawford."

He narrows his eyes. "You wouldn't be lying to me, would you?"

"If I am, would you tell my parents?"

"Help me with this blasted puzzle and we'll call it even."

I start to place my purse on the windowsill but quickly reconsider. I leave it strung across my chest, pinning it against my side with an elbow. He has made enough progress on the puzzle for me to recognize the finished result will be a hilly green landscape with a farmhouse and livestock. "Have you seen Connor today?" I ask.

"Busy with baseball," Gil says. "Coach Romanoff wants to move him to the infield, but my boy's better with the bat than the glove. Right field is where he belongs."

"A good bat gets you more scholarships than a good glove." I hope the words reignite memories of how proud he was when Connor earned a baseball scholarship to Purdue—take you to your favorite restaurant to celebrate proud, tears in his eyes proud.

"Ah, don't be so down on yourself. The Truman State scout was eating out of your hand last week. You'll get a scholarship."

"My father says I get it from him. All glove, no bat. I barely hit above the Mendoza line."

Gil tries to cram a piece into the hills, but the pale blue hue tells me it belongs in the sky. He resists my attempts to redirect his hand. He grunts and presses down on the piece with his thumb but cannot achieve the verisimilitude of it fitting.

"Mr. Crawford, when's the last time you saw my mom?"

His stare is equal parts earnest and suspicious. "How do you mean?"

"I just . . . I wondered if you'd bumped into each other." What I really want to know is if Gil can summon forth his last memory of my mother, if it will magically bring her into sharper focus for me.

"At the mailbox."

We lived two streets away from each other. "Are you sure, Mr. Crawford?"

He wets his finger with his tongue as if that will make the puzzle piece fit. "Maybe it was church. Yeah, yeah. She wanted to join the choir. She talked to the new preacher about it. Fella with the tumor in his neck."

It isn't a new memory. It's one from my teenage years. Joining the church choir had been one of my mother's short-lived hobbies undertaken during her periods of sobriety. She tried crochet but gave up halfway through a single sock. She tried drawing but broke all her colored pencils within a week. She tried birdwatching, but my father never allowed her to go further than the end of the street, and there were no birds in our trees because no birds wanted to nest near a house always erupting with shouts and screams. Her failure always drove her back to the bottle. She never even got to audition for the choir. My father forbade it.

"Do you think people are destined to become their parents?" I ask.

He cannot translate the question into digestible words. "Hmm?"

"I mean—do you see my mother in me? My father? Not that I'm going to be an addict or a . . ." None of the words I typically use to describe my father sound right. Lowlife. Monster. Beast. "There's no good in them. There's probably no good in me either. You can't plant a tree in salted soil and expect it to grow."

"Hmm."

"I don't know how I sleep at night," I say, more to myself than to him.

"Black widows eat their mothers. They sleep fine."

"But do they know it's their mother when they eat her?"

He abandons the ill-fitting piece. "Sure they do, but it's nature. Some babies are meant to eat their mothers. Some mothers are meant to eat their young. People don't eat their families—aside from the odd psychopath, I guess—but we take pieces from each other all the same. We cannibalize everyone we love until it's time for someone to cannibalize us."

"Knock, knock!" The chipper voice at the door belongs to Penny. From halfway across the room, I hear her smacking a wad of gum and smell the hot cinnamon on her breath. "Oh! Should I come back a little later? You two look like you're in the middle of something . . . important?"

"The sandwich had onions in it," Gil says.

"You asked for extra."

He covers the onion mound with a napkin as if the very sight is offensive. "No onions. Can't stand the things."

"You have to *tell* them no onions, Mr. Crawford."

"I did."

Penny flashes a tight-lipped smile as she relocates his tray to the dresser. "I'll make sure they look more carefully next time. Until then . . ." She guides him into a wheelchair. His prosthetic leg clanks against the footrest. ". . . we're going to bingo in the common room. Providence, would you like to join him? Mr. Crawford does better when he has a teammate."

"I should probably get—actually, I'd be happy to join. Is it okay—can I use the bathroom in here?"

"Of course. We'll be in the common room." Penny leans in closer to me and takes my hand. She weaves her fingers between mine. "And I'm so sorry about your mom. I know we were never close, but you have my number. When my mom died a few years ago . . . sometimes it helps to talk to someone who knows how it feels."

I count to five after they leave the room and slip into the bathroom, which is more barebones than I expect. No shelves, nooks, or crannies, completely without the ingenious little hiding places I was counting on. The cabinet beneath the sink is my only option. It's deep enough and cluttered enough to be a suitable hiding place.

I take the gun from my purse. I've already emptied the clip and wrapped the firearm in paper towels, fastened by rubber bands around the handle and barrel. I wedge it between the wall and a plastic shelving unit filled with razorblades and single-use flossers.

Come find it now, Josiah.

* * *

I am wandering through the aisles of the grocery store like a lost cruise ship passenger, arms full of off-brand cornflake boxes, when my phone rings.

"You have a call from an individual in custody at the—" The automated female voice is replaced by a garbled recording of Josiah. "—the Tillman County Sheriff's Department." The automated voice returns. "If you wish to accept, please press 1."

The line rings interminably. My imagination fires on all cylinders, jumping from one scenario to the next at breakneck speed until finally I settle on the one that brings me joy. I'm not the type to pray, but I shoot one into the sky anyway. *Please, God, let it be my father. Let it be the old man.*

"You're my one phone call, bitch. Get your ass down here."

"What did you do, Harmony?"

15

August 18th

12:12 PM

WE ARE IN the interrogation room at the sheriff's station. I know these cold, concrete confines. I see this room in my nightmares, where I am trapped like a caged animal and I claw at the walls until blood leaks from beneath my fingernails.

Harmony stretches her hands on the table between us, her wrists bound close in handcuffs. They're too tight on her. They were too tight on me too. By the time they free her, there will be deep, throbbing, red indentations encircled around each of her wrists, and she will keep her hands close together for hours, as if they are still chained.

"I was thinking about how the old man used to lock us in the linen closet after church. Pig."

Her words pull me back into the moment. "I've spent years trying not to think about it."

"It's boarded off. He's literally nailed wooden boards over that door."

"Mostly I think we're lucky he didn't do that while we were in there."

"I've been—" She tosses a glance over her shoulder at the unsubtle one-way mirror, where Josiah and company are no doubt observing us. She leans toward me. "I've been in here for *hours*. I'm so bored. I started to see if I could remember some of the verses he would make us recite in there, but I . . . you must remember some of them. You were always the best at Bible verses. All I remember is how morbid they all were."

"'And cast ye the unprofitable servant into outer darkness: there shall be weeping and gnashing of teeth.'"

"Do you remember one about an unpardonable sin?"

I shake my head.

"I've been turning it over in my head, since I've been *stuck in here for ages*!" Harmony shouts at the mirror. "Is there an unpardonable sin? Is there something so horrible even God can't forgive?"

"Blasphemy, now that I think about it."

She rolls her eyes. She starts to make a grand gesture with her arms, but the handcuffs stop her short, chains quivering with tension. "It can't just be blasphemy. Murder, rape, torture, animal abuse—and God picks blasphemy to be the bridge too far?"

"When are you going to tell me why you're here? How did you even get my number?"

"I like watching you chase your tail."

It is pointless to whisper, but I cling to our final vestige of secrecy. "You didn't kill her."

"You don't know shit, Providence."

"You expect me to believe you can't forgive me for what I did when you did the exact same thing? Why would you still be holding it over my head all these years later?"

"I always was a hypocrite," she says with a shrug.

"Did you get a lawyer?"

"I don't need one. I confessed. It's over. It's done. Best thing you can do for me now is give me pointers for prison."

"Why did you waste your phone call on me?"

"I called you because I need someone to go home and get my meds. I'll start bugging out if I don't have them. The sheriff said someone can bring them for me. I'm sure they'll confiscate it first to make sure it's not cyanide so I don't Eva Braun myself."

"Call your fiancé."

Another eyeroll. She's more nonchalant than Grace during her meeting with the principal, like this is all one big joke and she's waiting for me to finally laugh. "It'd take him forever to get here from Alliance. I couldn't call the old man because I don't trust him to actually bring me my meds, and I couldn't call Grace because she's still a kid. I didn't want to get her involved."

Something isn't right, but under the watchful eye of the sheriff, there is only so much prodding I can do. My gaze falls to her handcuffed wrists. "Where am I going?" I ask.

"I live in the apartments on Nilsen Road. Remember those ugly blue ones? Apartment six. Key's in the flowerpot. My pills are on the dresser in the bedroom. Bring me the Seroquel and the Depakote."

"Fine," I mutter.

"And please, *please*, don't talk to Grace."

"You want her to find out on the evening news?"

"In my ideal world, she never finds out at all. I just fade out of existence and she never has to know."

"She will find out, Harmony," I say.

"I don't want to her to hear it from you."

Her eyes are earnest, waiting for me to promise my silence, but I don't. I am not in the habit of making promises I have no intention to keep.

* * *

A dark, meaty cockroach skitters beneath the refrigerator when I turn the light on. Harmony's apartment is dank and filthy. The curtains probably haven't been pulled back in months. The scent of spoiled food permeates the kitchen, and I cannot tell if it is coming from the refrigerator or the mountain of dishes left in the sink. Her houseplants are all either dead or dying. A cat tree stands in the corner of the living room, its shelves occupied by heaps of dirty clothes and grease-splotched fast food bags, but there is, thank God, no trace of a cat suffering in this hell-hole. Each time I turn on a light, I close my eyes and count to three so any cockroaches will be gone by the time I open them.

In the bedroom, she has left a candle burning atop a copy of a self-help tome, its bookmark scarcely ten pages in. It strikes me as odd that the police haven't beaten me here. But then again, she confessed. They already found our mother's body. Open and shut case. Perhaps they see no reason to turn over her apartment. Then again, the Tillman County sheriff's department has never been lauded for its outstanding detective work. Scotland Yard they are not.

I tiptoe around the room like it's an active crime scene, touching as little as possible. As promised, the pills are on the dresser. They stand beside a picture of Harmony and a man who must be the mystery fiancé—a man I am, quite frankly, surprised to discover exists. They share a kiss in front of a tent and campfire, Harmony's left hand presenting her ring to the camera. There is a tear near the bottom of the picture, like she started to cut him out one day but thought better of it.

Her pill dispenser catches my attention next. Today is Monday, but her pills from Thursday onward are untouched. The oblong pills stare back at me from their clear pockets, a beast with two white eyes and one pink. She has too many pills left in the bottles too. She can't be in her right mind if she's taking her medication this sporadically. One missed antidepressant is enough to make me spiral, give me brain zaps, but these are the heavy hitters of psychiatric medication. I was on Seroquel once upon a time. The psychiatrist thought it might remedy my sleep disturbances. You don't quit an antipsychotic cold turkey unless you want a weekend at an inpatient treatment center. I might know that one from experience.

I sit on the unmade bed before I can worry about bedbugs. I can't make it add up. Say she killed our mother. Say she did so during a psychotic episode, maybe withdrawal-induced, maybe not. Why confess without a lawyer? Why wouldn't she capitalize on the one mitigating factor she has? It isn't like Harmony to fall on her sword out of some warped sense of honor.

Maybe I should let her.

If I really want this to be the end, it can be. This can be my closure. Deep down, I will know it's a lie, but you learn to live with the lies that help you sleep at night. Sometimes peace is more valuable than truth.

Not this time. No. I have to find out what really happened.

I won't let this be the end.

* * *

"Box Butte Fire Department."

I strip Harmony's bed as I talk. I have too much latent energy in my body to sit still. "Hi, this is—I'm looking for my sister's fiancé. I think he works with your fire department."

"Name?"

"My sister is Harmony Byrd."

"You're looking for Cal?"

"Sure."

"Hang on a minute."

We have very different definitions of how long a minute is. By the time someone returns to the phone, I've chewed flecks of skin from four of my knuckles. I wipe the blood on my bare thighs. "You're calling about Harmony?"

"I am."

"Which sister are you?"

"The one who tried to kill our mother."

"Hmm. Heard about you."

I lower myself onto the bed again. "Listen, I'm just calling because I'm worried about Harmony. I don't think she's been taking her medication, and I wanted to see if—"

"Hey, hold on a second. *For God's sake, Mark, I'm on the phone!* Sorry, go on."

"Does she do this a lot? Stop taking her meds?"

Cal's sigh hangs in the air like a storm cloud saturated with rain. "I see she hasn't told you. I . . . Harmony and I aren't together anymore. Haven't been for six months or so."

"She still wears her ring."

"It was my mother's and she won't give it back."

"Sounds like her."

"All due respect, miss, your sister has some real problems. I hope she gets the help she needs, but until then, I don't want nothing to do with her."

"Did she ever talk about our mother?" I ask.

"I don't really want—"

"She's in trouble. I'm trying to help her, and I don't have a lot of options. Believe me, I was mortified to even call you."

My admission of vulnerability is enough for him to let his guard down, just a little. The background noise on his end of the line ebbs and flows. "Mostly she talked about your dad. Your mom came up once in a blue moon. Good things, usually. Only thing I really remember is whenever she was working, she'd make a point to send money to your mom every month. Then, of course, she'd inevitably screw up whatever job she was at after a few months and whine about not having any savings, eventually find a new job, cycle would repeat. She was terrible with money. Blew hundreds of bucks on cigarettes every month. I tried giving her a vape to save her some cash and she threw it away, said it wasn't the same thing. Stubborn. The only person she ever paid reliably was your mom."

"Did she always do that when you were together?"

"All three years."

"Long time to be with someone you said has *real problems*."

"I did love your sister," Cal says. "When she was good, she was good. Nobody's ever made me laugh like Harmony. But she has a lot more bad days than good days. And the meds? She never took 'em regularly."

"Thanks."

"Hey, before you go? Could you try getting the ring for me? I wouldn't care if it was some dumb ring I bought, but my mom gave it to me before she died. She wanted me to have it for the right girl."

"I'll see what I can do," I say.

"For all the nasty things Harmony said about you, you don't seem so terrible."

"I have more bad days than good days."

CHAPTER

16

August 18th

2:46 PM

I CAN'T STOP SEEING it. The inside of the closet. The memory gathers dust in the far-flung recesses of my mind. Some memories I return to frequently because the triggers are impossible to avoid. A crying dog, a police cruiser, footsteps outside of my apartment door. Nothing ever forces me to return to the linen closet. It comes to me now in jolts like flashbang grenades. The single spiral lightbulb flickering overhead. The cold vinyl floor sticking to my skin. The smell of my sisters' breath, stale from two, six, ten hours without water. Baby Grace cocooned in my arms, unleashing deafening cries more beast than child.

Happy shall he be, that taketh and dasheth thy little ones against the rock.

By the time I get back to the sheriff's office, my hands are destroyed. I look like I lost a fight with a barbed wire fence, the skin at my knuckles completely torn away, dried blood smeared down the lengths of my fingers. I've never attacked my hands so viciously before.

The deputy who confiscates Harmony's medication crinkles his pug nose at my hands. "Miss, do you need a bandage?"

"Can I see my sister?"

"Wait here. Sheriff Eastman wants to talk to you."

I start suckling the dried blood from my fingers to clean myself up, but it only adds to my humiliation. The frizzy-haired receptionist gawks at me from across the room. She hovers one hand over her desk phone.

"I'm having a bad day," I say to her before I can stop myself.

"Sure."

"My sister was arrested."

"Okay."

I wait for her to pull her hand away from the phone, to give an indication she sees me as a person and not a nuclear reactor on the brink of a meltdown. "You know—you know, most people would say 'I'm sorry' when someone tells them something like that."

Nothing. She returns to whatever mind-numbing work her computer and her file cabinets have in store, and I focus on the rage frying a hole in my guts, the envy I feel for this ugly woman, her meaningless job, the microscopically small diamond on her wedding band. What has she done to earn this perfectly ordinary existence? The only thing separating me from her are shades of circumstance.

"Miss Byrd?" Josiah pokes his head out of his office. "Back here, whenever you're ready."

I am steps away from his door when the frizzy-haired woman speaks, her eyes glued to her computer screen. "I don't feel sorry for you."

"Excuse me?"

"I've heard about you and your family. I think it's horrible, the things that happened to you. But you could have made something of yourself. You didn't have to end up this way."

"End up what way?"

"Like trash."

My mind churns out a string of insults to kneecap this woman. You're supposed to take the high road, but sometimes you cannot resist the temptation to counter cruelty with more cruelty, like scratching an itch you've been ignoring for hours. If everyone takes the high road, no one gets their comeuppance. Maybe that's what Grace was trying to tell me when she asked why I didn't reprimand the loathsome woman in the principal's office.

I smile at her. "When you die, I hope your husband brings a date to your funeral."

If Josiah overheard our exchange, he doesn't let on. He stands behind his cluttered desk with his arms clasped behind his head. He is without his signature cowboy hat. "Just one question for you. Do you know where your sister's car is?"

"I assumed she would have driven it here."

"No. It's not at her apartment either."

"I have no idea where the car is." It sounds like a lie even though it isn't. More than anything, I wish I had Sara at my side to keep me from putting my foot in my mouth and inadvertently confessing to a crime before the conversation ends.

"It seems like she doesn't either," he says, "which, quite frankly, we're not willing to believe. Riddle me this. You confess to a murder, say you ran the woman over with your car, but you won't tell the police where the car is."

"Sorry, what am I riddling?"

"Does that make sense to you?"

"No. No, it doesn't. But if she isn't taking her medication, she—"

He interrupts me. "If Harmony tells us where the car is, between that and the confession, she could cop a decent plea deal. I'm buddies with the DA. I'd pull some strings."

"Is she not telling you or is she saying she doesn't remember?"

"Doesn't remember. The Indians have been looking all over the reservation. Hell, I've got sheriffs two counties away looking for the car."

"That's what I'm trying to tell you. I talked to her fiancé and Grace, and . . ." The nuances of mental health are not going to work on Josiah, a man from a generation that still sees mental illness as a sign of weakness. I need to sell it. ". . . without her meds, she was absolutely insane. She wouldn't have been in her right mind. She hasn't been taking them regularly, Josiah."

"We need to know where the car is. Bottom line."

Swing and a miss. "She never said anything about it to me."

"Then I need you to see what Harmony will tell you. She won't say anything to us, but she might to you."

"I think you're misremembering how close she and I are," I say.

"Then bring in Grace. Bring in your father. Bring in the fiancé. Hell, bring in twelve drummers drumming and eleven pipers piping for all I care. There's someone out there who can make her talk—and if she won't talk, I might have reason to believe she's lying. Maybe trying to take the heat off someone else."

"Why is this up to me?"

Josiah slides a plug of tobacco behind his lip. "It's not, but if someone can talk some sense into Harmony and spare her life in prison, I think it's a no-brainer. I'd bring Grace down here if I were you."

"I am not dragging Grace into this."

He furrows his brows, trying to make sense of my resistance. "It might just save Harmony's neck."

"She can decide for herself if she wants to be involved. She has a choice."

"Is this your way of trying to protect her?"

"You are the last person in the world who gets to give me advice on how to protect my sisters."

"I always tried to—"

Now it's my turn to cut him off. "To do right by me and my sisters? You'll have to forgive me if I find that hard to believe."

"Providence—"

But I'm already gone. I flip the bird at the frizzy-haired woman on my way out, bloody knuckles bared to the ceiling.

*   *   *

The conversation hangs over our heads like the guillotine's blade as we eat pumpkin ice cream. Grace and I exhaust mundane conversations to stay our execution—things like Bucket the cat, which of my tattoos are yard tattoos, whether Grace should try out for the cheerleading squad. She fills every pause. She knows something terrible is coming, and the moment she allows more than a beat of silence to elapse, her world will be rocked once again. I see the desperate plea each time our eyes meet. *If you love me, please don't do this. Please don't say anything.*

"Do you want a cigarette, Grace?"

She only accepts the offer once she sees we are alone. Since I last gave her a cigarette, she is more polished, crossing the boundary between casual and compulsive smoking. I can tell because she has a style now. She splays her fingers like the legs of a spider, inhales long but exhales short.

"Are you stealing Dad's cigarettes?"

"Ew, no. Why would you ask me that?"

I motion to her cigarette with my own. "Last time you coughed like a cancer patient. You've been practicing."

"Karishma bought me a vape. I lost my last one."

"Don't vape, Grace. They're terrible for you."

"Harmony said the same thing. She made me listen to her rant and rave about how much worse vapes are. Whatever. It's going to destroy my lungs all the same." She rolls her eyes. The cigarette fits perfectly between her gapped front teeth. "When did you start?"

"After prison."

"What was prison like?"

The same way you don't ask someone what they went away for, you don't ask them what it's like inside. I can't hide how much the question offends me. "I don't like to talk about it."

Grace shrinks into herself the way the dog would after my father kicked her. "Sorry."

"No, it's not . . . you don't have to be sorry."

Her eyes twinkle with ghoulish hope that I can be cajoled into divulging the details she seeks. I have those stories, of course. I can tell her about Sara teaching me how to fashion a toothbrush into a shiv my first week inside. I can tell her about being groped by the guards, male and female alike. I can even tell her about the week I spent in solitary for biting another inmate. But those horrors I have left behind. Their aftershocks have faded. It's the little things I can't free myself from.

"The worst part is it's never quiet," I say at last, ignoring how Grace's face falls when she realizes this is all I will give her. She doesn't understand how something so mundane can be so nightmarish. "You never have a second of silence, and then you get out, and you realize the real world is always quiet, but you can't live without the noise anymore."

Grace turns away to hide her disappointment. She still sees me more as a fascination than a sister—a bizarro exhibit in a museum rather than a human being—and when I fail to live up to those expectations, she doesn't know what to respond. I cannot indulge her with prison horror stories right before I tell her about Harmony. It would be unimaginably cruel, crueler than telling her the news itself. I could let her find out another way and relieve myself of this burden, but no one else will talk to her like an adult. They will sugarcoat it or lie about it, and she deserves more. What she decides to do with the information is her choice.

"We have to talk about something, Grace."

She meets my eyes reluctantly. She brings a spoonful of ice cream to her lips but cannot open her mouth. "I could tell."

"I don't . . . I'm going to say it all wrong, and I'm so sorry for that. I'm sorry for a lot of things, but mostly I'm sorry I don't know you and I don't know how to talk to you."

Grace releases a tiny exhale. "Okay?"

"I talked to Harmony a little while ago, and she's . . ." I stop myself from softening the blow with a euphemism. "She's in jail right now."

"Jail? For what?"

"She went to the police this morning and she told them she killed Mom."

"No."

"Grace—"

"No!" She springs to her feet. "No!"

"I'm just telling you what I was told, okay?"

"Don't tell me! Tell them!" She points in no particular direction, punching at the air again and again. "Tell Josiah Eastman that Harmony didn't do anything."

"I—"

The tears come hard and fast like a burst pipe, and she wipes them away with her wrist. When she thinks the valve has shut off, another torrent gushes forth. "What is wrong with you? Why didn't you stand up for her?"

"Because I don't know the truth," I stammer.

"She didn't do it!"

"I think she stopped taking her meds and—"

She cuts me off. "Why won't you listen to me?"

"What do you know that I don't?"

"Harmony would never hurt Mom," she says. "I know it in my bones, Providence. And she wouldn't have—she wouldn't have gone to the searches and faked it. She isn't like that. She can't bullshit anyone, and—and she has mental health problems, okay? She isn't well, but she's not a sociopath."

"Who did it then?"

The question takes her aback. "What?"

"If you don't think she did it, then who did?"

"I don't know."

"Doesn't it make sense if it's Dad?"

The question is a miscalculation. My visceral hatred toward him is something I share only with Harmony. The pain is different when you are no longer consumed by it. It becomes sharper as the years wear on, like a knife dragged across a whetstone a hundred times. I see it as proof of hindsight being twenty-twenty. I know now that my father is a villain, that I was horribly mistreated, that I did not deserve one single night without food or palm to the cheek or hand on my breast, but in the moment, I could always find a way to blame myself. It didn't matter why my imperfections were punished so sadistically: they were still imperfections, and all imperfections were worthy of punishment.

She immobilizes me with a scornful stare. The muscles in her face twitch as she clenches her jaw. "I don't even want to think about that."

"I'm only saying it's the easiest answer."

"The easiest answer is my dad killing my mom?"

I stop myself from saying yes. "Isn't it easier than Harmony doing it?"

Grace stubs out the cigarette in her melting mound of ice cream. Each time she opens her mouth to speak, she snaps it shut again.

"This can all be over," I say, "if we could find a way to show people he did it."

"What happens to me if he goes to prison? I'm a minor. Everyone's dead. We don't have any aunts or uncles or grandparents. Do I end up in foster care?"

"Someone would . . . Harmony would take care of you."

"She can't take care of herself," she whispers.

"I would take care of you then."

She has less confidence in those words than I do. She knows I would be a piss-poor substitute for a family. A feeble nod is her only acknowledgement of the offer before gazing into the distance, watching a young couple unload a horde of children from a minivan. Their triple-wide stroller barrels across the gravel parking lot like a tank. "How did Harmony say she did it?"

"With the car. She won't tell the cops where it is though."

"Because she didn't do it."

"I don't think she can take back a confession, Grace."

"You said she stopped taking her meds, right? She—she's not in her right mind." Her pitch grows higher, her tone more frenetic as she assembles an alibi for Harmony. "You have to tell them that. The last time she stopped taking them, she tried to kill herself. She was talking to herself all the time, and she—I bet they can call her psychiatrist and read all their notes. You have to tell them how much she needs the meds."

"Maybe you should tell them."

"How?"

"We can go to the sheriff's office. Maybe you can talk to Harmony and—"

She shakes her head. "Please don't make me go there."

"I won't make you do anything you don't want to."

"I can't see her. It will break me, Providence."

I reach across the table for her hand, but she ignores me. Another little rejection. I can't take them anymore, and so I suggest the unthinkable to prove my loyalty: "If you ever . . . if you ever wanted Dad to die, you could tell me."

"Then you're no better than him."

"It isn't the same," I insist.

"Violence is still violence."

But he deserves it. But the universe must be a just one. But the universe must mete out punishments to those most deserving. "I know the cops don't help. The neighbors are useless. I'm saying if you needed him to stop forever, I would do it."

I ache for her to say yes, not only because I want to play the hero, but because I need someone else to agree this is the only way our story can end. What is the alternative? For me to return to my meager existence, for my sisters to cobble together what pieces of a normal life they can still salvage, for the old man to die warm in his bed twenty years from now? Don't violent deeds deserve violent consequences?

"By next summer," she says, "I'll be gone. Karishma and I are going to the community college in Scottsbluff together. I can move on."

"You don't move on, Grace. You wake up at three in the morning and suddenly you can't breathe because you remember he's still alive."

She sets her jaw. "I'm not you."

"I—"

"I want to go home. I want to be alone."

*   *   *

I don't want to go home. I don't want to be alone. The cereal boxes I haul into Sara's trailer look like they have survived a tour in Afghanistan, crushed at the corners and bloated with air at the middle, the top of one torn open so I could shovel fistfuls of cornflakes in my mouth as I careened up the road to the reservation. Sara looks up from the couch where she toils away at a shapeless crochet project. "Jesus Christ, you look like you just walked through a minefield."

"I got you more cornflakes."

"I see that," she says slowly, discarding the yarn ball beside her. The shift disturbs Julius, who protests by grumbling and slinking to the tile in front of the back door.

"I didn't want you to think you had to cook for me every morning, and I knew we were out of cereal, so I wanted to buy you cornflakes."

"Why don't you set them on the table and then sit here with me?"

"Did you want cornflakes?" My voice cracks.

"You're freaking me out."

"My sister might have killed my mother."

Sara transfers the boxes into her arms and drops them on the table. Cornflakes sprinkle onto the shag carpet, but neither of us (nor the dogs) move to clean them up. "Tell me what happened."

"Harmony confessed, and it—it can't be her, Sara. I don't think it's her, and I can't let it be her either. It has to be my father."

"Daniel says his alibi checked out."

I spike the open box against the table. More cornflakes come flying out, confetti celebrating my suffering, and it is the final push I need to unravel. A piece of delicate, white flesh peeks out from beneath the shirtsleeve. The tantalizing vein throbs. "Fuck the alibi! I need it to be him."

"It's not him."

"If it's not him, he's never going to be punished. Not for this. Not for anything. He's going to live the rest of his life drunk and happy, and he'll never suffer one single consequence."

"He'll burn in hell," she says.

"I don't believe in hell."

"You have to. It's the only way some people ever get what they deserve."

I lower myself to the floor beside Zenobia. I wrap my arms around her and bury my nose in her dusty fur, the way I did with Annie when I was young. "I want him to die."

"I know."

"No, Sara, I mean—"

"I know exactly what you mean, and that's why I won't let you finish your sentence."

"Grace said it would make me just like him."

Sara shakes her head. "It's not the same thing. It's that if you go back to prison, he wins."

"He can't win if he's dead."

"Providence Byrd, don't."

"I got myself a gun."

"How?"

"Don't ask."

Her eyes simmer white-hot with fury. "If you brought a gun into my house, I swear to God I'll strangle you right now."

"It's not here."

"Where is it?"

"I'm not telling you." I send up a silent prayer that the gun is still safe in its half-assed hiding place. What the hell is nursing home protocol for finding a weapon in someone's room? "If someone comes asking, I don't want you to know."

The answer cools her rage to morbid curiosity. She lights a citronella candle on the windowsill. The mosquitoes will swarm soon. "You came here to kill him. That's why the sheriff wanted to look in your car."

I nod.

"So what stopped you? Why didn't you do it?"

I take too long to respond. Sara flits from window to window lighting the citronella candles. "You didn't really want to, did you? You knew deep down it wouldn't change anything."

"It's not about changing things. If he dies tomorrow, it doesn't undo every horrible thing he's done. But if I kill him, I hold him accountable. He answers for his sins."

"Destroying your life doesn't hold him accountable."

But I am scared my life was already destroyed at age seventeen, and I am scared I'm destined to feel like I'm suffocating until my father finally dies. I can't live like this. It is the sensation I get when I need to bite myself amplified a hundred times over, hot as the glowing coals of a fire, bitter as vinegar.

"I need this feeling to go away," I say quietly.

"Focus on something else. Focus on helping Harmony."

"How?"

Sara stoops down beside Augustus, ruffling the fur between his powerful shoulders. It doesn't rouse him from his deep sleep. His legs twitch like he is dreaming of chasing rabbits through a field. "Finding her a good lawyer, for a start."

CHAPTER

17

August 19ᵗʰ

9:02 AM

As I HURTLE past the state line into Annesville, I spot one news van. There is one more in the Burger King parking lot in Carey Gap. That's it. My dead mother is only worth two news vans. It would hurt less if there were none here at all.

I stare at myself in the rearview mirror, quizzing myself on every question I think an enterprising reporter might ask, from Annie the dog to why I am dressed for the cold in the dead of summer. Eventually, I have been looking into my eyes so long that my pupils morph into tiny oval slits, like a snake, my irises shifting from tawny to pure yellow.

My car rattles as I drift over the center line. A minivan swerves to avoid me, the bleat of its horn echoing between my ears long after it's gone. When I look into my eyes again, I see two round pupils shrinking to pinpricks in the sunshine, the way they should.

I need to escape. I need to be someone other than a woman with a murdered mother, and so I take refuge in the quiet of the nursing home. It is removed from time and space, its own galaxy strung together by the distorted realities of the residents. The worlds they inhabit exist only inside their heads, and like the unsung extras in a Broadway show, the nurses quietly uphold the verisimilitude. The televisions are tuned to game shows and black-and-white movies, the reading material divided between word searches and outdated magazines whose covers promise to divulge the secret to keeping the lushest garden on the block. In the common area, teenaged volunteers lead a game of bingo. Two girls at the front of the room alternate announcing numbers at breakneck speed while a handful more whisk from resident to resident, racing to help them scratch off one number before the next can be called.

Gil has graduated from puzzles to chess. Captured pieces stand at attention alongside the board. I watch from the doorway for a moment as he contemplates his next attack, tapping his fingers against an empty can of 7-Up. When he remembers how to correctly move the knight, my heart skips a beat, and I indulge myself in the naïve hope that the Gil I love is not gone forever—just lost in a fog, ready to emerge at any second.

He dashes that hope when he says my mother's name. "Elissa! You look well. Summer suits you."

He always said that to my mother when they crossed paths. No matter what time of year, no matter how haggard she looked, he would smile and say the season suited her. "You look well too, Gil," I say, and I wonder if anyone has tried to tell him that my mother is dead. Is it crueler to let the illusion continue or to shatter it?

"I'm glad you happened by."

"Do you need a chess partner?"

Gil looks down at the board, his face lax with confusion. He plucks the rook from the queenside corner and closes it in his fist. "I have something to give you."

"My birthday is in May."

"Bah. It's important."

"Gil—"

But now he is on a mission, rummaging through his nightstand drawers like a raccoon through an open dumpster. He tosses items onto the bed and the floor when he realizes they're not what he's looking for. I reach for his elbow and then he yells. "No! No!"

I flinch.

He isn't going to hit me. But I flinch because my body remembers what happened the last time someone yelled at me like that, and the time before, and the time before. I jump backward, out of his reach, and try to catch my breath. He continues narrating his search like nothing happened. He even cracks a joke when he finds his dentures case. I wait for a nurse or a nosy resident to peek into the room, but no one comes. Like always, no one comes.

Finally, Gil finds what he's looking for. He presses a bundle of cash into my hand.

"What is this?"

"It's for Providence," he says.

I leaf through the bills, all hundreds with a few fifties and twenties mixed in. Ten grand, easy, probably a little more. It is an unfathomable amount of money to be holding in my hand. Even after my best days tattooing, I've never had a bundle of cash this thick. "No," I say, shaking my head. "No. No. I can't."

"Even when she gets the softball scholarship, Truman State will still make her pay for the dorms and the food. She shouldn't have to worry about the debt, Elissa. Not for the first year or two anyway. She's still a kid. Let her play softball and have fun."

"You can't give me this much money. What—what about Connor?"

"Connor's taken care of."

I thrust the money toward him, but he slides his hands into his pajama pockets with a sly smile. "Tom would kill me. He'd kill you too," I say. "He won't accept charity."

"Then it's a good thing he doesn't need to know."

"Where did you even get all this cash?"

Gil laughs as he returns to the chessboard. The rook he nabbed is nowhere to be seen. "Nothing untoward, if that's what you're implying." He pauses. "Marjorie had a nest egg. I paid off the house, Connor's got something . . . I wanted to give a little of what's left to Providence."

"I can't take this."

"Please, Elissa. I insist."

I try one more time to give the money back, but he shakes his head and advances the white bishop across the board. I promise Gil I'll be right back and duck out into the parking lot. My hands tremble so intensely I can barely handle my phone. Connor picks up on the first ring.

"Your dad just gave me ten thousand dollars."

"He what?"

"He thinks I'm my mother." I wait for the nurse on her smoke break to go back inside before I continue. "He said it's for me when I go to college. I—I can't take it, Connor."

His exhale crackles on the line. Water runs in the background, followed by the clinking of plates and silverware. "If he wanted you to have it, take it."

"Not under false pretenses. I'm not too proud to turn down money, believe me, but it's a lie. He thinks I'm going to play softball at Truman State. He thinks I'm going to be an astronaut. If he was lucid enough to remember what happened, he'd never give me thousands of dollars."

"The man visited you in prison. He'd still give it to you. He loves you."

"I'm practically robbing him."

"Then think of it as a gift from me," Connor says. "Think of it as my way for saying sorry—for the past, for being a shitty friend, everything."

"You're a teacher in Nebraska. Don't act like you couldn't use ten grand."

"Don't worry about me. Use it for Harmony. Get her a decent lawyer." The water stops. "Are you going to watch the press conference?"

My heart stutters. "What press conference?"

"The sheriff," he says. "You didn't know?"

"Of course not. Why would anyone tell me anything?"

"Shit, I'm sorry. It's about your mom and Harmony. I figured . . ."

"It's fine," I say, even though it isn't. Another cold reminder that while I am a Byrd by blood, I am not a Byrd in spirit. An impenetrable pane of glass separates me from the rest of my family—usually for better, but today for worse. "Could I come to your house to watch it? I don't think I should be alone right now."

"Anything I can do to help," he says quietly.

*   *   *

I refuse to sit on the couch when the press conference finally comes on. The camera is trained on an empty folding table. It boils my blood to think of people settling into their living rooms to consume my mother's tragedy. They think of themselves as bystanders, but they're fiends, nourishing themselves with someone else's suffering. There is nothing Americans love more than butchered women. Nothing captures our imagination so completely.

The Crawfords' house remains remarkably intact, as if my childhood memories have been gouged from my mind and brought to life. The furniture is lumpy and musty, the shag carpet so blue it gives me a headache. His parents' favorite wedding picture, a candid shot of them laughing during a dance, still occupies the place of honor on the mantle. As the story went, Gil's prosthetic started squeaking to the rhythm of the song ("You Make My Dreams," Hall and Oates) as they danced, and after the first chorus, Marjorie dissolved into a fit of giggles. She snorted when she laughed, which in turn made Gil laugh. They were laughing too hard to finish. It was a story they loved to tell together, like comedians rehearsing their favorite skit. At the end, they would share a conspiratorial smile, the two of them the only ones in on the joke, and Gil would kiss Marjorie's cheek.

I see ghosts like this in every corner. I see the alcove where the Christmas tree stood, teeming with so many presents they spilled out beneath Gil's desk and atop Marjorie's piano. I see that same piano too, and if I hold my breath, I hear "Lorena" carrying down the hallway, reverberating from the floors. I smell stargazer lilies in bloom. I feel the notch in the top of my bishop as I slide it across the chessboard, the crenellations atop my rook. The little memories are the ones that eat me alive.

On the TV, a man clears his throat. Josiah and company take their seats. He sits at the center, a deputy on either side, with Daniel relegated to the furthest chair, only half of his face in frame. His all-black uniform makes him stand out from the Nebraska deputies, all outfitted in tan. I feel sorry for him the way you do for someone who arrives at a masquerade party without knowing they needed a mask.

"He does that a lot." I point to the screen as Josiah busies his hands with paperwork. To my disappointment, his hands are steady. No sign of nerves. "He always shuffles his paperwork, like he can't keep still."

The camera pans out to reveal dozens of empty chairs and only four reporters. One of them even looks asleep. Connor told me the conference was closed to the public to prepare me for the possibility of low turnout, but this is worse than I could have imagined. The universe is sending me an unmistakable message: *your mother is not worth anyone's time or resources.* Had my mother been prettier, had she been richer, had she been younger, had she never used drugs, the room would be full of people demanding justice for her murder. Josiah's face falls when he sees the low turnout. He reminds the reporters how personal my mother's tragedy is not just to the community, but to him as well. "I've known the Byrd family for going on forty years now," he says. "Our daughters went to school together."

There is all of one high school in a thirty-mile radius, but never mind that.

"On Sunday, our pastor in Annesville shared a verse from Psalms I think we all needed to hear. 'The Lord is near to the brokenhearted and saves those who are crushed in spirit.'"

"Always with the Bible verses," I mutter. "He recited one of the beatitudes to me when he was done questioning me."

"Man of faith," Connor says.

"Only when it suits him."

As Josiah reconstructs the timeline of my mother's murder and disappearance, I notice the tobacco in his lower gums, protruding like a tumor. The microphone picks up the viscid sound of him swallowing. Again and again, his mouth clots with saliva and he has nowhere to spit. He pretends to sneeze into a handkerchief as the floor opens to questions.

Connor turns to me, a question he hesitates to ask on the tip of his tongue. "Do you think she did it?"

"I don't like stories when they're too perfect."

"Parallel, maybe. Not perfect."

The piano bench, weakened by years of disuse, creaks as I sit down on it. I bump the keys with my elbow and drown Josiah out with the strident melody. "You don't think it's too perfect? One sister tries and fails to kill her mother, and then thirteen years later, the other one tries and succeeds?" My sigh does nothing to relieve tension. My body is a screw tightened one twist too far. "I think she's not in her right mind. Even if she did, it was an accident. I don't think she's a murderer."

"Is it just a feeling?"

"I did time with a couple murderers. You can tell. There's a void in their eyes."

One reporter asks how thin the search for my mother has stretched the department and if a budget raise should be considered in the next election. When I look at Connor, his face is tight with disappointment. Clearly I have given him the wrong answer. He never liked Harmony, always suspected something was wrong with her.

"Do I have a void in my eyes?" I ask, long after the moment passes. I angle my face toward him so he can examine my soul, appraise it like a jeweler does a precious gem.

"No."

"You didn't even look."

He dismisses my question as a childish distraction. "I know what your eyes look like, Providence."

Cold, flat, dark. Like a snake. I imagine them transforming again.

Another reporter speaks. "How closely did your department look into the oldest daughter, given her history of violence?"

"We are confident Providence was not involved in her mother's death." When the reporter starts to talk again, Josiah cuts him off. "No, no, let me be more clear. We definitely ruled her out very early in the investigation. I'd like to remind everyone that regardless of the past, now she's a young woman grieving the loss of her mother. I hope you all keep her in your prayers, same way you do with the rest of the Byrd family."

The exoneration borders on theatrical. It is his good deed for the day, announcing my innocence to the world and reminding them of my humanity.

I want to be grateful, but I'm not that big of a person.

CHAPTER

18

August 19th

9:40 PM

The unanswered questions buzz through my head, loud and hideous like June bugs. Why won't Harmony tell the police where the car is? Does she know where it is at all? Who was the first to suspect that my mother was missing? How long did they take to report her absence to the police? And where, where, *where* are the shoes? I can't get them out of my mind. A dozen cops combed the woods for hours, but somehow the shoes eluded them.

Killers like to keep trophies—locks of hair, severed body parts, mouthfuls of teeth. A pair of cheap shoes wouldn't be the sexiest souvenir, lower risk but also lower reward, but it might scratch the same itch.

When I tell Sara we need to search my father's liquor store, a devilish smile splits across her face. She grabs her keys from the coffee table, swings open the front door, and gestures grandly to the threshold. "After you, my lady."

So here we are, parked in the parking lot of the abandoned post office, steeling ourselves for the crime we are about to commit—or, more accurately, *I* am steeling myself. Sara jitters with anticipation like a prize racehorse at the starting gate. She assures me we have nothing to worry about: this is Annesville, after all. The liquor stores here get broken into every other week.

"There's witnesses everywhere," I say. Lining the sidewalks are the local drunks, the homeless people with nowhere else to go.

"I have cash. We give them twenty bucks, they won't say shit—and besides, do you really think they want the cops to show up?"

"Fuck, this was a bad idea."

To my surprise, Sara nods. "I haven't felt this much adrenaline since the last time I stole a car. I forgot how addictive it is."

I committed a crime of passion, but Sara committed crimes of adrenaline—*crimes*, plural, because she had stolen more than a dozen cars before she was finally caught. She targeted junkers and jalopies, cars that wouldn't exceed the value threshold for her crime to escalate from a misdemeanor to a felony. The first time she fucked up was her first time stealing a car on the Nebraska side of the state line. Dirty and beat-up on the outside, nothing to write home about, the Volvo boasted thousands of dollars in custom engine modifications. The owner used it to street race down in Scottsbluff. Class IIA felony, same as me. Our sentences were identical.

Hot air billows through the car when she opens her door. Unlike the last few nights, there has been no relief from the heat after sunset today. I steal the claw clip from Sara's cupholder and twist my hair into a pathetic excuse for a bun to keep it off my damp neck.

"And you're sure we can just waltz right in? The door won't be locked?"

"I know where he keeps the spare key," I say as we start walking.

"That was years ago."

"He hasn't moved his recliner since then. I can't imagine he'd move the spare key."

Most of the men (all of them are men—not a single woman among them) on the sidewalk ignore us or nod politely when we pass. They slump against the cinderblock wall in sweat-soaked shirts, beer cans and whiskey handles at their sides, passing the hours with games of cards, dice, and dominoes. The only man who bothers us is squat and curly-haired, holding a cloudy-eyed chihuahua in his arms. He thinks his vulgar comments about my body will shock me, but they won't. I've heard them all before.

On his wrist is a tattoo of five dots. I gesture to it. "How long were you away?"

"A nickel," he says. Five years.

"Me too," I reply.

"Yeah? What for?"

"Aggravated assault."

I lift the hem of my shirt just enough to show him my quincunx tattoo, tucked beneath my ribs, right where you might try to shank me. Four dots to signify the prison walls, a single dot in the middle to represent the prisoner. Kiera's offered to cover it for years, but I'm too fond of it. Baby's first ink. I traded a whole book of stamps for it.

A tenuous understanding emerges between me and the man with the chihuahua: we are part of the same terrible club. He spits into the gutter and staggers toward the men playing dice. The dog yips at me and Sara or, more likely, at nothing at all, just the void of its blind eyes.

We round the corner and slip into the narrow, lightless alleyway between the liquor stores and the auto repair shop's junkyard. There is someone snoring in a sleeping bag and someone masturbating furiously near the dumpsters, but otherwise, we're alone. I grab the metal rod leaned up against the wall, which is just long enough to extend above the awning over my father's door. I flail blindly for a while before I hear metal grating against metal, then yank the pole back toward me. The keys fall into the weeds without a sound.

I was with my father one day, maybe eleven or twelve years old, when he retrieved his spare keys from atop the awning. I can't remember why I tagged along with him to the liquor store that day. He pressed a finger over his lips and *shh*'d me as he poked around the awning with the metal rod, and the gesture filled me with treacherous warmth because it was the first time my father had asked me to keep a secret that didn't involve hurting me. By then I was old enough that my fear of him was beginning to calcify to hatred, but not old enough to resist my biological hardwiring. Part of me still remained hungry for him to love me in the innocent, wholesome way other fathers loved their daughters.

"It's the opposite of hiding the keys under the doormat, butterfly," he said when he finally got the keys. "Out of sight, out of mind."

"You really can't teach an old dog new tricks," Sara says as I ease the key into the lock. I expected it to resist, as if it could somehow sense that I was an intruder, but the door glides on its hinges like they're buttered. We steal into the storeroom, nothing but boxes of liquor and old paperwork piled high on the wobbly desk shoved against the wall. A box fan hums in the corner. "I wish we could burn this fucking place down," she says.

"I am not going away for arson."

"Let me dream, okay?" she whispers. "What are we looking for?"

"I'll know it when I see it."

"Explain for those of us who won't know it when they see it."

"Her shoes, her jewelry, anything that looks like it belonged to her. Some piece of her that he has no business having." I let out a heavy sigh. "Sara, I know you said his alibi is solid, but I need to make sure it isn't him."

"I'll take the storeroom if you want the register."

She wants the storeroom so she can rummage through my father's paperwork, but I don't force the issue. We keep the lights off to maintain what little secrecy we have; the slivers of moonlight lancing between the blinds will have to be enough.

It resembles every other liquor store I've been in, snack aisles in the middle and liquor aisles on the fringes, tiny shot-sized bottles of liquor filling the endcaps. I consider drinking one but think better of it when I remember Sara is only ten feet away. Cigarettes are locked up behind the cabinet (locked in the most literal sense of the word, with a heavy chain and padlock strung around the glass cabinet). Between shelving units drilled into the walls are glossy posters of women in bikinis eating burgers, women in bikinis posing on monster trucks, and women in bikinis with crisp American flags cloaking their shoulders. The posters make me queasier than the mothball-mixed-with-piss odor in the air.

The cash register is locked, but every other drawer is ripe for the picking. I comb through colorful lotto scratchers and crumpled receipts, old to-do lists and fast food burger wrappers. Two bullet casings rattle around the bottommost drawer, but I don't let myself get excited by the discovery. My mother wasn't shot. Some other poor bastard was. Mitesh Jadhav.

In the end, I find nothing to connect my father to my mother. I find something much worse instead.

Hidden in the shadows behind the cash register, thumbtacked beneath a calendar of swimsuit models, are three pictures I've never seen before. Left to right: me, Harmony, Grace. We're all frozen at sixteen or seventeen, not quite girls and not quite women, posed in front of the gnarled oak tree in the backyard. The hemlines of our dresses ride high. Our dark hair waterfalls over our shoulders in tight, springy curls. It would be less violating to be one of the women in the calendar.

The memory bubbles to the surface, my hair sizzling as my mother wraps it around her curling iron. The pink babydoll dress I've been instructed to wear belonged to my mother once upon a time. It was designed for a narrow, lean body. With my curves, it looks obscene. My mother pauses after every lock of hair to sip her drink and swallows her ice cubes whole. "Just a few pictures," she says. "It'll make your father happy. It'll be over like that." She punctuates her sentence with a snap and a smile.

A fourth picture has fallen to the floor. My mother. My mother at sixteen, wearing the same pink dress, smoothing the fabric over her modest baby bump. Radiant and sun-soaked, she smiles at her unborn baby. She vows that they will share a lifetime of unquenchable love, but this promise, like all her promises, is too easily broken. There will be gin bottles strewn throughout the house, blankets stained by bodily fluids, doorless bedrooms, and broken cheekbones. There will be a car pitched into reverse on a tepid March morning before church. There will never, ever be enough love.

My father may not have been the one to end my mother's life, but he killed her all the same. The happy girl in this photo died a long time ago.

It is not sadness that envelopes me then but rage. The emotions are more alike than you think, sharp at their edges and black at their cores. The difference lies in how long you can tolerate them. Sadness will live inside of you forever, but rage demands to be acted upon to its fullest, most terrifying extent.

* * *

Our search, just like every search for my mother's body, yields no helpful clues. We've come full circle.

Once we're back on the reservation, I ask Sara to make a pit stop at her brother's trailer.

"Please don't tell me you and him are buddy-buddy now," she grumbles as we turn off the main road. We jostle violently over a pothole. "That would put me in a coma."

"I'm thinking maybe he can tell me something I don't know yet. He's the closest thing I have to a friend in law enforcement."

Five minutes later, we pull up to his trailer. I'm relieved to see the front porch empty and curious how I failed to notice the snowflake-shaped Christmas lights strung along the eaves last time I was here. Sara starts to get out of the car with me, but I shake my head. "I want to go alone," I tell her, "in case I need to charm him."

"For my sake, don't elaborate."

I'm perfectly happy to let her believe I'm talking about flirtation instead of blackmail. I promise to be back in a few minutes and jog to Daniel's front door.

He answers the door with that same *WORLD'S BEST DAD* mug in hand, which he hurriedly sets on the end table. "Most people call before showing up at someone's house." Then more quietly, a plea, "My daughter is here, Providence."

"I can hear you talking about me."

Defeated, Daniel invites me inside. The trailer screams *bachelor pad* with its movie posters on the walls (he is apparently the world's biggest fan of *No Country for Old Men,* with not one, not two, but three iterations of Javier Bardem staring blankly across the living room) and cheap, mismatched furniture.

A teenage girl with fuchsia-streaked hair paints her nails on the couch. She is thin and ungainly, her limbs stretched like taffy. She blows on her nails before toggling her fingers at me in a bashful wave.

"Scarlett, this is Aunt Sara's friend, Providence. Providence, this is my daughter Scarlett."

Scarlett's smile reveals two rows of fluorescent orange braces. "I really like your name."

"I like yours too."

"My dad doesn't like it," she says. "Apparently my mom went rogue when she filled out the birth certificate. They were supposed to name me Lauren."

"We're divorced," Daniel explains.

I have to get this conversation back on the rails. I'm dangerously close to getting the entire verbal family tree. "It's nice to get to know you better, but I need to talk to you alone. It's about my mother."

Daniel motions for me to follow him down the hallway. I boil with jealousy at the wholesome pictures on his walls: him cradling Scarlett as a baby, him with Scarlett on his shoulders in front of the elephant exhibit at a zoo, him holding Scarlett's tiny hand as she's dressed in a bumblebee costume for Halloween.

I hesitate infinitesimally at the threshold of his bedroom but step forward anyway. Involuntary response. My brain can't help but short-circuit at a man inviting me into his bedroom, unable to interpret it as anything other than a fly hurtling toward a spider's web. The air in here is antiseptic with alcohol. Coffee mugs everywhere. The bed is unmade.

"I want to see the files you have on my mom."

"Sheriff Eastman is—"

I interrupt him with a sharp shake of my head. "I know you must have something. Please, Daniel."

"I can't share confidential documents with you just because you're my sister's friend."

"Please don't force my hand."

"Providence, I don't know what you think—"

I tap my nails on the handle of an abandoned mug. "I think you went to rehab once upon a time, which means you're not just having a few drinks on the down-low. You're an alcoholic. I think your sister would never recover if I told her you were drinking again. I think . . ." The next hit is below the belt, so cruel I almost let my sentence fizzle without launching this final barb, but I came here on a mission. I refuse to be derailed by imprudent pangs of sympathy. "I think you have a daughter you should consider. Scarlett must remember you going to rehab. I bet it'd crush her to see you do it again."

His face remains steady, handsome features turned to stone, but his eyes betray the fury churning beneath his stoic surface. "Fuck you."

"Don't play chicken with me, Daniel. You'll lose every single time."

"You want the files?" He yanks the drawer of his nightstand so hard that the handle pops off. He keeps the handle squeezed tight in his fist, knuckles whitening, veins in his forearms bulging obscenely. "Here. You can have them if it means I never have to see your face again."

The fat manila folder thrust into my arms is bound shut with rubber bands: *BYRD, E.—HOMICIDE (COPIES)*. I look at the treasure trove in my hands and swallow my budding guilt. I have the vague sense that my mother would be disappointed in me for doing this.

"And Providence? Don't you dare say my daughter's name again."

* * *

The documents cover my air mattress. Copies of everything. Copies of interview transcripts, copies of handwritten notes, copies of every report from every database my mother was entered into, copies of pictures taken throughout the years, copies of the medical examiner's report, copies of copies of copies clipped together like a Russian nesting doll. Once I start, I cannot stop.

I find the original missing report. It was logged by a deputy whose name I don't recognize, but his signature is alongside Josiah's at the bottom of the paper. It reveals nothing new. My mother was last seen leaving Bible study. She arrived on foot. She was wearing a long blue dress with white polka dots, white kitten heels with a plastic ribbon on the toes, and a rose gold

crucifix. All of this I already know, but the three lines conclud-
ing the report, thoughtless data entry to the deputy who typed
this up, send a chill down my spine.

   *LAST KNOWN CONTACT: THURSDAY, AUGUST 6TH,
APPROX. 7:30PM*
   REPORT ENTERED: AUGUST 7TH, 5:48PM
   REPORTING PARTY: GRACE BYRD
   Grace.

CHAPTER

19

August 20th

1:14 PM

GRACE WAITS FOR me beneath the chokecherry tree on the lot with the burnt-down house. The branches sag with bunches of glossy purple fruit, bruises against the brilliant blue sky. My favorite thing about chokecherries is that there is no universal rule as to when they are ripe. It varies tree to tree and bush to bush. Some are ready to be picked as soon as they deepen from green to red, but others must blacken before they are ready to be eaten. It's a prosaic mystery, but one I always found delight in.

My mother knew every chokecherry tree in Annesville, which ones could be harvested at red, purple, and black. It's why her pie always tasted so heavenly. When she shared the recipe with Grace, she must have imparted her knowledge of the fruit too, and as I look at my sister, my stomach cramps with envy for the secret my mother entrusted her with.

Perhaps that's what my mother thought about as she was dying. *At least someone else knows about the chokecherry trees.* It was her pearl of wisdom, the only thing she could pass down to her daughters.

"Is it ripe?"

Grace looks up from her phone and into the crown of the tree. Sunlight falls to her face in jagged golden pieces. "These ones are," she says, taking a quick pull from her vape. "Big and purple, like they should be."

I pluck a tangle of chokecherries from the tree. The bunch is round and thick like a Christmas ornament. When I bring the first berry to my lips, Grace shrieks and scrambles to her feet. "What are you doing?"

"I've only eaten a slice of toast today."

She bats the chokecherries to the ground. Her face is stark white. "They have cyanide in them! They'll kill you if you eat them raw!"

I can't contain my laughter. "It's just the pits, Grace. You can spit them out."

"But . . ."

"That's why Mom always made us pit them when she baked a pie."

She shakes her head. "She told me you can't eat them raw at all. If you did, they'd poison you and you would choke. That's why they're called chokecherries."

I was sixteen. My mother was sober. Juice squirted into my eye while I was pitting the chokecherries, and as I flushed my eye in the kitchen sink, I started crying because I was sure I would go blind. "If the raw ones can kill me," I said between sobs, "then I'm sure the juice will make me go blind." She cupped her hands around my face and asked me to open my eyes. She said, "They won't really kill you, Providence. I told you that when you were little so you wouldn't choke on the pits."

"So they're not dangerous?"

"No."

"But they're called chokecherries."

"That's my favorite thing about them," she said. "They sound like they'll kill you, but they're harmless."

So, to dispel the myth for Grace now, I say the same thing: "They sound like they'll kill you, but they're harmless, Grace." I try to channel my mother's cadence—the fanciful rhythm to her words, her voice airy as if she had been relieved of a grave burden—but it falls flat.

Grace rolls her eyes. "What a stupid thing to lie about," she says.

"She didn't want us to choke on the pits."

"The pits are, like, the size of a pea."

Now the recollection has been soured for both of us, an eye for an eye, another happy memory of our mother ground to dust. Grace's dress pools around her as she lowers herself to the earth again. She holds the chokecherry bunch in her hand like Snow White with her apple, the stems and berries lacing between her fingers. "What did you need to talk about?" She utters the question in a single breath. I pretend like she isn't eager to get away from me. "Dad'll be home for lunch soon."

I think about my mother showing Grace which trees have ripe fruit. I think about them harvesting bunches of chokecherries with wicker picnic baskets. I think about them painstakingly extracting the pits, holding their breath because they are nervous about wasting too much good fruit.

"Why did you wait to report her missing?"

Exactly as I feared, I see the wheels in her head spinning, plotting out her next move. "I'm sorry, what?"

"You waited a whole day. Why?"

"Sometimes she just didn't come home. I didn't think anything of it."

"She always came home. She wasn't even allowed to leave overnight for funerals."

Grace does her best to meet my stare, but the confidence rings hollow, no more real than a little girl trying on her mother's high heels for the first time and thinking she's finally a grown-up. "Well, things have changed," she manages.

"Grace, please. If you know something, tell me."

"What are you accusing me of?"

"Lying," I fire back.

"I didn't do anything! I talked to the cops. I talked to them a hundred times."

"She always came home. He wouldn't give an inch on that." Every time I try to say *Dad*, my tongue loses its way.

She pulps the chokecherries in her hand. The juices trickle down her forearm in rivulets. She squeezes, squeezes, squeezes until the berries are no longer berries, only purple paste oozing between her fingers. "I didn't do anything."

"Then tell me why you waited."

Flies are drawn to the sweet fruit remnants. Two of them buzz around her in erratic circles, their flight noiseless and weak as if they will die without this meal. "Because she was running away."

"She never would have run away."

"You didn't know her as well as you think, Providence."

I am a believer in the classic truism that people do not change. They might evolve around the edges, but who they are at their core will always remain the same, constant as the sun rising in the east. My mother was never one to upset the status quo. Decades married to our father instilled in her that the only way to survive was to be seen and not heard, shrinking yourself as small as you can possibly be. After all these years forcing herself to be small, what finally made her drum up the courage to leave my father?

Courage. The word has teeth I don't expect. Whatever courage my mother mustered, it was only enough for her, not her and Grace both. Grace is the girl forever left behind, drawing love from wells that have long ago run dry. We were born in the wrong order. It should have been Grace first, so the sister who deserved the most love would have been given the most love.

"How do you know she ran away?"

"She told me," Grace says, voice cracking, "not when or where, but that she was going to. She made boxes for Harmony and I to remember her by, just little trinkets and birthday cards, nothing special. Harmony didn't even care. She thought Mom was getting rid of old keepsakes from the attic. When she didn't come home, I figured she finally decided to do it. I didn't worry." She pulls her knees to her chest. "She told me she would call when she got to Rapid City. There's a women's shelter there. So I waited. And then she didn't call. A whole day went by, and I knew something was wrong."

She snivels and begins to tremble, and although my duty here is to comfort her, my mind snags on the wrong thing. Grace and Harmony got boxes. Grace and Harmony got goodbyes. I didn't even get a voicemail. My mother opened her mouth to speak to me and died before she could say a single word.

"Was there a box for me?"

"I—I don't know. She didn't show one to me." The answer is *no* and she is too kind to say it. *No* will cleave me in two.

"Is that really everything, Grace?"

"It's everything."

"Because if—"

She cuts me off. "I swear on Mom's ashes. There's nothing else."

"Did you tell the cops she ran away?"

"No, but it's because I've heard on all the podcasts—literally every single one I listen to, I swear—they don't look for run-aways," she says. "It's not illegal to run away, so the cops care less. I thought if I told them, they wouldn't look hard enough. They would think, *well, there goes another local drunk*, and close the case."

As I join her on the ground, her head heavy against my shoulder, her hand clammy in my own, I speculate about

Harmony. If she found out our mother was running away, maybe she felt betrayed, and maybe the natural response to such an inconceivable blow to the psyche is an equally inconceivable crime. We forget what a mortal wound it is to be forsaken by someone whose blood you share, a person whose existence is inseparable from your own, bound to you by cosmic divination rather than choice. You exist within them and they within you. They echo through your marrow eternally.

In my mind's eye, I answer my mother's phone call. She says, *Stop haunting me, Providence*, and then she hangs up. I call her back again and again, but the number has been disconnected. Instead of my mother's voice, there is only a dial tone.

Grace turns to me with a drawn mouth. It's the first time I have been close enough to see the faint freckles spattered across her nose and cheeks. I see so much of myself in her that I want to apologize. I hope her resemblance to me does not condemn her to a similarly doomed life. We come from the same parents, from the same home, share the same appearance—and can a rosebush ever grow any flower but a rose?

"I need to go home." Grace uses the tree trunk to pull herself to her feet. She dusts the dirt and twigs from her dress, but nothing can be done about the chokecherry stains. "If I'm not there when Dad gets back . . ."

"You don't have to explain."

"I know."

As she takes her first steps back to the house, my heart catches in my throat. "Grace, wait."

"What is it?"

"Can I give you a hug?"

The smallest of smiles warms her face. "Of course. I love hugs."

It is the first time in years a hug has brought me joy. She hugs me tighter than I expect, and once I steady my breathing, I surrender wholly to the embrace. I never want to let go.

She speaks into my shoulder, her voice a half whisper. Maybe she doesn't want me to hear it, but I do. "I wish it was you here instead of Harmony."

* * *

At the sheriff's office, I anticipate resistance when I ask to see Harmony, but the deputy smiles, nods, and guides me to the shoebox-like visitation room without a word. I'm relieved not to be in the interrogation room again. I never spent time in the visitation room because no one came to visit before my sentencing, except the overworked public defender in such a rush to see me before the day ended she forgot her purse at the jail in Alliance and couldn't go more than two minutes without mentioning it. "It was Louis Vuitton," she said, "brand new, leather." She wanted me to thank her for the valiant sacrifice. I never did.

Harmony's jumpsuit is candy apple red. The way she shuffles into the room makes me think she is cuffed at the ankles too, but no, only the wrists. "I'm touched," she says as she takes her seat across the metal table. "I thought you'd have run back home and long forgotten me by now." She walks her index and middle fingers across the table.

"Sorry to disappoint."

"Bite me," she says. "I was being genuine."

"Even when you're sincere, you sound like you hate me."

Her hands are cuffed just far enough apart for her to crack her neck, a motion she makes with enough speed and force to sever her spinal cord. She allows her head to loll forward and rotates in a semicircle from shoulder to shoulder. Her vertebrae never stop crackling. "You want something," she says. "What is it?"

From here on out, I have to tread with caution. I'm certain our conversation is being monitored somehow, and I can't let it slip that Grace withheld information from the police, even if those details have ceased to be relevant. Odds are, no one is going to bring down the hammer and charge her with obstruction, but I need to keep her as far from the fray as possible.

"Have you been up to the attic lately?"

"Oh, all the time. Weekly seances and everything. Summoning our dead grandma from the urn on the mantle. She says hi, by the way."

It's not a question of Harmony being smart enough to realize I'm speaking in code, but whether she is shrewd enough to understand why I need her to play along. "I was thinking about it the other day," I say. "I'm sure all of our old keepsakes are up there."

"Yeah, like the old man's favorite belt to hit us with."

"His favorite Bible to preach fire and brimstone from."

Her laugh singes the air. "King James Version."

"Do you think Mom would ever give us any of the old shit?"

"She cleaned out the attic a few weeks ago. Spring cleaning in the summer. You know how she was. She gave me a box."

"Something to remember her by?"

"No. Just old school projects, birthday cards, so on. I guess it was nice she cared enough to keep it. I always thought she threw it away." She pauses and stares at me, an actress waiting for her scene partner to remember their lines. "I had a feeling she was cleaning things out. She had a box for Grace too."

So she knew our mother was making a break for it. No one told her, but she put two and two together. "Was there a box for me?"

"I don't think so, but honestly, what did you expect? You tried to kill her. If she had nothing to give you, nothing to say to you, that's her right."

I push a knuckle into my mouth, my teeth grazing a healing scab. A crust of flesh falls beneath my tongue. "She called me five times the day she died. She had something to say."

"It doesn't matter now. She's dead."

I return to my mind's eye. When I answer the phone this time, my mother says, *I'm going to die, Providence. Are you happy? You always wanted a dead mother.* Then the dial tone.

"Easy for you to say. You got closure."

"You're barking up the wrong tree for sympathy." Harmony releases the loose bun atop her head. Her hair is so greasy it looks damp. "I have my own shit to worry about. My arraignment is tomorrow."

"Are you pleading guilty?"

"Depends what my lawyer says. Depends if the DA offers me a good deal."

"Don't plead guilty until they've given you a deal. They'll work with you if you tell them where the car is."

She curls her fingers without quite making a fist, like a witch preparing to cast a spell. "Oh, my God, stop asking me about the car!"

"You either don't know where it is, which means you confessed for kicks, or you really don't remember, which means you weren't in your right mind and that's your defense."

"Where'd you go to law school, again?"

"Harmony—"

"You want to talk about doing things for kicks? How about meddling in my life? Pretending like you give one single fuck about what happens to me?"

The door swings open, and the affable deputy who escorted me to the visitation room peers in. We straighten up immediately, like we used to when our father caught us digging into dinner without saying grace first. "Yelling usually means trouble. We good in here?"

"Peachy keen," Harmony retorts, oblivious to the deputy's concern being for my safety, not hers. He only leaves the room once I nod.

Alone again, I try a new approach. "I don't think you grasp what is going to happen to you."

"I did a stint in the county jail. I'm not Mary Poppins."

"The county jail is not in the same dimension as the prison in York."

"How naïve do you think I am?"

"Did you know there are no mirrors in prison? There's polished metal you can just about see yourself in if you squint. I forgot what I looked like by the time I got out. And as much as you change, the world changes without you. It took me months to figure out how to work the new cell phones. There was a new president. All my favorite TV shows were over. And you forget you have choices in your life. The first time I had a real cheeseburger when I got out, I cried. I literally sat there in a crappy diner in Grand Island, and I cried into this overcooked hockey puck of a burger. I could put whatever I wanted on it. I had such little control over anything for five years that putting mustard on a cheeseburger brought me to tears. And I'm telling you the little things, Harmony. That's not being sucker-punched in the yard, or being groped in the shower, or having pages torn out of a book you're reading during a search just because a guard thought it would be funny to torment you, or spending a week in solitary and having people slide food through a slot on the floor like you're an animal."

I can't tell if my soliloquy is cruel or merciful, if I am giving it for her benefit or mine. It's the most I've ever talked about prison outside of therapy. Harmony chews on her fingernails until the skin around her nailbeds turns red. Eventually, she peels her eyes away from me to stare vacantly at the floor, perhaps immersing herself in the nightmare I have thrust upon her.

"If you have any sense at all, tell them where the car is."

"What if I really don't remember, Providence? Have you considered that possibility?"

Her face is inscrutable. I cannot distinguish sincerity from vitriol. Every word she says is laced with venom. She could make the classifieds drip with sourness. "Then tell them what they need to hear. Tell them about the meds. Tell them you lied about your fiancé. Tell—"

"Did you call Cal?"

"Jesus Christ, Harmony, you are so far from the point."

"No, this is exactly the point: you meddling again, galloping in with your stupid, misguided savior complex." She rips the engagement ring from her finger and stows it in her bra. "And if Cal fed you some sob story about the ring being his mother's, it's a lie. He bought it at a Kay Jewelers in Omaha. I was there."

"I don't give a fuck about the ring," I snap. "Where is the car?"

"Don't worry your Botoxed little head about it."

"Harmony, please."

She yells for the deputy. He whisks her out of the room, down the short hallway to the cells. I shout at her one last time before she makes the turn.

"Where is the goddamn car?"

20

August 21ˢᵗ

7:46 AM

THERE IS A lottery for spectators to get into the courtroom. The line weaves around the courthouse and into the parking lot it shares with the local drugstore, each person clutching their ticket like they're hoping to tour Willy Wonka's chocolate factory, not watch an arraignment that will last all of five minutes. I can tell they're all locals. The press may not be interested in my mother's death, but the people of Tillman County are.

The courthouse is a blocky brick building. Local folklore credits God himself with its construction in the late nineteenth century. The bricklayers ran out of bricks before they could finish the walls, and to complicate matters further, all the fuel stockpiled for the kiln had washed away in a thunderstorm. Dejected, defeated, staring down the black throat of winter, the bricklayers went to sleep in their tents beside the unfinished building—but when they woke the next morning, conveniently Easter Sunday, they saw threefold the bricks they needed to finish the courthouse.

The miracle inspired them to build the second story. (God may have rested on the seventh day when he created the earth, but on the seventh day in Tillman County, he produced bricks out of thin air.) While everyone agrees on this facet of the story, there are no records as to when the marble statue of Lady Justice—blindfolded, armed with her scales and sword—was placed in front of the courthouse doors.

"Did I ever tell you the roof started leaking during my arraignment?"

Sara and I are waiting at the crosswalk. We parked almost half a mile away, and the kitten heels she let me borrow pinch my toes with every step. I've borrowed yet another dress from her, this one tea length, long-sleeved, and the same shade of rich blue you see on the rooftops of houses in Greece. This morning, I'd been paralyzed thinking of how precisely to make myself presentable not just for the courtroom, but for onlookers who would recognize me and the reporters who might take my picture. Sara took charge and styled me, and though I now look like the wife of a youth pastor, I am grateful to have one less distraction to contend with.

"You never mentioned it," I say.

"Water started dripping onto the stand. It was a few drops at first, but by the end, it was coming down so hard it splashed the judge in the face." Sara smiles up at the overcast sky, as if to thank the clouds for their cooperation. "Maybe the same thing'll happen for Harmony."

"God willing."

"Are you okay? You look pale."

I shake my head as we cross the street. "I'm going to puke."

"Let's sit for a second," she says.

"I don't want to be late."

"We've got time. You don't want to vomit while she's making her plea." Sara steers me toward a bus stop bench, occupied at one end by a woman reading a romance book with a shirtless, chiseled man on the front. She wedges a plastic bag of groceries between herself and Sara. "Talk me through it. What are you thinking?"

"You've heard the phrase 'crossing the Rubicon'?"

"My dog is named Julius."

I want to chuckle, but the most I can muster is a sharp exhale through my nose. "My father used to say it. We're going to go in there and she's going to cross the Rubicon. She can't come back from whatever she does here."

"Did she say how she'd plead?"

The woman leans closer, still pretending to flip through her book.

"No," I say.

"She likes to keep people guessing, doesn't she?"

"She's always had a flair for the dramatic."

A leathery hand gropes my shoulder. I jump like I've received an electric shock. My father has never looked this sophisticated, not even in the pictures I've seen of my parents' wedding. His salt-and-pepper hair is slicked back, heavy with pomade, and his oxford button-up is free of wrinkles and creases. To anyone who doesn't know him, Tom Byrd looks like an average man, and his averageness will be captured in photos, disseminated to people who cannot fathom the evil beating inside. They will sympathize with him as an ordinary person caught in the crossfire of larger-than-life tragedies, trapped in a waking nightmare. *First his daughter*, they will say, mouths agape, *then his wife, and now his other daughter?*

"Fancy seeing you here, butterfly."

Grace peeks out from behind my father's shadow like a mouse snared in a trap. The sleeves of her plum-colored shirt flutter in the wind. One hand grips the hem, pulling the fabric down to keep it from riding up and exposing her midriff. A familiar crucifix necklace adorns her neck. I recognize Jesus's tarnished body lashed to a rose gold cross, the crown of thorns upon his bowed head. Our mother's necklace.

"But Mom," I say, ten years old, as we walk out of church, "what about the two thieves crucified next to Jesus? Why don't we make jewelry for them too?"

My father notices me staring at the necklace. He caresses our savior with his thumb, his other fingers relaxing on Grace's collarbone. Her skin revolts against his touch by turning crimson beneath his calloused fingertips. "Your sister looks beautiful in rose gold, doesn't she? I think it brings out her eyes."

"That was Harmony's favorite necklace."

"Harmony has enough jewelry. You've seen the rock on her finger." He focuses on Sara, who has not yet faced him. She busies herself with a cigarette. The smell, somehow, does not drive the eavesdropper away. "And who is your friend here?"

"I'm Sara Walking Elk. You don't know me, but I know you."

"And how's that?"

She angles her head enough for him to see her profile. She refuses to do the courtesy of meeting him in the eyes or shaking his outreached hand. "You make your blood money selling liquor to my tribe."

"As long as their money's green, I don't turn 'em away. Just trying to make an honest buck."

"You should come to Long Grass sometime, Tom. You can see what your honest buck looks like from our side."

He rubs the back of his neck and smirks. "All due respect, I can see you've got an axe to grind. Your quarrel isn't with me."

"You're exactly who my quarrel is with."

"How is it you know my daughter?"

"I shared a cell with her."

This is the last straw for the woman with the romance novel. She drops her book in her purse and hurries down the street, grocery bags swinging from her arms like wrecking balls. In the distance, the clouds swell and darken with rain.

"Then you'll forgive me if I'm a little hesitant to take morality lessons from a criminal."

"From what I hear, you're no paragon of virtue yourself."

I trifle with the hem of my dress so no one can see me cringe. Sara is using ammunition that is not her own, my pain dimmed so hers can shine brighter. When I'm in my father's presence, I like to pretend none of it ever happened. I don't want him to have the satisfaction of knowing he still haunts me.

My father's hand returns to my shoulder. "I want us to go in there together, butterfly, all three of us. Harmony needs us to be a united front."

"I'm sitting with Sara."

"She's not your family."

Sara starts to say something, but I drive my elbow between her ribs before she can toss another match into the fray. "I'm not sitting with you," I say.

"Gracie and I insist, butterfly."

They will pack us into the courtroom seats like cattle into the slaughterhouse chute, not an inch of space between us. An entire side of my body will press against my father's, and I will leave the courtroom smelling like his aftershave. I will scrub my shoulder raw where he touched me. I want to slough off every inch of my skin at the thought.

"You should go," I say at last. "I'll see you when I get in there."

"Stubborn as an ox, like your mother used to say."

"She said you should go." Sara tries to take my hand, but I recoil.

Grace starts toward the courthouse, but my father won't leave until he launches his Parthian shot. "She'd be disappointed in you. You never gave her one goddamn thing to be proud of."

"She's dead. She doesn't give a shit anymore."

"Don't speak to me that way about your mother."

A lightning bolt streaks through me. I leap to my feet. "She's dead! She can't be disappointed in me anymore because she's dead. I never loved her and she never loved me, and I will talk about her whatever fucking way I want because I have the right. I have the right to hate her and I have the right to grieve her. You can't take any of that away from me."

I picture every word as a physical blow, hooks and jabs and uppercuts, because the high I get from losing my temper in front of him is almost as gratifying as a real punch. He says nothing, only smirks. He takes Grace by the arm and pulls her down the sidewalk. Just as the crowd absorbs them, Grace's shirt lifts to reveal a bruise unfurling across her hip, dark like necrosis.

"Good for you." Sara stands close to me, her hands opened awkwardly like she suspects I'm going to chase after them and she'll need to pinion me. "Good for you. He deserved that, and you deserved the catharsis." The encounter with my father has given her a taste of what she has craved for so long, like a parched desert traveler offered a tiny sip of water. She bounces on her toes in hopes of seeing them in the crowd. "Are you ready to go?" she asks.

"I'm not. But I can pretend to be."

* * *

I tell security that Sara is my wife. I even hold her hand and kiss her cheek to sell it. I can't tell if he knows I'm lying, or if the repulsion plain on his face is from the idea of two women "tainting" the definition of holy matrimony. Regardless, he allows us in.

The courtroom is too full. The bailiff escorts a dozen people out before the proceedings begin because they've exceeded the fire marshal's maximum capacity. The unnatural crowdedness reminds me of the way church pews fill up at Easter and Christmas but never for a regular Sunday service in March.

I scour the room for familiar faces. My father and Grace are two rows in front of us. I can see him talking to nearby neighbors, accepting condolences, yucking it up for the few local reporters on the other side of the aisle. Smile and smile and be a villain—isn't that Shakespeare? His arm rests behind Grace's head. He smooths her hair and pretends he does not know about her gruesome bruise. By an inexplicable divine error, Coach Romanoff won one of the lottery seats. He at least has the decency not to grin about it. There is no Zoe, no Connor, no Gil, the latter of whom I didn't remotely expect to see, but whose presence would have put me at ease.

Sara waggles a stick of gum beneath my nose. The peppermint stings my nostrils. "Peppermint is good for nausea. Take it."

"I'm fine."

"You keep gagging."

"All rise. The Tillman County District Court is now in session."

It's not the same judge who sentenced me. This is a heavyset, middle-aged woman whose glasses hang from a bejeweled retainer around her neck and bounce against her chest with every step. The box-dyed blonde hair suggests a mother, but the gray roots sprouting from her part suggest a grandmother. Though she pretends not to see the small press gaggle at the back of the room, she strikes her gavel for their attention. Her role in their stories, however significant, is small. She is part of the supporting cast. If she gives them a bit of spice, hams it up, offers them something to remember her by, she might even see her name printed on the front page.

Her voice sounds artificially deepened, like she has lowered it an octave for dramatic effect. "This is the case of *People of the State of Nebraska v. Harmony Byrd . . .*"

I fade in and out as the judge talks. There isn't a flicker of emotion from Harmony. She looks as pretty as one can while incarcerated, where makeup is scarce and restful sleep a distant memory. Clean hair transforms her into a different person. To me though, the engagement ring, somehow polished to a sheen, is what attracts the most attention. She props her hands on the table and tilts the left until her marquise diamond catches the light, as if to ask how bad can she really be if someone wanted to marry her.

I can't picture her sauntering down the aisle in white, a man awaiting her at the altar. She would find the flowers wasteful, the dress gaudy, and the vows cheesy. Even as a young girl, she never saw the beauty and romance in playing dress-up.

The judge races through a prescribed list of questions: name, date of birth, ability to understand the English language, when she was arrested.

"Are you currently under the influence of drugs or alcohol?"

"Seroquel and Depakote."

Some of the crowd recognize the medication names and titter. The rest exchange appalled glances, certain they have just been introduced to a new strain of marijuana.

The public defender (the same woman who defended me—the gaudy Louis Vuitton purse gives her away) brings her manicured fingers to her temples. "She misunderstood the question, Your Honor. Those are prescription medications."

Harmony can't help but be pleased with herself, getting a joke off right beneath the judge's nose, upstaging her on her own turf. She purses her lips to hide a smile.

"Are you under the influence of any *illegal* drugs or alcohol?"

"No, ma'am. Sorry—Your Honor, I mean."

The judge glares at Harmony over the rim of her glasses. "The grand jury has charged that on or about August sixth of the current year, you—Harmony Byrd, the defendant—used a deadly weapon—that is, a vehicle—to incapacitate and ultimately end the life of Elissa Valerie Byrd, and later used said vehicle to transport Elissa Byrd's body to a remote location on the Long Grass Indian Reservation for disposal. The charges against you are murder in the second degree and unlawful disposal of human remains. If tried and convicted of these charges, you may be sentenced to life in prison."

When my mother was murdered, she was a person. When she was disposed of, she was human remains. There is a purgatory between those two acts, the desolate drive through the reservation, when she was both.

"Do you understand the charges as I have read them to you?"

"Yes, Your Honor."

"How do you plead?"

Harmony soaks up her last moment in the limelight. She draws her shoulders up when she inhales, down when she exhales, a runner on the track waiting for the starting gun to fire. "Not guilty, Your Honor."

All the air escapes my lungs, another layer to the susurrus filling the courtroom. My father locks his hands behind his head. I want to see his face, if he is angry or relieved. Regardless of what he feels, he doesn't share it with Grace. Instead, he claps a hand on the shoulder of the anonymous man beside him, a decidedly masculine gesture of affection. Probably a drinking buddy who will commiserate with him over stouts at the pool hall.

The plea blindsides the everyone, but no one more than Harmony's lawyer. They exchange words shielded by hands around their mouths. I glean a sliver of satisfaction from having known Harmony might plead not guilty before her own lawyer did—more than a sliver when I consider that I was the one who persuaded her. For the first time in my adult life, I've done something a big sister is supposed to do. We're supposed to be the guiding lights for our little sisters, their shoulders to cry on, their older and wiser confidants, and I don't have to remind anyone how spectacularly I have failed to live up to those expectations. I steered Harmony away from suffering and protected her from danger. Finally, *finally*, I've gotten it right, and even if I get it wrong for the rest of my life, I have at least tasted redemption today.

The judge sets Harmony's bail at half a million dollars. She ends the session with another righteous rap of the gavel. Grace shoots me a pointed look as she hurries out of the courtroom, and I know to follow her. We have minutes, maybe even seconds, before my father whisks her away.

In the bathroom, she blots her tears with paper towels, running the sink behind her to drown out her sniffles and snorts. "I'm crying because I'm relieved," she says before I can speak. "Now there's a chance. I—oh God, I can finally breathe."

"I saw the bruise on your hip."

"This isn't about me. I'm fine."

I crank the knob of another sink and check over my shoulder to make sure we're still alone. "I meant what I said, Grace. He deserves to die."

"You don't get it! You're just like him if you do that. You think your motive makes it just, or pure, or right, but it's violence all the same. We've had enough violence for one lifetime."

"The motive is exactly what makes it different. It's why we can fry serial killers in the electric chair and then have a good night's sleep afterward. Deep down we know it's right. Some people don't deserve to walk the earth."

Grace clenches her eyes shut. "Maybe you could sleep at night, but we're not all you."

"You don't sleep at night as it is. You lie awake for hours and you hold your breath and you pray you don't hear him walking down the hall." I pause. "Don't you wish he was dead?"

"Of course I do! I wish it every day! I want to walk into the living room and see him slumped over on his recliner, clutching his chest."

"It's no different than what I want to do."

She grips the counter, rocking back and forth on the balls of her feet. A pregnant woman comes through the door, but, sensing the gravity of our conversation, immediately turns to leave.

"It's not on your conscience, Grace. It's on mine. It would finally be over—for you, for me, for Harmony, even for Mom. It's not over until he's dead."

"You don't need to kill him," she whispers.

"Then I'll take you back to Missouri with me."

"I wish I could, but I can't—I can't—" She rips another fistful of paper towels from the dispenser and buries her face in them. Makeup streaks across her face like the erratic brushstrokes of an abstract painting. "I'm not your responsibility. I can't ask you to rearrange your whole life for me. It's not fair to you."

"You can't stay here, Grace. I know I'm late, okay? I should have tried to connect with you years ago, and I'm so sorry I never did. I thought it was better if I stayed far away from you. I was always trouble. Nothing good ever came from being around me."

"Providence . . ."

"It's late, but it's not too late," I plead. "Grace, please. Come to Missouri."

"He'll never let me leave."

"Maybe he's finally tired of it all. Maybe he just wants to have the house to himself so he can get drunk in peace. Maybe everything with Mom, with Harmony—maybe I could make him see reason."

"Reason with him? You can't reason with the devil."

Women stream through the door before I can reply. One recognizes us and offers condolences, rubbing her hands between our shoulders like we are colicky babies to be soothed.

Grace flees the bathroom before I can say goodbye.

*   *   *

The rain is steady like a drumbeat all the way to the reservation. The roads are slick. We nearly fishtail at the state line, one brake pump away from belting off the highway and through the grainy picture of Mount Rushmore on the *Welcome to South Dakota!* roadside sign, Teddy Roosevelt's woolly mustache the last earthly thing we see.

Sara preens in the visor mirror, wiping away mascara flakes and smoothing flyaways made frizzy from the rain. Her septum piercing is crooked, but she leaves that imperfection as is. "I can't tell if you're not talking because you're sad," she says, gripping the handle above the window as we come to a stop, "or you're concentrating on the road."

"I'm not a good driver."

"Tell me how you're feeling."

Instead of ruminating on my encounter with Grace, I've been replaying Sara's conversation with my father in my head, the recollection growing hazier and more distorted with each recitation, like a tongue twister you've attempted too many times. I want to tell her she hurt me, but I also don't want to explain why such an insignificant remark, one I'm sure she doesn't remember, meant so much. The longer I'm here, the more I crave a return to my regular life, where I pretend to be a fatherless daughter everywhere except the four walls of my therapist's office. I wanted him to know I pretended like he was dead. I had hoped it inflicted a psychic wound upon him, an agony he could not escape but could also never place. Now, he can pinpoint exactly where the pain comes from, and he knows it isn't real.

A homeless woman pushes a shopping cart across the intersection. The seconds click by with only the pattering of rain to keep us from silence. I want to hurt Sara the same way she hurt me.

"Your brother is drinking."

The noise Sara makes is a cross between a laugh and a gasp. "What do you mean?"

"Bourbon in his coffee."

"I don't think you know what you're talking about."

The homeless woman muscles the shopping cart over the curb and onto the sidewalk. I drive above the limit so we can get back to the trailer and I can hide from the fallout of this conversation. I can't help but be relieved to finally throw this secret from my back. "I'm sorry I didn't tell you sooner."

Sara's face is taut. Her breath strains through her lips in tense, controlled breaths. The emotional relief delivered by my spiteful remark is eclipsed almost immediately by shame, like when you make yourself vomit after a night of drinking to stave off a hangover, only to still feel like death warmed over the morning after.

I pull into the driveway and leave the wipers on high. They squeal against the windshield as the rain lightens. "How long have you known?" Sara stares straight ahead.

"Not long," I say.

"How long?"

"A few days."

She flips her visor up. My clip-on air freshener falls to the floor from the disturbance. She pins the plastic, daisy-shaped holder beneath the toe of her shoe and takes it hostage. "So why didn't you tell me?"

"He was willing to tell me about my mother's case if I didn't say anything."

"So your pain matters more than my pain."

"It wasn't like that."

She brings the full force of her shoe down on the air freshener. The holder cracks like an eggshell. "I don't see what else it was like."

"It was about protecting you too. I didn't want you to hate him, Sara. I know how you feel about alcohol, and when you told me about him going to rehab, how you stopped speaking to him, I thought it'd ruin your relationship if you found out he was doing it again. I thought about you ending up like me, estranged from my sisters, and I just . . . I didn't want that to happen to you. It's horrible."

"You know what would really ruin my relationship with Daniel? Him dying."

I try to meet her eyes, but she refuses. "I'm so sorry, Sara."

"Did you know you're like a sister to me, Providence? I will never have the same relationship with anyone else that I have with you—and I love you, you dumb, selfish bitch. You've been through horrible things, okay? I have too. We've both experienced enough trauma for a dozen lifetimes. So we look out for number one, right? It's how we survive. But the difference is, I know sometimes I need to put other people first, and you are so used to looking out for yourself that you can't put anyone else first."

The words are etched into my bones, branded into my skin, with one bigger and bolder than all the rest. *Selfish.* My first instinct is to refute the epithet, tell her what I said to Grace in the courthouse bathroom, but then my mother's voice knells through my head. *Most people call a spade a spade, Providence,* she says as she pours a splash of gin into her water bottle, *and even if they're just being mean, there's usually a grain of truth in it.*

I don't know if it's a memory or a figment, but I cling to it all the same. It is already washing away like kelp pulled back into the ocean by the tide, the same as all my recollections of my mother, doomed to fade with time.

"I'm not kicking you out, because I know you don't have anywhere else to go, but I need space." She looks at me from the corner of her eye. "*I love you.* But I can't even look at you right now."

"I love you too, Sara."

"I wish you'd learn a better way to show it."

Her phone lights up. Her dark eyes tick-tock back and forth as she reads.

"Is everything okay?" I ask.

"Speak of the devil." She shows me the text, Daniel's name on the screen. "Harmony gave up the ghost on the car. It's on the reservation."

* * *

I idle outside the trailer for hours, waiting for a text, a phone call, a news alert, a carrier pigeon, *some kind of update.* I watch the sun burn off the clouds and then I watch it dip below the horizon and then I watch the sky turn deep blue, speckled with stars like crushed velvet. The mosquitoes feast on my bare legs. I smack one as it attacks the skin around my moth tattoo, so ferociously that when I examine my palm, there is no longer any trace of its existence beyond a smear of blood.

Citronella candles appear on the windowsills. Sara came outside to bring me an ashtray a few hours ago, which I mistook for a peace offering, but has otherwise left me to frantically pace in silence. The dogs have taken her side in the fight and ignored me all day.

My hands are raw from so much wringing, my face warm from a sunburn, my bare feet blackened from dirt. One more lap around the trailer, I tell myself, just to burn off more anxious energy, then I'll go inside and pack my things. I'll find a motel to stay at for a night or two, and maybe once—

I shriek when my phone buzzes. I nearly fumble it out of my hands twice. "Hello?"

Josiah needs no introduction. The wet mouthful of tobacco is enough. "Providence? Sheriff Eastman here. I, ah . . . well, I can't tell you too much, but I wanted you to know we found Harmony's car up on the reservation."

He tells me about the unmarked dirt road, the copse of dead trees (charred by a brushfire, he adds) in which the car had been concealed. It was almost forty miles away from where my mother's body had been found.

"Was there anything in the car? My mother's shoes?"

"Just Harmony's personal effects. Mints, a vape, a scone covered in mold. The front of the car was mangled like she hit something."

"A vape?"

Karishma gave me a vape. I lost my last one.

My stomach lurches into my ribs, my heart into my throat. Suddenly, I can feel every part of my body. I feel my bones straining against my skin. I feel my teeth rooted in my gums. I feel every blood vessel and every nerve ending catching fire.

"Providence? You still there?"

I am grateful beyond words that the sheriff cannot see my face right now. "Yes. Yes, I'm here. It's—I'm—sorry, I wish I could stop stuttering."

"I know it's a lot to take in."

"Did she take the plea deal?"

"Fifteen years, possibility for parole after ten. Plead down to manslaughter."

"She's going to prison."

"She's going to prison," he echoes.

"Maybe I should be relieved."

"I would be."

What sweet relief it would be for all of it to be over. For Josiah, it is. Case closed. Car recovered. Plea deal signed. Confession affirmed. Sentence handed down.

But it's all a lie. A giant fucking lie.

I run inside for my purse and my keys. Sara is in the bedroom with her door shut, sparing me the further pain of telling her what's happened. I will combust if I have to explain myself to anyone. I beg myself to wait until I'm in the car before I really put the pieces together and draw the terrible conclusion I am careening toward.

I only have one sister who vapes.

It's not Harmony.

21

August 21st

8:52 PM

"GO HOME, BUTTERFLY. You're not welcome here."
"I want to see Grace."

My father throws his empty beer bottle into the front yard. I can barely hear him over the television. *Top of the order for the Rockies as we head to the eleventh inning . . .* The light flickers through the sheer curtains. There are beers on the coffee table and a bag of Doritos on his recliner. "I said go home."

"It's an emergency."

"I don't give a shit."

"Grace!" I call into the house. "Grace!"

He shoves me back. I scrape my leg against the splintered wooden railing as I tumble down the steps, my full weight crashing against my hip as I hit the earth. My leg looks like it's been fed through a shredder. Dried grass and dirt stick to the blood. The pain is enough to double me over, but I scramble to my feet anyway. He will always have the physical advantage, but I will always have more willpower.

"I saw the bruise you left on her."

"You don't know what you saw," he says. "Get off my property. Get out of Annesville. Go home. You wore out your welcome ages ago. Next time I see you skulking around my house, I'll shoot you like a dog. If I hear about you talking to Grace again, manipulating her with your bullshit, trying to turn her against me, I'll shoot you both."

"Not if I shoot you first."

"Oh, butterfly. I'd like to see you try."

*   *   *

Mitesh Jadhav answers the door with a shotgun. The skin on his neck reminds me of a shriveled fruit peel. A perfectly round scar the size of a nickel marks the spot where the bullet flared through him. He assesses my disheveled state and lowers the gun, but doesn't put it away.

"Little late to be knocking on doors unannounced, Providence." He is one of few people who can make my name sound pretty. His accent softens its syllables.

"I'm sorry, Mr. Jadhav. It's—" I gesture broadly at myself to acknowledge that I am aware how unhinged I look. My hair is matted from the rain, and my leg is still bleeding, and I am barefoot, and my feet are black from dirt. "It's an emergency. I wanted to talk to Karishma."

"About what?"

"Grace."

He finally sets the shotgun down. "I don't want my daughter dragged into any trouble."

"I don't either."

Mitesh shakes his head and massages his bullet wound, as if to remind me the mere existence of my family means trouble. "You've been through a lot—you and Grace both—in the last few days, and I'm sorry for all of it, but I don't want Karishma involved."

"Mr. Jadhav, please. I'm trying to look out for Grace. I wanted to ask Karishma if she could keep an eye on her at school. She's taken everything so hard, and I need to know someone is looking out for her."

He sniffs out my lie immediately. "I'll pass that along."

"I'll only take a minute."

"Good night—and again, I'm sorry about your mother."

I idle on the front porch after he shuts the door like an abandoned pet hoping their owner will have a change of heart, sure if I wait long enough and seem desperate enough he will relent, but my hope amounts to nothing. I get back in the car, turn on the engine, and scream until my throat is raw and my ears are ringing.

*   *   *

There's only one place for me to go. Only one place I want to go. One person I want to be with. When she picks up my call, the crush of relief is so immense that it floods my eyes with tears.

My phone routes me south to Carey Gap, then east for a few miles along Route 20, the night black as pine tar and the highway apocalyptically desolate. I peel onto an unmarked dirt driveway. There is no name or address number posted on the mailbox, but there is a red-and-white sign warning me that trespassers will be shot and survivors will be shot again.

Towering hackberry trees line the driveway. My car trundles forward until the trees part to reveal a jute-colored Queen Anne house, three stories tall with a circular tower reaching up from the front corner of the house. The perimeter is awash in porch lights to atone for the darkness of the driveway.

My first thought: Clutter family. If someone fires a shotgun on the prairie and no one is around to hear it, did anyone fire a shotgun at all?

I bury the morbid image as soon as she steps onto the porch. I don't want to entertain a universe in which Zoe could suffer such a fate. Even dressed for bed, she still takes my breath away. Dewy skin. Milkmaid braids. Pillowy lips, sticky with balm. She offers a one-armed hug before inviting me inside.

The interior exudes Victorian glamour with its botanical wallpaper, dark wood molding, and heavy velvet curtains—and while I find it charming, I also can't dispel the feeling that I am appallingly out of place here, a pigeon among peacocks. Zoe escorts me into a parlor room with stained glass windows. A chandelier twinkles from the rosette sculpted into the ceiling. We sit on chaise lounges opposite each other, and as I settle into the cream-colored upholstery, I have the humbling thought that this piece of furniture probably costs more than my rent.

Zoe appraises my appearance thoughtfully, like an art collector who suspects a forgery, her mismatched eyes inscrutable until they reach the dried blood crusted on my calf. They pop open wide enough to fall out on stalks. "Sweet Christmas, Providence, let me get you a washcloth."

"It's not as bad as it looks."

"Don't be silly."

Zoe disappears down the hallway, returning a minute later with a handful of damp rags and pouches of alcohol wipes. I reach for her supplies, but she shakes her head and sits on the hardwood floor. She wraps her hand in a rag and, slowly, gently, with the care my mother should have tended my wounds with, wipes away my bloodstains. The wound itself looks like something left behind from the jaws of a rabid animal, with half a dozen shallow, ragged cuts surrounding one that runs longer and deeper than the rest. The shallow ones must have been the splinters. The deep one, I can only assume, was from a nail. It missed my solar system tattoo by centimeters.

My dress is also ripped along the hem. Something else I've ruined for Sara.

She doesn't warn me before the alcohol wipe. I inhale through my teeth and yank my leg away. "Jesus, Zoe!"

"It hurts less if you don't know it's coming."

"Debatable."

"Give me your leg again."

I do. I curl my nails into the cushion when she reapplies the alcohol wipe. "Aren't you going to ask me what happened?"

"I can put two and two together."

"He wouldn't let me see Grace."

"Of course not," she says. "How can he have iron-fisted control over her if he lets her have a relationship with someone who escaped that house?"

"I need to talk to her. I have this feeling—" I stop myself. It would unburden me to share my fear with someone else, but the stakes are too high. This is not Grace withholding details from the police. This is not a minor infraction or a well-meaning hiccup. This is catastrophic, and no one else can know, at least not until I'm sure.

"You have what feeling?"

"Nothing," I tell her. "The usual horrible feelings I have when I think about my father."

Zoe pastes bandage after bandage over my wounds, and when she's done and she goes to the kitchen to wash her hands, only one thought pours through my head. *Please don't go. Please don't leave me.*

But she comes back. She reclines on her chaise lounge and drapes her porcelain legs over the top of the seat. Her lavender baby tee rides up above her ribs. The beauty mark beneath her breast winks at me, and she smiles coyly when she catches me admiring her. "What are you thinking about?" Zoe asks.

"My mother."

"What about her?"

"How I'll never speak to her again."

"My parents aren't dead, but they may as well be," she says. "We haven't spoken in thirteen years. They aren't allowed to speak to me since I was disfellowshipped. Even if we were all in the same room, they'd act like I wasn't there. Anyway, once I went to college, I used to spend every second hoping they'd call so I could hear their voices again, just be reminded we lived on the same planet, but they never did. I spent years waiting for the phone to ring, and then one night, I was getting in bed and I realized I didn't think of the phone at all. All this to say: one day the wanting just goes away."

I clutch a throw pillow to my chest, my fingers dancing along its intricate embroidery. I find a pattern that feels like the letter *E*, then *L*, then *I*, so on, so forth. *Elissa*. The wanting is all I have left of my mother. The void she left behind and everything I hoped would fix it. "You know she called me five times the day she died? I didn't answer. It'd been so long, I didn't even recognize her phone number."

"Providence, you couldn't have known any of this would happen."

"Even if she had nothing to say to me, I would know nothing had changed between us. That would have been closure in itself. Now I have to wonder for the rest of my life if she had a change of heart."

She knows better than to trot out a platitude about how my mother loved me or remind me of the unconditional love a mother has for her daughter. "What would you say to her?"

"I keep asking myself and coming up empty. Maybe it means there isn't anything for me to say."

"We always have one last thing to say."

But I don't think I do, and that's because it doesn't feel like she is really gone. My mother lives inside of me. She will forever be within me. There is no end to our story. She is my lungs and my beating heart. Without her, I cannot breathe. I cannot exist.

There is no Providence without Elissa. She is Alpha and Omega, the first and the last, my beginning and my end.

* * *

Things I understand to be inevitable: taxes, heartbreak, the heat death of the universe. When Zoe invites me to her third-floor bedroom for a shower and a change of clothes, we begin to feel inevitable too. Something between us shifts, the way the air feels distended just before rain. You know what's coming. All there is to do now is wait for the heavens to split apart.

The walls here are pine green and accented with ornamental moldings, the bed vast enough to drown in. Propped between pillows is the cherished stuffed puppy she's had since she was a baby. He resembled a golden retriever once upon a time, but his yellow fur has turned gray, and the stitches of his smile have come loose. She relocates him to the wingback chair on the far side of the room, his arms and legs crossed demurely upon his throne.

She has matching pajama sets in every color of the rainbow. My hair is still wet from the shower as I hunt for anything that might fit me (I've always been noticeably thicker than Zoe). Meanwhile, she preens in her full-length mirror. Her hair, free from its braids, tumbles down her back in a glossy waterfall of blonde. I'm certain there are men who vote for her just because she's beautiful and single. How tantalizing to think that you have a chance, however slim, to fuck your congresswoman.

Every time I glance at her, her eyes remain fixed on her own reflection, and the longer she withholds her attention, the more I need it, the more my need evolves into a real thing. It pulsates with memory, a heartbeat all its own.

I exhume a long-sleeved shirt from the bottom of the drawer. It squeezes me like a corset, tight enough to make my breasts ache, but at least it conceals my scars. She's never seen those. The biting only started once we ended.

Zoe smiles meekly at me through the mirror. She asks me to watch TV with her for a little while. She doesn't want to be alone yet.

We slink beneath silk sheets and rest our pretty heads on silk pillowcases. We find a rerun of *Friends*, the episode where Monica thinks Chandler is jacking off to sharks. With every burst of canned laughter, Zoe sidles closer. Skin meets skin, her forearm brushing mine, her thigh against my own. Girls are so soft. It's the best thing about us.

When her lips find mine, I taste her heartbeat. She kisses me like I am water, like I am air, like I am breath. Like I am inevitable. My body fizzes with desire like a can of shaken cola.

It is an emotional bloodletting, a return to a place long forgotten in the fog of memory. The topography of our bodies has changed—mine most drastically, sculpted and sanded beyond recognition—but the choreography of our desire has not. Legs entwined, spiraling around each other like vines. Hands in hair. Mouths on necks. *Do you still like this?* Yes, yes, always yes, Zoe. Her breath, my breath, mingling hot and golden together, smoldering. When she peels my shirt off, my bite mark scars glow silver in the television light. She doesn't ask.

Touches, featherlight. The curl of a finger, the flick of a tongue. Her body is delicate and birdlike, enchantingly different from my own. She wants me to tell her she's a good girl, and I do. *There you go. That's it.* She tastes like saltwater and pennies when she comes on my tongue. Contrary to all the poetry you've heard, women never taste like nectar or candy. I wouldn't have them any other way.

She is on top of me with one finger inside me, then another, and her smile is incandescent. *The face that launched a thousand ships.* She tells me I'm beautiful when I finally come. It is a reward for both her patience and mine. She slips her fingers out of me and brings them, still glistening and slick, to my lips, and

I take her fingers into my mouth and taste myself, and then I bite, just forcefully enough to make her gasp.

The ecstasy is agonizing. So is the comedown, quick yet deep like the slash of a pocketknife. Nostalgia is no match for reality.

Our heads return to their respective pillows, a valley of mattress now separating us. The heat between us cools to shy indifference. A different episode of *Friends* is on, one I don't recall, and we feign interest in the plotline to avoid talking about what we've just done. I want to ask her if this means anything to her, but I don't. I already know the answer.

In five years, Zoe will have a wedding band on her finger and a husband in her bed. He will be generically handsome, good at polite conversation but mediocre at oral sex. She will smile at him over a dinner spread of dishes that she cooked singlehandedly and tell herself this is good, this is right, and when she thinks back on this night, how pretty I looked beneath her, she will shudder and remind herself it was just a phase. I am merely a waypoint on a journey that will take her far away.

I lock the bathroom door behind me. The walls are thin enough that I can still hear the studio audience's guffaws. I stare at my naked body in the mirror, every scar and tattoo coloring my skin, and wait for my eyes to fill with tears that never come. I imagine unzipping my ribcage and cupping my hands at my sternum, ready to catch the sadness when it pitches out of my chest, only to look down into my palms and find them traitorously empty. As if this encounter did not mean anything to me either.

Zoe is a waypoint for me too. Zoe is not my destination.

A younger version of myself stares back at me from within the mirror. Underneath the plastic surgery, the tattoos, and the bite mark scars, there is a teenaged girl with amber eyes and crooked teeth. She keeps her hair chopped to her shoulders so no one can yank it. Her nails are bloody from being gnawed to the quick. Greenish veins spread like cobwebs across the hollows of her eyes. Her smiles fall short of her eyes, and she fidgets with her clothing to make sure her bruises and scrapes remain covered at all times.

The girl in the mirror is me, but she is Grace too.

I know what I have to do.

CHAPTER

22

August 22nd

7:50 AM

I'M PARKED DOWN the street from the high school in Carey Gap, hoping my presence does not look as sinister as it feels. Colorful backpacks stream past. Piping laughter takes flight on the wind. A gang of teenage girls, the scariest creatures of all, are clustered a few feet away from me, passing a vape around their circle. Smoke plumes above their heads as if from tiny chimneys.

The silver sedan I've been waiting for barrels around the corner. Karishma emerges from the passenger seat before the wheels have stopped moving. She snakes a crossbody bag over her shoulder and waves a shy goodbye to her dad. I watch his car pass mine. I count to three.

I pounce.

Karishma's dawdling pace means I barely break a sweat to intercept her at the flagpole. When she hears me calling her name, she turns away from the nearby gaggle with carmine red cheeks. She lowers her head as she shuffles toward me, as if her acknowledgement of my presence poses an existential threat to her social status.

She tucks her arms beneath her ribs and rocks on her heels. "Is it even legal for you to be here?"

"I need to talk to you about Grace."

"Okay, well . . ." Karishma gestures to the locker hallway, where students bottleneck at the doors in their rush for first period. "I have physics in, like, six minutes."

"What would it take to convince you to get in my car?"

"You're insane."

Insane? No. Hell-bent. But they look so much alike. The warning bell shrieks. The bottleneck at the locker hall vibrates with frenzy, everyone jostling their way toward the double doors. Six minutes has become five will become four will become a missed opportunity, gone up in smoke.

"Karishma, Grace needs you. If you love her at all—and I know you do—you'll help me help her. Tell me what it would take to get you to come with me."

Her frantic eyes dart like dragonflies, from the sidewalk to the students' bottleneck and then to the weather-worn American flag atop the flagpole, before finally settling on me. She chews the inside of her cheeks for a long time before she finally speaks.

* * *

Karishma's conditions are simple: one hundred dollars and a cheeseburger with extra tomatoes. She reminds me about the extra tomatoes several times. When she unwraps the burger from its greasy paper, she expresses disappointment at only having five tomato slices. She extracts one from between meat patties and places it on her tongue like a sacramental wafer.

As we pull into the empty nature preserve parking lot, she shifts in her seat and chuckles nervously. "You swear you're not murdering me, right?"

If I was planning to skin her and wear her flesh as an over-coat, I might just get away with it all the way out here, where no one would hear her scream. The preserve promises no breathtaking natural beauty, only a few crudely maintained trails cutting through the brown sandhills. Informational signs advise of the local flora and fauna. We park closest to one showcasing a blown-up picture of a tarantula, the hairy abomination cradled in a woman's palm to prove even hideous creatures are worthy of love.

She mistakes my silence for sulking. "I'm sorry. I shouldn't have said that, with your mom and all. I'm being insensitive."

"I have thick skin."

"I know you came by my house last night. My dad was really weirded out."

"What'd he say?"

"Nothing. He's—well, you don't know him that well. My dad isn't great with people, especially strangers."

Especially Byrds. I roll down my window for reprieve from the greasy air. "Did you buy Grace any vapes?"

Karishma removes another tomato slice from her burger, folds it in half, and sucks it into her mouth like a spaghetti noodle. "Why are you asking? It's just a vape."

"I'm not trying to get anyone in trouble. I'm not buddy-buddy with the cops."

"I'm eighteen. She's not. I've bought her a couple."

"Did she lose one recently?"

It's too on the nose. Karishma's alarms have been raised, but she is not quite wily enough to sell me the necessary lie. "I don't think so." She plays it too cool. Like every teenage girl, she thinks she's a good liar, and maybe she is about trivial things, finishing a homework assignment or coming home after curfew. But she has never lied about anything with real stakes. I think back to when our paths crossed at the church. If she had lied to her father about the joyriding or simply pretended it didn't happen, she wouldn't have been there. That tells me she isn't good under pressure. It's a matter of finding the right buttons to press.

"I think you know something about my mother," I say.

"No."

"I think Grace told you what happened."

She wants her laugh to sound incredulous, but I only hear jangling nerves. "This is weird, Providence."

I don't like this. I don't relish the opportunity to intimidate a teenager. It's like I'm back in prison, preying on a weaker inmate to preserve my rank in the hierarchy, feeding the sadistic streak I wish I didn't have. "Grace waited to report our mother missing because she killed her. Harmony didn't know where the car was because she didn't drive it. Grace did. Grace ran over our mother, and she was too panicked to realize she left her vape in the car when she abandoned it, and I think you, me, and her are the only three people alive who know this."

When she lifts her eyes, their strength surprises me. She holds my stare unblinking. "What you think happened didn't happen."

"Then tell me what did."

"I can't."

"Bullshit. There's no reason you can't tell me."

She discards her burger carcass into the paper bag between her feet. She pushes it as far from her as possible, like the mere sight will make her vomit. "What you think happened," she begins, enunciating every word, "didn't happen."

"You were there. That's why you won't say anything."

It's a bluff. I don't think she had anything to do with it—or at least, that's what I think until she turns away. I have the fleeting thought that I should lock the car doors to keep her from bolting off into the sandhills, but then she'll really think I'm going to hurt her.

I am walking blindfolded through a maze, looking for answers about my mother, and every turn I take brings me closer to disaster than peace.

"What is it worth to you?" she asks.

"What's it worth to me?"

"My dad has a lot of medical bills from when your dad shot him." She wrings her hands. "I'm tired of watching him buy groceries with spare change."

"You'd rat Grace out to me for money?"

Karishma rakes a hand through her bangs. Her fingers snag on a tangle, but she yanks them through anyway, the follicles ripping from her scalp like Velcro. "I'm telling you what you want to know, aren't I?"

I want to warn Grace that her best friend may not be who she thinks she is. Her best friend's loyalty has a price. In a less dire situation, this would be a teachable moment, a lesson for a teenage girl experiencing her first real betrayal. But is it a betrayal to put flesh and blood over her friend? Is it a betrayal to love your parent so much? No. I wish I was so devoted to my father. Such dedication is exactly what nature intends. *Honor thy mother. Honor thy father.*

"How about a grand?" I ask.

I know from the way her eyes pop she would have taken a couple hundred, but if her intention truly is to make a dent in Mitesh's medical bills, giving her less seems insulting—and if she's fleecing me, so be it. There are nobler hills to die on.

I take the money from my purse to prove I'm good for it. "Tell me and it's yours."

She stares into her lap, willing herself to find the courage to speak. "We took Harmony's car. Stole it, technically, I guess."

"Why?"

"There's an abortion clinic in Casper. It's the closest one."

"For you or for her?"

"For Grace." Karishma is relieved that I didn't clutch my pearls and launch into a moralizing screed. She loosens up the tiniest bit. "But you can't—"

"I would never tell. I swear on my life, Karishma."

Her face darkens with shame when she looks at the money again. "It was a whole ordeal to get out there. And I mean—she was too scared to even look up clinics. I did it for her. She was scared of your dad, but I was scared of the government. I worried I'd wake up and find out abortion was suddenly illegal and we'd be hauled off to . . . well, you know. York. I figured we'd have to go to Denver or Omaha, but the one in Casper was new, and we could get there and back in a day."

"So you stole the car."

Her story is breathless. "First she got a fake ID so she could say she was over eighteen—don't ask me how she got that or the money—and then yeah, we stole the car. Harmony knew it was us. We've done it before because we know where she keeps her keys. It was the day your mom went missing. We ditched school and told our dads we were hanging out together after, and then we drove to Wyoming. The procedure was outpatient, really fast, but on the way back, I hit a deer. It was . . . God, it was awful, the sound." Karishma forces the words through clenched teeth. She is remembering every noise the animal made. "But the point is, we damaged the front of the car. So when we brought the car back that night, it had a big dent, one might say a *human-sized* dent, and Harmony must have thought . . . She never asked. She *never* asked. She dumped the car. If Grace knew she was going to confess, she would have told Harmony where we were. I know she would have. She would have stopped it before it went this far."

"Harmony wanted to protect Grace," I say, more to myself than to her. *Honor thy sister.*

"Harmony never could keep a secret." She relegates Harmony to the past tense with ease, the way you write out a minor character who has ceased to be relevant to the story. "She got drunk once and told your dad about Grace's boyfriend. He was so angry that—"

"Don't finish your sentence."

"Grace insisted on not telling Harmony," Karishma says. "She didn't trust her to keep it a secret."

"And if my dad found out, he'd hurt her."

"That's why I never said anything, not until right now."

"The police never questioned Grace's alibi?"

"I was her alibi," she says. "I said she was with me."

"Harmony is going to prison for a very long time for something she didn't do."

Karishma pinches her nose until the skin blanches white. "We didn't make her confess! She's the one who made the decision! The lie is too big now. There's no undoing it."

The ultimate act of selflessness collides with the ultimate act of selfishness. Harmony falls on her sword, and with her own neck on the line, Grace lets her. She is a liar, but she is no murderer. What Karishma said is true. The lie is too big. A house of cards. Move one and the rest will fall. Grace and Karishma are both guilty of very real crimes—obstruction at the very least, more for Grace with the fake ID, even more depending on how she got the money. With the local attention my mother's death has brought, they would certainly go to jail, maybe prison. And all of this is to say nothing about my father's wrath. He would hurt her if he found out she had an abortion. I believe it in my soul. I think he would even kill her.

I hand her the money. "So if Harmony didn't do it, and you and Grace didn't do it, who did?"

"I have no clue," she whispers. "I—I think it was just a random act of violence and now we've all made a fucking mess of it."

"And you swear you don't know where she got the money?"

"All she said was her sister had friends in high places. I didn't ask how Harmony knew anyone in high places."

Karishma has the wrong sister. Harmony does not have well-connected friends, but I do. I have one in particular.

* * *

Zoe commands a legion of interns and assistants, most of them women, all of them white. They have converted the old auto insurance office on the main street in Carey Gap into a campaign headquarters humming with too much life to be stuck in mid-nowhere Nebraska. They peck dutifully at their keyboards and field phone calls with aplomb, half-eaten lunches left to shrivel on desks so visitors understand how busy they are. It appears all of them are obligated to have a red *ZOE MARKHAM FOR CONGRESS* sign affixed to their cubicle.

"It's reelection season," Zoe explains as she closes her office door behind me. One window looks out at the sea of cubicles, the other into the parking lot they share with a hardware store. "It's not usually this busy, which—and I don't mean to be rude, really—means I don't have a lot of time to talk. And if it's about last night, I—"

"It isn't."

She softens at this. We sit on the cracked leather couch, facing each other but not quite touching. I want to savor the moment, her closeness, because I have the nagging feeling this is the last time we will speak, but I've come here on a mission. All I need is an answer, and then I can go. "Why did you help Grace?"

"Help her with what?"

"Zoe, please don't. I already know."

Her smile wobbles. "No, really. What are you talking about?"

I hesitate to use the exact words in case anyone is listening in, if her office is somehow under surveillance. "I don't care that you did it. I just have to know why. For myself."

Zoe gets up and stands before the map of Nebraska hanging on her wall. Every county is shaded a different color, but Tillman County has the distinction of being encircled by a heart. "If I did do something, it would be because I wanted her to have an adult in her life she could trust," she says, her back to me, her expression hidden. "It would be because I saw how much you needed that adult in your life when you were her age. Maybe if you had someone, things would have turned out differently."

"I had that adult," I say. "I had Gil."

"But I think you needed more. Someone you could really talk to and confide in, not just a respite away from home."

"I didn't think you knew Grace so well."

She finally faces me to pull the blinds looking out into the office shut. She is as impassive as ever. "I don't, but she—*if* she came to me, because I'm not saying anything happened, it would be because she needed me, and I had the means to help."

"Did she tell you what she was using the money for?"

She nods, then continues like she has read my mind. "It doesn't matter how I feel about someone else's abortion. She wanted one. I didn't need her to tell me more than that. She knew exactly how her life was going to play out if she didn't have one." She pauses. "She's like you, actually. She doesn't want kids at all. She started going on about it, and I thought about you saying the same thing to me at her age."

"Birds of a feather."

"You can cry, Providence." Her voice is silky, notes plucked from a harp.

"I don't want to cry anymore."

"But you can, if you need to." She sits beside me again and offers her shoulder, but I don't take it. I'm so tired of crying.

We don't say anything for a long time. I hear the phones ringing outside of the office, the staff's chatter seeping through the walls. My world has crumbled, yet life carries on for everybody else. I resent the normalcy of their lives and how they can speak their traumas aloud. You can talk about a divorce. You can talk about a cheating spouse. You can talk about the death of a loved one. You can talk about the bank foreclosing on your house. But I cannot talk about what I know, and I am condemned to bear this secret forever. The only person other than myself who will ever know the full story is Grace, and now I am bound to her, more hopelessly entangled with her than I will ever be with my mother. I am furious with Grace for making this mess and dragging so many people into her web, for leaving me to piece it all together, and yet I still want to hold her in my arms and comfort her because none of it was intentional. It was a single flame that grew into a roaring wildfire.

"I want to kiss you." Zoe's fingertips are icy against my jaw, her mouth parted in invitation. The soft light turns both of her eyes green.

"No," I murmur.

"The door's locked. A couple more minutes won't—"

"I have to let you go, Zoe. This isn't fair to either of us."

Her wounded expression startles me. "I know I mean a lot to you," she says. "That's why I'm saying you can."

"You do mean a lot to me, but I don't mean a lot to you anymore, and that's okay. Part of me can't let go of what life would be like if I hadn't gone to prison. I picture you in that life. I picture us happy, in a big house on a lake, like we always talked about. You'd teach me how to swim. We would sit on the porch and drink lemonade. We'd have a few chickens and ducks. Do you remember?"

"Oh, Providence . . ."

"I want us to be happy. I wish it could be with each other, but it can't. I have to learn to be okay with it."

Her hand slides further up my cheek and I cannot help curling into it. Her lotion smells like honey. "You'll be happy. You're too stubborn to not end up happy."

I kiss her on the cheek, and then I leave, lighter and heavier at the same time.

23

August 22nd

8:08 PM

THE POOL HALL is quieter than a graveyard at noon. I blame it on the Rockies being trounced, twelve-zip in the third inning. Their manager looks to be on the brink of an aneurysm, which is not unlike how I feel as the boyish bartender brings me what is supposed to be a Tom Collins but has the distinctly battery acid taste of a gin and tonic.

But no, that's not true, is it? That knifelike pain in my head has nothing to do with a botched drink order and everything to do with the supercut of childhood memories playing in my head. First the good, the pure: chokecherry pies, baby sisters bundled into my arms, Annie the dog, flying high on the rusty swing set. When the horrors resurface, I am not angry, or frightened, or distraught. I am only tired.

I am so, so tired.

"Mind if I join you?"

Josiah's hat casts a shadow over his face. He approaches me coolly, like a bounty hunter finally tracking down an elusive outlaw. Unlike my father and his compatriots, loyal to their beers, Josiah nurses a clear drink garnished with basil leaves. "Unless you're expecting someone?" he asks, gnawing on an ice cube.

"I'm leaving when I finish this."

He sets his drink down on a damp clump of napkins. He whistles for the bartender's attention. "Another one when you get the chance, son?"

"Fancy running into you here," I say to Josiah.

"They let me out of the station every once in a while for some fresh air."

I chuckle into my glass and hope he doesn't notice. I don't want him to confuse my amusement for a ceasefire. He fishes another ice cube from his drink to swallow like a pill. "Five years until I retire, God willing and the creek don't rise. I'm ready to get the hell out of Nebraska."

"Don't come to Missouri. It sounds like *misery* for a reason."

"You got a fella waiting for you at home?"

"I'm a lesbian," I deadpan.

The bartender drops off a fresh drink for Josiah. He transfers the soggy basil leaf from the old drink to the new. He sips and grunts approval at the flavor before blindsiding me: "My daughter is too."

"*Penny?*"

He laughs. "Only one I got."

"I'm surprised you're okay with that."

"What's there to be okay with? She's happy and healthy. That's all a father can ask for."

It's all I can do not to choke on my own envy. "My father would beat me bloody if he knew about me."

"I owe you a proper apology, Providence," Josiah says. He removes his hat as if to underscore his sincerity.

"I don't need it."

"Can you do an old man the favor of hearing him out?"

"Don't come to me for absolution."

"You don't have to forgive me. God knows I don't deserve it. I'd just like to say my piece."

I slam my glass down with too much force. The bartender jumps like I've fired a gun. "Please don't, Josiah. The only thing I want is to never see you or speak to you again. That can be your apology," I say. "It's too late for anything else."

"There's nothing I regret more than not standing up for you girls. It haunts me every day."

"It should."

He motions the bartender over and hands him cash to pay for my drink. I want to tell him to take his ten dollars and shove it up his ass, but a free drink is a free drink. "Harmony is getting transferred to York at the end of the week," he says. "If you want to say goodbye, I'd do it sooner rather than later."

"Sounds like I'll have at least ten years to visit her."

"York isn't too keen to let former inmates come back for visits."

"I'm never done repaying my debt to society," I say with a brittle laugh. "I never get to move on from something I did when I was seventeen years old, and yet my father gets to walk this earth free as a bird. He gets drunk and watches baseball games like every other man. You know what the difference between him and me is?"

"Me."

"All you ever had to do was arrest him. Stick one charge on him."

"I'd do it very different if I could now. I know that's no consolation."

"Why didn't you do it different?"

Josiah waits for me to meet his eyes. "Because I was a coward. There's no nicer way to put it. Tom scared me to death when I was young. Sometimes he still does. I've never met a man like him before, where you look in his eyes and you know he's got no soul. Every time I'd start to think he didn't scare me, he'd do something to remind me why I was scared in the first place. Shot my dog once, you know."

"Slept with your wife."

"Now, that's just a nasty rumor."

"Penny doesn't look much like you."

"You could tell me the stork dropped her at the doorstep and I'd still be her dad. The rest is background noise."

I coax the dregs from the bottom of my glass. The straw bores into my gums like a dental instrument, and I dig it in further to sharpen the pain. "I wish I was a big enough person to forgive you, Josiah."

"If you ever think of anything I can do to make amends," he says, downing the last of his drink, "please tell me. I can't undo anything, but I'd like the chance to set something right with you."

"Don't bet on it."

He tips his hat to a young couple playing pool and saunters through the open door, the midnight darkness consuming his burly frame as he crosses the parking lot. Just as he disappears from view, I remember one thing he can do for me—one thing he can give me and my sisters. He nearly flattens me beneath his Jeep as I intercept him in the parking lot. The top has been removed from the car. He doesn't even need to roll down a window to yell at me. "Sake's alive, Providence!"

"Can you make sure my mother gets a grave at the church?"

"It's up to your father what he wants to do with her remains."
He pulls the emergency brake even though the parking lot is
flatter than a ruler. His brown eyes are warm. "He's her next of
kin. If he wants to keep her ashes, there's not much I can do to
stop him."

"I know you can't take her ashes, but you could make sure
there's a headstone, a plaque, anything. Just somewhere to
mourn her that isn't the mantlepiece in that horrible house."

"I'll see what I can do," Josiah says.

"It would mean a lot to me and my sisters."

This brief interlude of usefulness is the closest I can come to
forgiving him today. Certain grudges, like the one I hold against
my father, will fester inside me until I die. Even if my father
escapes judgment from everyone else—even the law, even God
himself—I can never forget. I can't allow myself to completely
move on. There must always be one place where his sins are
unforgiven, and if that place is my heart, then so be it. But one
day, even if it is years from now, long after my hair has turned
gray and he's become food for worms, I'd like to think I could
forgive Josiah.

He exhales, slow and deliberate, and I worry he is going to
try apologizing to me again. "I can call in some favors," he says.
"I'll get Elissa a headstone."

"That's the first time anyone's mentioned my mother to me
by name."

"I guess we always find it easier to define people by what
they mean to others rather than who they are alone."

His truism sparks another request. "Can you make sure they
don't write anything like *wife* or *mother* on the headstone? I want
her to be Elissa for once. Even if it's a fancy rock in a cemetery,
she should have something that's her own."

"You'll want something on there. Something more than
just her name." When he sees me racking my brain, he adds,

"Sit with it. You don't have to come up with anything right now."

"What about a beatitude? 'Blessed are the poor in spirit: for theirs is the kingdom of heaven.'"

Josiah smiles. "I think that's perfect."

24

August 22nd

9:59 PM

ANNESVILLE HAS DEVOURED my mother. I settle on this as the cause of her death because it's the only resolution to this saga that brings me any peace.

As I detour through Annesville's darkened streets, I tell myself this town morphed into a monster—a real, sentient, bloodthirsty beast—in search of easy prey to feed on. Its five dirt roads became veins, its mailboxes became teeth, its condemned houses became eyes. And at the very center, its throbbing red heart, are the liquor stores. It intuited my mother's plan to escape, and as soon as no one was looking, snapped her between its powerful jaws. It knew no one would come looking for her until it was too late.

When I turn onto Maple Street, the door of the Crawfords' bungalow is wide open. My stomach freefalls at the sight, and my mind latches onto the image of a blood-soaked crime scene with my friend's pallid corpse at its center.

I park across the street and run across the clover-covered yard. Constant motion is imperative: if I stop moving, I'll think about the danger I may be walking into. But when I enter the house, nothing is amiss. No blood, no signs of a struggle, no dead bodies. There's even a fresh zigzag pattern in the carpet from the vacuum cleaner. What made Connor leave in such a hurry that he—?

No.

No, no, no.

Gil.

It takes four calls for Connor to pick up. We're both breathless when he finally does. "I can't talk right now, Providence."

"I was driving through town and saw your front door wide open. I thought you'd been murdered."

"I—fuck, no. I'm fine. I was in a rush. It's my dad. He slipped in the shower and hit his head. It's bad. I'm walking into the hospital right now. Penny says it's a concussion, but I wouldn't trust that nursing home to diagnose someone with a head injury if their brain was halfway out their ears."

Gil's brain, already shriveled like flowers in a waterless vase, swells and bruises as we speak. Does he know where he is? Does he understand why his head hurts? I pace from the piano to the kitchen and back again. "Is he at least conscious?"

"Providence, I don't know anything."

"I'm sorry. I—I'm—" In my mind, Gil's brain swells obscenely, pressing against his skull until its blood vessels pop. "I'm just worried about him."

"I know you are," he says. "Stay at the house for a few minutes and catch your breath, okay? I'll call you in the morning."

He hangs up before I can ask another question. Gil Crawford may have been a surrogate father to me, but he is not my real father, and the only person with the right to rush to his bedside in the dead of night is Connor. I convince myself it isn't personal. There may be medical decisions to make, tearful goodbyes (God forbid) to exchange. Those moments are not for me; I can only wish they were.

But there is a sense of impending doom I cannot quell—thoughts of Gil in the morgue, thoughts of him in a vegetative state, a machine drawing breath instead of his lungs. I've already lost my mother. I can't lose Gil too. Part of me thinks the universe can't be so evil that it would make me suffer another paralyzing blow, but another part remembers I am a lightning rod for tragedy.

I won't leave until Connor returns. I don't care that it's unforgivably selfish to claim this pain as my own. If I wake to a voicemail telling me that Gil died in the night, I fear I will never recover.

I turn on the TV and crank the volume on the home shopping network. Perfectly banal, like an anesthetic straight to the brain. The host extols the wonders of a plumping lip gloss as if her lips have not been enhanced with filler. I rot on the couch, fingers between my teeth, and allow my mind to drift until my thoughts converge on the need for a cigarette.

As soon as I step outside, creatures scutter through the grass, the bushes, along the branches of the mighty oak tree buckling the earth with its roots. I use the rusty birdbath as an ashtray. Not my finest moment, but better than setting Connor's backyard ablaze. I gaze at Gil's old woodshop in the corner of the yard. I can hear the shrill whine of his circular saw and smell the powdery traces of sawdust, a scent I always found more delightful than I should have.

The door grates as I open it. Everything is in its right place, exactly as I remember it. I imagine Connor standing here, surveying Gil's favorite hideout, unwilling to part with his father's favorite things even if he has no use for them. Perhaps he stands here and considers taking up carpentry himself. There is an unfinished chair felled on the ground, missing its fourth leg. I lean it against the wall, beneath his array of carpentry tools.

My cigarette has burned nearly to the filter. I extinguish it beneath my slipper, hoping I remember to dispose of the remains later, and walk to the shelf where Gil keeps the trinkets he used to whittle, hunks of wood carved into the vague outline of animals. By his own admission, he was more adept at the bigger projects. *These hands are ham hocks*, he would say, *the less detail, the better.* They face east toward the rising sun, paired off in predator-prey couplings: the bear eats the deer, the bird eats the snake, the alligator eats the turtle. The only predator without an assigned meal is a wolf at the far end of the shelf. I wonder if Connor would notice if I pocketed it.

As I approach the workbench for better lighting, I trip over something. The wolf skids across the concrete floor and disappears beneath the workbench.

I stop. I look down. I have tripped over a pair of shoes. Women's shoes. White heels with plastic ribbons on the toes.

My mother's shoes.

*   *   *

I wait on the couch, the shoes on the cushion beside me, my spine rigid like I've run a steel rod through it. When I glance at the shoes, I can't think of anything but my mother's mutilated foot, the fraying cords of muscle straining to keep it attached to the rest of her leg. I try to remember how she looked in these shoes, and when I fail to do that, I just try to remember her alive, walking, breathing. But now, in every memory, her foot is bloody and falling off, and she is dead.

Connor sees the shoes as soon as he comes in the house, almost midnight, but he isn't alarmed. He reacts with little more than a long sigh.

"Why do you have my mother's shoes in the workshop?"

He reaches behind him. He takes out my pistol.

"Why did you hide a gun in my dad's room?"

"You killed my mother! If I want to hide a nuclear bomb in your dad's room, you can't say shit to me about it." I sound like I'm on the verge of tears, but it is fury—thirty years of it coming to a hilt—that runs my voice ragged. "You killed my mother and then you had the temerity to act like my friend. You stood there and you comforted me when they found her body!"

"I did not hurt your mother, Providence."

"You're a liar."

"My dad did, and it was a fucking accident, I swear to God. Let me explain, please."

"You don't run people over on accident!"

"You do when you have Alzheimer's and you don't know how to use a car anymore. You do when you forget that the old service road out to the water tower isn't the highway to Scotts-bluff. He called me in tears, Providence. He knew he'd done something awful."

The service road. My mother's favorite shortcut to church, the only snatches of time she was a free woman. I stand, which he sees as an invitation to approach me. "I'll break your nose if you take another step toward me." I draw my arm back so he knows I mean it.

"I would never hurt you."

"Just like you'd never hurt my mother, right?"

"How do you think he got to the church the first day you got here? He didn't walk twenty miles! He's done it before: takes some nurse's keys, gets in her car, and comes back to Annesville. He can't leave Annesville behind. Sometimes it's the church, sometimes it's the house, once it was—"

"But you hid her body."

"Yes. Yes, I did."

"You threw her away like trash!" I cry. "You dumped her in the woods, and you let the vultures eat her eyes and the coyotes mangle her feet, and then you held me when I saw her body."

"I was protecting my dad."

"He killed her!"

"It was an accident. A freak accident—a one-in-a-billion accident. You think I would have done that if I knew he did it on purpose? He called me, and he cried, and he begged me for help, so I did what I had to do to keep him safe. He's still a person. He's still my dad."

"And what was my mom?"

"Your mom was a person too, but not my person."

"I'm going to the police."

Connor lifts the gun. The safety is engaged. "You do that and I'll tell them about the gun."

"How did you find it?"

"I went to the nursing home for his meds. I found it next to his goddamn Namenda bottles."

"Who says it's mine?"

"No one else comes to see him," he says.

"Your fingerprints are on it too, dumbass."

"And who are they going to believe? Me or the felon?"

"I'll take my chances."

I am bluffing when I head for the door, but he falls for it. He blocks my way like a linebacker. "Don't do this to him, please."

"And I should let Harmony go to prison for something she didn't do? I should sacrifice my family for yours? How noble that would be."

"It's noble to save someone you love. Someone who loves you. Don't kid yourself about the relationship you and Harmony have. She's never going to want you around, but my dad loves you like a daughter. He doesn't even know how to move a bishop half the time, but he knows who he loves."

To choose one sister over another is a decision of blood, but to choose Gil over Harmony can only be a betrayal—and yet, at some level, even though I hate him for it, Connor is right. It boils down to love. Gil loves me and Harmony does not.

People love me. I am lovable.

"He's an old man." Connor is close to tears. "He's not well. He never would have hurt your mom on purpose, God as my witness. I was only—damn it! Damn it!"

The sobs strangle his breath, but I will not comfort him. I watch him weep, watch him collapse to the floor, watch him bury his head in his hands, watch him crumble into pieces. It boils my blood. He hauled my mother's body to the woods. He left her body beneath the leaves for the little boy to find. He comforted me when I saw her body.

Body. Body. The word snags in my brain. He is the reason she is a body and not a person anymore.

"It never had to go this far. You could have called the cops."

"He doesn't deserve to die in prison."

"He has Alzheimer's. They'd send him to a care facility."

"Half their dads and granddads were in the KKK. You think those good ol' boys wouldn't jump at the first chance to throw another Black man in prison? They don't give a shit about the Alzheimer's. They'd still lynch him if they could." He runs his teeth over his bottom lip, his chest trembling from the force of his exhale. "What if it was Grace? You'd have done the same thing. I saw it when you came to the school that day, how you would have taken a bullet if it meant she'd be safe."

And he is right, about all of it, but I can't give him the satisfaction. "Give me my gun."

"No."

"It's my gun."

He thumbs the tears from his cheeks. "I'm keeping it. You go to the cops and I will too. You don't and we have no problems."

"Maybe I'll go to them anyway."

"They won't believe you."

"I have her shoes," I say.

"They're just shoes. Maybe they were my mom's. Only so many places to buy shoes around here." He does not intend to be snide, but it still sounds that way. He is three moves ahead of me.

"The car. If he hit her with a stolen car, then—"

"I tore the engine apart. The nurse had to scrap it for parts. It's gone."

"My God, if you had put half the effort into getting my mother medical attention as you did covering your tracks and hiding her body, she would still be alive. Did you hear her breathing, Connor? Was she still gasping for air when you left her to die? Did she beg you for help?"

"I thought she was dead, I swear to God. If I'd known—"

"Fuck you, Connor."

I storm out of the house. One more word and I will be sick. One more word and my universe, already splitting at the seams, will collapse completely. I stop in the driveway and look back at the house.

I take the deepest breath I can manage, *one two three*, and then I throw my mother's shoes through the window.

CHAPTER

25

August 23rd

3:43 AM

Sungila Lake is quiet and dark. I will jump into its unknowable water. I will sink down until my feet touch the bottom, and then I will spring up and haul myself back onto the dock, safe as houses.

My clothes are folded on a dock piling. I've texted Sara that I'll be coming back to the trailer in a little while to sleep. Should I overestimate my innate swimming prowess and drown, at least someone will come looking for me. Regardless, a watery death seems unlikely. The dock reaches only twenty or so feet out from the shore. Even if I can't pull myself back onto the dock, I'm sure I can drag myself to dry land.

I run down the dock and jump. I am suspended in the air for a small eternity before I plunge into the water. The cold chokes out all the air in my lungs. My first instinct is to breathe. I have to clamp a hand over my mouth to keep from inhaling water. Once the panic subsides, I lift my arms upward and allow myself to sink. The water moves around me in a delicate embrace, a dangerous slow dance in the blackness.

Mother, I wish you had taught me how to swim.

Mother, I wish it could have all been different.

Mother, I failed you and you failed me too.

Mother, I hate you, yet I would sacrifice anything to run into your arms one last time.

And Mother, Mother, I am sorry. I have never said it before, but I am sorry for what I did to you. I'm sorry it was you and not him.

My feet touch the bottom, and I realize, with immense relief, that the water is not as deep as I feared it would be.

* * *

Only the dogs welcome me when I come back to the trailer. I reward their loyalty with treats. Sara's bedroom door is shut, but if the graveyard of fresh cigarette butts in her ashtray is any indication, she hasn't been in bed long. I want to wake her, to sit at the foot of her bed and cry in her arms, comforted by the friend I love most in this world, but that is what ghouls do. It feeds our misery to share it with others.

My sorrows are my own.

I count my breaths in the pitch black. Zenobia paws at the door and joins me on the air mattress, stretching her legs as far as she can before going limp with exhaustion. Occasionally she smacks her lips to reassure me she is still alive, and I twitch my foot to return the favor.

Sleep comes to me in fits and starts. When the dog shifts, I jolt awake because, for a split second, I can trick myself into thinking it is my mother on the bed, come to sing me to sleep.

26

August 23rd

10:21 AM

N O TIME TO mourn, no time to grieve. Life marches onward. Blessed are they that mourn, but cursed are they that withdraw and take private time to do it. The anger and sadness suffocate me—brutal, prolonged, spine-chilling suffocation, like a plastic bag has been thrown over my head and I am writhing hopelessly for a gasp of air, but I have no time to process any of my emotions. Today I see Harmony.

The red jumpsuit flatters my sister. The khaki she will be forced to wear in York will wash her out, consuming her frame and identity in equal measure. As the deputy shepherds her into the room, both hands gripping her bicep as if she is the Hulk, liable to turn green and burst free from her handcuffs at any second, I try to imagine what she will look like at her first parole hearing ten years on. She will be thinner, older, her cheekbones more sunken and her complexion more sallow. A life of confinement will age her more rapidly than a thousand cartons of cigarettes or gallons of liquor. The only thing prison will ravage more than her appearance is her spirit. She walks into this room with her chin held high, but she will lower it more with each passing year. Once her chin drops, her eyes will soon follow, and then her shoulders will slump, her gait will slow. She thinks she is strong enough to withstand the systematic crushing of her soul, but she isn't. No one is. Prison is an institution designed to break you piece by piece, like eyelashes ripped out one at a time.

Graceless like a ragdoll, she lands in the seat. She flings her arms in the air to protest the deputy's roughness and sticks her tongue out at him as he leaves. "Flinging me around like a sack of potatoes."

"You look all right."

"Liar. I look—what did the old man always say? Rode hard, put away wet." She rakes her hair back with a hand. "They messed with the timing of my meds. They're making me take the Seroquel in the mornings. I feel like a zombie."

"When do they send you to York?"

"Thursday."

"Long bus ride," I say.

"Yeah, and I don't even get a book to pass the time. I get to stare out the window at the world-famous natural beauty of Nebraska."

"You'll have plenty of time to read soon enough."

Harmony scowls. "If that's your idea of a joke, save it for another audience. Why'd you come here anyway?"

I want to tell my sister she is brave and stupid, noble and reckless, that I am at once frustrated by and in awe of the walking contradiction she has become, but those precise words reveal too much, and the deputy lurks nearby with golden ears. Today, I can offer only tepid praise. "You're a force of nature, Harmony."

A crooked smile flashes across her face. "Tell me something I don't already know."

"I'm not sure if I'll be able to visit, but I'll try to get cleared. It'll probably take a few months."

"You don't have to do that."

"I'm telling you I want to."

"Providence, *I* don't want you to visit."

An incredulous laugh escapes me. "You'll be dying for company, I promise."

The emotion on her face vaguely resembles remorse. She brushes her fingers through her hair again, her hands gliding up from her ears until they converge in a rat's nest atop her head. "I appreciate your offer, but I don't want to see you."

"Can I ask why?"

"I don't need this relationship."

She mistakes her clinical words for a clean break. She thinks she is amputating the limb, but she is tearing it violently from my body. "You really don't mince words," I manage.

"I never understood the point of beating around the bush."

"Is it Mom?"

"I can't forgive you. I wish I could, I really do. I've gone 'round and 'round with my therapist, with my psychiatrist, with Grace, and I . . ." She clenches her fists and then releases them, her palms turned to the heavens. "I can't do it."

"It was thirteen years ago, Harmony. I regret it every day, but I can't take it back."

"You know Mom never hugged me after you tried to kill her? Never once. She stopped loving me the same time she stopped loving you. She was just waiting for me to turn into you. She got over it by the time Grace was older, but me? As far as I'm concerned, you did kill her. You took her away from me. She had shortcomings— she drank, she was an addict, she was miserable, she had no business raising a kid, let alone three. But you're the reason she couldn't love me anymore, and that's what I can't forgive you for." Harmony's eyes are empty, two vast oceans, the depths of which cannot be charted. "You turned her into this cold, lifeless creature who loved painkillers more than she loved me."

"Did Mom ever tell you the real story? About the day I ran her over?"

"She was standing at the end of the driveway and you put the car in reverse, unprovoked." Her voice is colorless, like someone repeating the punchline to a joke they've heard a hundred times before.

"No," I say. "He was the one I wanted to run over. He'd cracked her over the head with a beer bottle, and I . . . remember what you said to me in the house? That I should kill the right parent this time? I tried, Harmony. I tried to kill the right parent back then. She pushed him out of the way at the last second."

Her frown deepens. "I don't believe you, and I don't forgive you."

"I'm sorry. For doing it, and for everything that happened to you after."

"Okay."

My moment of madness still echoes through all three of our lives. An eye for an eye and a tooth for a tooth, but I never considered that by taking eyes and teeth from my mother, I would be taking them from my sisters too. Their suffering, like mine, is an existential torture: sorrow for the lives we never lived, grief for the people we were never able to become. It is Harmony's right to deny me forgiveness for everything I've stolen from her.

But knowing she doesn't have to forgive me makes this no less painful.

I blink back tears. I wish I had no more left to cry. "Even if—I mean, I can still send you money, if that's okay. Maybe books. I won't write letters or anything. I can give you things to help the time pass."

"No letters."

"I promise."

She studies me for an ulterior motive before nodding. Behind her, the deputy observes us through the glass insert of the door. "You can send me a few things, long as you don't do it out of pity."

Every book I send and every dollar I deposit in her name will be an apology for a different sin, further blurring the line I draw between altruism and guilt. I will send her things throughout her sentence, even if I never hear a word of thanks. I don't want the only kindness I've ever shown Harmony to be contingent on her forgiveness.

"There is one thing you can do for me," Harmony continues.

"Name it."

"Please look out for Grace."

"What happened to leaving her alone?"

"Well, I won't exactly be around, will I?" When she sighs, her breath smells of the stale remnants of sleep. "Someone has to stick around and look out for her. You're not my first choice, but who else is there?"

"I'm going to go home soon, Harmony."

"Take her with you."

"She's seventeen," I say. "It's kidnapping if I take her across state lines without our father's permission."

Her upper lip curls. "You can't leave her with him."

"I told her—" I stop myself when I catch the deputy again, looming at us from the other side of the door. I finish my thought in a frazzled whisper. "I offered to *help* if she needed to get out. Whatever she needed. I told her just to say the word."

"She doesn't know how to ask for help. You and I never did. Why would she be different?"

"The only option is . . ."

Her eyes are ferocious. She knows exactly what I am saying. "Finish what you started."

"I'm not that person anymore."

"But this time, it's righteous, isn't it? Listen to me, Providence. We are both lost causes, but she isn't. If you can get her out of there and help her have a chance at a normal life, do it."

"And traumatize her all over again?"

Her patience hangs by a thread. Every movement she makes is quick and twitchy, like insects are crawling on her. "Grace doesn't hate you now, but I promise the second you drive out of town and leave her behind with him, she will. She will never forgive you."

"What if something happens to me? What if I die? Then who does she have?"

"Is it fun for you to think of everything that can possibly go wrong?"

I speak softly enough for the incessant chugging of the air conditioning unit to drown out my words. "She will be fucked if something happens to me. You are gone. Mom is gone. We don't have aunts or uncles or cousins. There is no one now that you're going away."

"She's fucked if you leave her with the old man."

"She doesn't want it to end like this."

"You can't ask her to make the decision," she says. "She won't get there on her own, even if she wants it. She's a sweet girl. You take the burden on your conscience, not her."

"Harmony—"

She pushes her chair away from the table. The legs screech against the concrete floor, a sound so sharp I feel it in my teeth. "Do it, Providence. Do it. It's the only way he's ever going to stop."

"You don't have anything to lose."

"And you do?"

I swallow the *fuck you* on my tongue because I don't want it to be the last thing I say to her. "She said it would make me the same as him."

Harmony shakes her head. "All three of us know that isn't true."

"If you feel this strongly about it, why didn't you ever do anything?"

"Because I didn't learn how to stand up for Grace until it was too late, and I've been scrambling to make amends ever since. I'm a lot like you that way, always looking out for number one."

"Sometimes people just need to hear 'I'm sorry' for them forgive you."

"She's forgiven me," she says. "I haven't forgiven myself."

We stare at one another, trying to commit our faces to memory, but we already doomed to forget. As soon as I peel my eyes from her, she begins to fade, like a photograph exposed to sun until it blanches white.

"I'm going to go now." Abruptly, Harmony is on her feet. The handcuffs are looser than the last time I visited. If she manipulates her wrists just so, she could slide right out of them. "I need a nap. The Seroquel . . ."

I want to keep her in our slice of purgatory forever, but this is done. We will forever share blood, but we will never again be sisters. "Good luck, Harmony."

"I'm a force of nature, remember? I don't need luck."

Cued either by a secret signal or by eavesdropping on our conversation, the deputy glides into the room. Harmony shoots me one last smile before being escorted from the room. I watch the back of her head until she rounds a corner. I hold my breath until I can no longer hear her footsteps. I tell myself not to cry because she will not cry, and because she would not want me to shed a single tear. She has given me the gift of closure. She jettisons me from her life with ease, and though it will not be as painless for me, now I must do the same to her.

It is the last time I ever see Harmony. I will tick the days of her sentence off my calendar, her absence a primal lack in my life, like hunger or thirst, but I will never speak to her again. In the future, when I think of her, a precious serenity will wash over me, and I'll know she's thinking of me too.

*   *   *

I follow Sara around the trailer like a shadow. When we go outside to throw tennis balls for the dogs, I finally break our silence. I want to tell her everything—how extraordinarily fucked up my life has become, how I am choosing to uphold a grievous injustice, how I am indeed the selfish and stupid bitch she thinks I am—but it would be another act of selfishness on my part, more emotional waterboarding that my friend does not deserve. As we settle into her metal patio chairs, all I can tell her is: "You're in my will, Sara."

She wipes the slobber from one of the tennis balls onto her sweatpants. "Gee, fantastic. That's not ominous at all."

"I thought you needed to know."

"Providence . . ."

The dogs confuse the pause in our game of fetch for ending it entirely. Left to entertain themselves, they roughhouse in a patch of dirt. Every time it looks like one of the boys has her pinned, Zenobia breaks free and turns the tables. "If I had a house and a yard, I'd steal Zenobia from you. I like her."

"Don't try to distract me."

"You've always been in my will. I have no one else to leave anything to."

"What about Grace? Harmony?"

"Harmony and I are not going to have a relationship."

Her frown softens into pursed lips. "Did something happen?"

"Everything and nothing. She doesn't want anything to do with me, and I'm going to do my best to respect that."

"You can still leave things to Grace when your time comes."

"I mean if something were to happen soon," I say as I fish a cigarette from the carton in my lap, "before I could change anything. I don't have much, but everything goes to you."

"Why are you giving me a verbal suicide note?"

"I have to get Grace out of that house, Sara. If it's the last thing I do on this earth, I have to do it."

She withholds her lighter, as if denying me a cigarette will make me see reason. She flicks the flame on and off. "You're going to kill your dad," she says at last.

"I'll try to reason with him first."

"Oh, I'm sure you'll get real far with that."

"Stop acting like you know him the way I do. You weren't raised by that monster."

Sara relents by lifting both hands like a criminal apprehended at the end of a manhunt. She drops the lighter in my lap. The metal, still hot from the intermittent flames, scorches the moth tattoo on my thigh. "If you're only planning to 'reason with him,'" she says, sharpening the words with air quotes, "then why are we talking about your will?"

"Because I think he's going to shoot me when he sees me. He said that's what he'd do if he saw me again, and he said if I talked to Grace, he'd shoot us both." I exhale an unsteady breath. "And my gun is gone."

"*Gone?* Did it grow legs and catch a bus to Denver?"

"The less you know about the gun, the better."

She shakes her head. "You have got to be kidding me."

"As fucked as you think this is, multiply it by a thousand."

"And Grace is a minor, so you can't just run off with her like a thief in the night."

"That's kidnapping, and I'd get twenty years, easy." The first drag of my cigarette calms my racing heart. I wish I could find this comfort elsewhere, preferably in a way that isn't going to give me cancer untold years down the line, but nothing ever comes close. Simple pleasures. I've relied on them to keep me going for a long time.

"When's her birthday? Maybe you wait it out."

"January."

Sara lights her cigarette with the cherry of my own. "When I said you were selfish, I wasn't asking you to die for someone to prove me wrong."

I don't want to die either, but I'm also not scared of it. I have too many bruises and badly healed broken bones to be scared of death. "If I leave her with him, then I'm just as much a monster as he is, and Harmony . . . she has never asked me for anything, but she's asking me for this."

"You're not obligated to fulfill Harmony's last wishes because you're sisters, same way she's not obligated to forgive you or love you."

"I can't tell you why, but I owe this to Harmony."

We finish our cigarettes in silence and watch the dogs bounce around the yard, connected at the hips to form a multiheaded beast, like a Hydra from Greek mythology. They separate to drink water and catch their breaths. Julius and Augustus flop down on the porch while Zenobia lies down at our feet, her head on a swivel to monitor the perimeter.

"If something does happen to me," I begin, "will you please be there for Grace? I know legally you can't do anything, but I want there to be a safe person for her to go to if she needs it. And—and you're the only one in my will, but I want you to give some money to Grace. I don't have much. Tattoo artists don't get life insurance." I smile, but the levity does nothing for Sara. "She mentioned she wanted to go to the community college in Scottsbluff. Maybe enough money to help her with that."

"Please don't die on me."

"Just in case, Sara. Please. Promise me."

She closes her eyes and chews on the words. "I promise."

Before I can impose another demand upon her, she marches into the trailer. One by one, citronella candles appear in the open windows. I practice an apology in my head. I refuse to end this conversation on anything but good terms, because if I do die, I don't want my best friend's final memory of me to be a bitter one.

She reappears a minute later and presses a cool, slender object into my palm. As my thumb passes over the telltale button on its handle, she tells me what it is. "My switchblade."

"What would Daniel say?"

Sara holds her arms across her chest. "Nothing. They're legal for felons to carry in South Dakota."

"Is this your blessing?"

"Clearly I can't talk you out of this," she says, "so it's me making sure you have a snowball's chance in hell at fighting back."

I hit the button. The blade jumps out. Sunlight glints along the polished metal.

CHAPTER

27

August 24ᵗʰ

11:11 AM

"I UNDERSTAND YOUR FRUSTRATION, ma'am, but we've been asked to limit Mr. Crawford's visitors to only his son for the time being."

The horse-faced nurse behind the desk engrosses herself in paperwork to avoid eye contact, as if I will disappear if she ignores me long enough. I set down the bouquet of pink and white stargazer lilies I brought for Gil. I went to three different florists before I finally found them, then shelled out fifty dollars for a dozen limp flowers and a cheap vase for them to wither in. "These are his favorite flowers," I say.

"I'm really sorry."

"I'm never going to see him again. I brought him flowers."

She simpers and tilts her head, looking just past me. "And that's very thoughtful of you, but I'm afraid there's nothing I can do. I don't make the rules, unfortunately. That's what I like to call above my pay grade."

"How much money will make you look the other way?"

This gets her attention. She draws a hand to her chest and gasps like I've suggested we infiltrate the Louvre and steal the *Mona Lisa*. "I'm insulted you would even—"

"Everything okay here?" Penny joins the nurse behind the desk, standing close behind her, hands cupped over the nurse's broad shoulders. The gesture is too intimate to be platonic. The horse-faced nurse unclenches at her touch, and when Penny's hands push aside the fabric of her scrub top to massage her bare shoulder, she doesn't recoil. This woman has probably met Josiah, shaken his hand, eaten dinner at his table, held Penny's hand and kissed her cheek in front of him.

Penny smiles at the bouquet. "Beautiful, flowers, Providence. Stargazer lilies?"

The horse-faced nurse rolls her shoulders until they pop. "I'm trying to explain, *politely*, that Gil Crawford can't have visitors other than his son."

"Did something happen?"

"I'm going off the notes in his chart."

"I'm leaving town soon," I say to Penny as she reads the computer screen through squinted eyes. "I'm probably never coming back, so I wanted to say goodbye."

Penny strokes a petal with her thumb, then brings it to her nose and breathes in the scent left behind. "It's probably a precaution from the concussion," she says "You know how Dr. Bart is. Gil's doing great."

It probably has nothing to do with the concussion and everything to do with me telling Connor to drop dead. If he was willing to cover up my mother's death to protect his father, he wouldn't bat an eye to blackball me from the nursing home. "Connor mentioned the concussion," I say. "It sounded pretty minor."

"They happen a lot here," the nurse says.

"Slips and falls every day of the week," Penny adds, turning to her colleague. "I don't see the harm. He's been lonely the last couple days, anyhow."

She shrugs again. "You're the one who'll get yelled at."

Her smile still plastered on, Penny hands me the bouquet and leads me down the hall. She leans close to me like a high schooler with a titillating piece of gossip to share. "Not like they can fire me. We're four nurses short as it is."

We avoid a wet-floor sign and the janitor mopping up a yellow puddle. The door to every room is open, allowing the competing cacophonies of their television channels to spill into the hallway—radical right-wing news channels, gunfire from old western movies, has-been celebrities shilling reverse mortgages. There is no bingo in the common room today. The French doors are fastened shut by a bungee cord around the handles, a handwritten sign taped to the door asking residents to join them for a gin rummy tournament at seven.

"Has Connor been back to visit since his fall?"

Penny's cheerleader ponytail whips the back of my neck when she shakes her head. "He's busy. He comes as much as he can."

"If Gil was my dad, I'd be here every day."

"You wouldn't," she says. "This place sucks the life out of you. You go in and the person you love can't even remember your name. It's painful. I don't blame people who can't handle it more than once or twice a year."

Chastened, I hold the flowers tighter against my chest.

Penny announces our arrival in a singsong voice. "Mr. Crawford, look who came to see you!" She ushers me through the doorframe in a dramatic sweeping motion, as if she's welcoming me onstage for a game show. The gesture strikes me first as childish, but when I see the tenderness in her face, I realize this is the bright spot in her day of feeding people who cannot feed themselves and cleaning people who cannot clean themselves.

Gil is too engrossed in setting up his chessboard to greet us. He wears a gauzy bandage above his temple, the top edge of which has unpeeled from his skin and flopped over like a dog's ear. I start to bring him the flowers, but Penny gestures to the dresser. I make as much noise as possible, clearing my throat and shuffling my feet, but Gil never looks up, and the stargazer lilies are thus sentenced to a short, sunless life.

"Maybe your friend could join you for a game of chess, hmm?"

My name is on the tip of his tongue. I will him to say it and I will him to never speak it again, to find peace in its clumsy syllables and to turn to stone as soon as they pass his lips. He sputters, stuck on the first syllable. *Prov—Prov—*and every word he could make pours through my mind. Providence. Provide. Provoke. Proverbs. *Let us swallow them up alive as the grave; and whole, as those that go down into the pit.*

And then it comes, "Providence," just as splintered as the man before me. My lungs ache like a giant fist is squeezing out all their air, my ribs caving in on my heart.

Penny guides me to the chair across from Gil and spins the chessboard. "Maybe you can be white, Providence," she says. "White goes first, doesn't it?"

"That sounds good to me," Gil says.

As she leaves, Penny turns on the radio. A staticky country station bleats at us from the corner.

"You should move this one." Gil taps the queen's pawn. His smile warms my face like the first ray of sun after a thunderstorm. "Got to control the center."

I move the king's pawn instead. "Maybe this one."

"Remind me to teach you the Caro-Kann one of these days."

"I already know it."

"Who taught you?"

"You did, Mr. Crawford."

He strokes his whiskered chin. "Bah. I'd remember if I did."

"It was the summer with all the tornados," I say. "You knew we didn't have a storm cellar and you'd always wait for me to come before you closed it up."

His laugh is empty. He knows something is wrong, something is missing, but he no longer has the faculties to identify the absence. The world is sharing a delightful joke, and he is on the outside looking in. "Between you and me, I always thought your dad was a prize idiot, not building a storm shelter all those years."

My head snaps up at the past tense, the whisper of memory carried within. Now I see two versions of Gil. I see the Gil who hugged me on Christmas mornings, who cooked me macaroni and cheese with diced jalapenos mixed in on my birthday because it was my favorite thing for dinner, who taught me to play chess, who cheered me on at softball games when my parents were too drunk to attend—and then I see the Gil who crushed my mother's bones, who tore the life from her body, who wept over something he knew was horrible but could not explain why. I wish I could force these two versions of Gil to fight to the death so one could prevail, and then I would know how to feel. Either I would hate him or I would love him. Nothing in between.

But there are not two versions of Gil. There is one man, one soul inhabiting the husk across the chessboard, and I love him and hate him in equal measure. The memories live on like a fruit rotted on its skin but still bright and juicy inside. In the end, this is all we have. People are only the tally of their memories.

"Can I ask you something serious, Mr. Crawford?"

He twirls a pawn between his fingers. "Shoot."

"How come you always let me go home?"

"How do you mean?"

"The bruises. The welts. You saw them, but you always let me go home."

He reaches for the wrong cheekbone. "Is it your face?"

By now I know it is fruitless to evoke memories. Gil's memories are no more real than dreams, figments that disintegrate just as soon as they appear. And so, one last time, I join him in his distorted piece of reality. "He hit me with the Springfield again."

"We should get you ice. I'll—I'll call Marjorie, have her get you an ice pack."

I grab his arm as he stands. He is so frail that my fingers encircle his wrist, the carpentry calluses that once studded his palms sanded down to the sere skin of an old man. "I don't want ice," I say. "I just don't want to go home."

"You'll stay for the night then."

"No, Mr. Crawford. I don't ever want to go home."

"Oh, Providence," he says, "I wish I could make that happen."

A pinch in my throat. "There's nothing stopping you from trying."

"In a perfect world—"

"In a perfect world, my father doesn't hit me when I make an error in a softball game."

"You don't deserve it," he says.

"Why do you always let me go home?"

It dawns on me as Gil's mouth hangs ajar that in all the years I spent at the Crawfords' house, I never once asked this question—not aloud, not even in my own head. It was enough to have my bruises iced and my wounds bandaged, to know that no matter what pain I was in, Gil Crawford would find a way to ease it. There were always ice packs and hot soup, even arm slings and walking boots exhumed from the attic. But then I went home and it happened again. A cycle of violence enabling a cycle of love. There are only so many times a bird can have its broken wings mended before it can no longer take flight.

"I don't want to make more trouble, not for you or your mother." The crackle of the radio dwarfs his voice. "Keep you here, make Tom mad. Call the cops, make Tom mad. I don't think it's doing the right thing if I'm just putting you in more danger."

"I'm already in danger. Every second I'm there."

"I know."

"You could do more for me."

"I wish I could."

"No, Mr. Crawford." I clutch his hand. "You could. You could, right now. Just don't make me go home."

"There's nothing I want more than a universe where you never feel pain. Not a stubbed toe, nothing." Now it is Gil whose words tighten with tears. When he tries to castle, he knocks over a pair of his pawns. "But certain things you can't make right."

"But it's the trying that matters."

"Maybe. Maybe I've never tried hard enough."

I weigh his action against his inaction, every tenderhearted letter and worn paperback he sent me in prison against all the nights I returned to Cedar Street alone. The Crawfords were just as scared of my father as everyone else in Annesville, but they laced their acts of kindness with defiance. Piecing me back together was their *fuck you* to him. And yes, it's more than anyone else ever did for me, but more isn't enough.

For most of my life, I've worried I am unlovable, a creature so repugnant that even my own mother never smiled at me warmly or cradled me in her arms. I thought that I was born unlovable the way some people are born deaf or blind, a simple fact of my existence. When I ran over my mother, it felt like fulfilling my birthright. Deprive me of love and I will deprive you of life. But I'm starting to understand I was not born unlovable. I grew into it because I was never given a chance to be anything else.

People love me. I am lovable.

Every time Gil sent me home, he stole another chance from me.

No, Providence. No, there's nothing more I can do. No, my love for you has limits.

He could have sent me home ninety-nine times if only he let me stay on the hundredth.

Yes, Providence. Yes, I see you. Yes, I love you.

And Gil, I love you too, even if it was never enough.

The bones of his hands are slight like toothpicks when I squeeze them. My voice betrays me with a quiver. "Do you remember the words to 'Lorena,' Mr. Crawford?"

"Remember them? Ha! Marjorie'll have them inscribed on our headstones."

"Can you sing it for me?"

Gil chuckles. "I've never been much of a singer. Wait for Marjorie to get back. I'll sound much better if she's on the piano."

"She won't be home for a little while, and I have to go soon. Please, Mr. Crawford. I want to hear it before I leave."

His smile reveals a newly missing tooth. He must have knocked it out when he fell. "You always come back."

"I do. But let's just think about right now, okay? Let me hear the song one more time."

And it's true—he isn't much of a singer. His voice is hoarse and thin from age. But he remembers every word and every note, and his hands drum the keys of an imaginary piano. When I close my eyes, Marjorie is here, Connor too, all four of us in the living room. The open windows invite spring into the house, the air redolent with budding flowers. The carpet is blue. The stargazer lilies reach toward the sun. The chessboard is ready, and Gil plays white.

*   *   *

I'm not sure how long I've been sitting on the curb outside the nursing home, barely breathing, certainly not moving. "Lorena" resounds through my skull beginning to end. Each time I begin the song anew, I lose one more word, one more layer of the melody, until it is pared back like a church hymn.

People pass, their conversations interrupting my song, but no one dares disturb me. They assume I am grieving a loved one in the facility. In a way, I guess I am.

As I contemplate the walk to the car, my phone buzzes.

"Karishma?"

"Grace hasn't been at school in a couple days," she says quietly. "I don't know if you've talked to her, but I haven't heard anything, and . . ."

"You think she's in trouble."

"I do," Karishma says. A man's voice rumbles in the background. Mitesh, I surmise.

"I'm going to take care of it," I assure her. "This time tomorrow, it's all going to be over. I'll be at his liquor store right when it opens. I'm going to end it."

"That sounds a little . . . I mean, don't do anything stupid. Like, don't go back to prison."

"Don't worry about me. Grace is going to be okay. That's all that matters."

Karishma's sigh crackles in my ear. I wait for her to protest again, but nothing comes. We hang up after a few moments of silence, and I lift my face to the sky, committing the warmth of the summer sun to memory.

CHAPTER

28

August 25th

7:18 AM

I WAKE WITH THE sun. I smoke half a pack of cigarettes on the trailer porch as I watch it rise over the nearby grove of trees, dandelion yellow. One hour until the liquor store opens. Every second is a bullet.

I am caught between preparing to die and fortifying my resolve to live. It seems foolish to bet on either outcome. He may shoot me on sight. He may do me the courtesy of a conversation before shooting me. He may mortally wound me. He may leave me with only a flesh wound. He may be sensible and listen to me. He may trick me into thinking I've persuaded him and shoot me in the back when I turn to leave. He may really kill me. The possibilities are horrifying in their endlessness. My father is a grenade with the pin already pulled. There's no telling when he will explode and how much carnage will ensue when he does, and the uncertainty is what frightens me most. If I knew I was going to die, I could at least say a prayer for my soul.

And as it is appointed for men to die once, but after this the judgment.

I picture my father sprinkling my remains in a landfill. What a sick twist of fate that if I die, my ashes will belong to him.

I dump the dregs of my coffee onto the lawn. I scratch Zenobia behind the ears. I slide the switchblade into my bra.

And then I drive to the liquor store.

* * *

Most of the vagrants on the street are still asleep, some in sleeping bags, some on cardboard slabs laid across the sidewalk. A small group plays blackjack on the curb, substituting bottle caps for chips. The dealer wolf-whistles at me when I pass.

I tell myself I am no longer seduced by bloodlust, no longer intoxicated by the thrill of revenge. I tell myself this is strictly business, a loose end demanding to be tied up. I'm not sure if I believe it, but I am leaving violence as the last resort, and surely that counts for something. It must mean I've changed, even a little, that I see a different means to my end.

The bell on the door chimes when I walk in. My father is not behind the counter, but he calls out from the back stockroom. "Be with you in a minute!" He grunts and groans over the bottles clanking together.

I snatch a shot-sized bottle of vodka from an endcap and down it in a single gulp. It burns on the way down and sours my stomach instantly, the liquor pooling in my gut like an oil spill. I fight to keep from retching as I put the bottle back where I found it, among a graveyard of empty friends. I'm the umpteenth person this week to do this. My final *fuck you* to my father isn't even unique.

His footsteps are leaden. He stops in the doorframe, a beer bottle in his hand. We look at each other like a deer spotting the hunter who has it in the crosshairs. I don't know who is the deer and who is the hunter.

"You must be deaf, butterfly. Clearly you didn't hear what I said when you crawled onto my porch."

I keep my voice even and calm. I can't be weak, but I can't be too strong either. "I came to talk."

"You and I got nothing to say to each other."

"You don't, but I do."

"That's the problem with you: always looking to have the last word." He gathers his greasy shirt above his holster to remind me of his Springfield. My cheekbone throbs at the sight of it. "If it's so important, spit it out."

"Grace should come to Missouri with me."

I mistake his pause for contemplation, but it is mockery. His laughter rattles between the liquor bottles. "And what other wishes can this genie grant you?"

"I only want her."

"It's not a custody arrangement," he says, setting down his beer. "She's my daughter. End of discussion."

"She's my sister."

"What happens if she goes back home with you? She sleeps on the couch in your shitty apartment while you're drawing on people to pay the rent? Oh, what a dream life you're offering her, Providence."

"Aren't you tired of raising your daughters?"

"I've been tired fifty-seven years, daughters or no daughters."

"Don't pretend like your children are the great joy of your life." I soften my words with a chuckle forced from the bottom of my throat. It sickens me to show him even an imitation of joy. "You're an old man now. You want to drink your beers, watch the Rockies lose, sometimes go play pool in Tyre. If Grace comes with me, you can have the life you always wanted.

This whole thing'll be done. That's the best thing that could happen for any of us."

"Family isn't a rotten tooth. You don't just yank it out when it starts to hurt."

I train my eyes on his holster. "Normal families, sure, but when was this family ever normal?"

"You had a roof over your head and food on the table. You had nothing to complain about."

"Do you really believe that? Can you look me in the eye and tell me you honestly don't think you did anything wrong?"

He can. "I never did nothing to you that my old man didn't do to me or my sister, God rest her soul. It didn't break us: it made us tough as nails. I wanted you girls to be tough. None of that crying over a scraped knee bullshit. No back talk, no sass. It never did me any harm, and you don't look any worse for wear. I made you strong. That I won't ever apologize for."

"You made me scared."

"Fear is a choice," he says. "Look at Harmony. You think she was ever scared?"

"You were always too drunk to hear us cry."

"You only think that because you were the weak one. I never saw you be strong, Providence, not once. Look at what you've done to your arms. It's a weakness."

"I keep myself alive. I'm a survivor."

My father waves his hand like he's batting away an insect. "Don't get philosophical on me."

"Please, I am begging you. Let me take Grace."

"No."

"One word?" I lift my hands. "That's all I get?"

"The answer is no."

"She's going to go to college soon anyway."

He shakes his head. "She's not. She'll go when I think she's ready for it."

"You can't be happy unless you're making someone else suffer, can you?"

"Providence, I am giving you one last chance to turn tail and get out of my store. You said your piece and I heard you out. It's time for you to go."

I step closer to him. "Give Grace a chance at a normal life. Give her one reason not to wish you dead. One thing to be grateful to you for."

"Are you finished?"

"No."

"Walk away."

"I'm not finished. I won't—"

Pain rips through my thigh, hot and fast and bloody. I hear a scream I barely recognize as my own, even recognize as human, a noise not unlike the one my mother made beneath the wheels of the car. I am on the ground before I realize he has shot me.

He shot me. My father shot me.

He walks toward me, gun still drawn. I stare down the barrel. The muzzle is agape in an eternal shriek. And the wound— it burns, God it burns, and I am paralyzed. I cannot even move enough to press my hands on the wound to stop the blood gushing from my leg. The pain radiates to the furthest reaches of my body. It screams up my spine, into my brain, the roots of my teeth, down to my toes, all the way to my fingertips.

"Run," my father says. "Get up and run."

No words form. My mouth is numb. It is all I can do to keep breathing. The world has gone blurry.

He stoops and grabs a fistful of my hair. Something cool nuzzles against my shoulder—not the gun, no, that's in his other hand. It's his wedding ring. And I suddenly think of my mother dressed in white, committing herself to this vile brute who calls himself a man.

He fires the gun at the ceiling from beside my ear. The ringing is so loud it doubles me over. "I told you to get up and run. Will you listen to me now? Get up! Get on your feet!"

I don't have time to reach for the switchblade. I do the only thing I can think to save myself.

I rear up and bite his nose. I taste the blood and I feel the chunk of flesh I've taken with me. It rolls between my gums like a pinball as he falls backward, his hands clamped over his face. The gun planes across the floor.

"Fucking bitch!"

I claw my way on top of him and bear my full weight down upon his chest. Now is my chance. I am so desperate to breathe that I choke on the air. Before I can reach for the switchblade, he rams a fist into my solar plexus, and now I am wheezing, my vision turning green at the corners, so starved for oxygen that I would tear a hole in my own throat for a single gasp.

The gun skids to a stop in front of the pyramid of twelve-packs. He bear-crawls toward it.

I use the shelves to pull myself to my feet, but I collapse as soon as I straighten my wounded leg. The blood courses down my leg like honey from a forbidden hive, thick and sticky and somehow unbearably cold.

Get up, Providence. Get up.

One more time. I drag myself upright. He inches closer to the gun.

I reach for the switchblade as I drag myself down the aisleway, bottles of liquor shattering against the ground in my wake.

And I don't think twice.

I throw myself down on him.

I plunge the knife through the back of his neck.

The knife hitches as it severs his vertebrae. He collapses beneath me, and I sense the moment the life leaves his body as he goes limp on the floor. And it is delicious. One more thrust,

I tell myself, just to make sure, and this one is cleaner, slicing through with ease. I stab him until the tip of the switchblade clatters against the floor and bounces away from me, until his blood mingles with my own. It coats my hands and soaks my shirt. It is a lifetime of rage finally exorcized from my body. You'll shoot me like a fucking dog, will you? I'll eat you like a fucking dog, you sick, sick man. And me, I'm sick too. Sick for doing this, sick for delighting in it so brazenly, sick for pretending I was not driven by revenge or fury, the sadistic desire to end another person's life. But that's okay. I have the right to the last laugh. I get the last fucking word.

This is my pound of flesh.

Finally. Finally.

Harmony, Grace, I've avenged us. It's over now. We're free.

The pain roars through me again, stronger now than before. Everything goes white.

*   *   *

The world resurfaces in fragments as I fade in and out. A crowd. The same man who wolf-whistled at me uses his shirt as a tourniquet on my leg. An ambulance. *I haven't seen that much blood since my granddad showed me the old slaughterhouse in Gordon.* A hospital. They jostle me around on the stretcher, and they aren't running, which I find funny because I'm certain I am about to die. An operating room. The doctor smiles as me as I fight against an anesthetic sleep and beg him to save my moth tattoo. *Count backward from ten, all right? You're in good hands, miss.*

And it turns out, he's right. I wake up in a barren hospital room, mummified in blankets pulled up to my chin. The curtains are drawn, but the room is lit by the blinding hallway fluorescents and the artificial glow of the machines at my side. Oxygen tubes dangle from my nose and IVs sprout from the crook of my arm.

I peel the blanket back to look at my wrists. No handcuffs.

A nurse comes running when I hit the red button on my bedside. She checks my vitals, blinds me with a little flashlight that she asks me to follow with my eyes to make sure my brain is still intact. The surgery was a success. They removed the bullet, she tells me, and I'm very lucky it didn't hit bone. She says more, but I still can't hear out of my left ear and I'm too shell-shocked to tell her so. I am convinced this is a dream, a hallucination from the edges of a coma, and when I do wake up, it will be in a prison hospital, bound to the metal bedframe by my ankles and wrists, a khaki jumpsuit at the foot of my bed.

"The doctor . . . soon. . . . . . important . . . someone else . . . talk to . . . let him in?"

I nod at her piecemeal question. She leaves the room and not ten seconds later, Josiah comes in. He bears his cowboy hat in his hands like he has come to pay his respects at my funeral.

". . . okay?" He pulls up a chair at my bedside and I hide my hands beneath the blankets.

My mouth is dry. The words won't come. Josiah offers me a plastic cup of water and I drink from it in tiny sips, a dove at a birdbath. He is too polite to comment, but he gawks at my scarred arms.

". . . lot of . . . to see you."

I tap on my ear. "I can't hear very well."

He repositions his chair to the other side of the bed and leans toward me, keeping his words soft. "The nurse said the hearing loss is temporary," he says. "Lots of folks came to see you. They're all in the waiting room, whole pack of 'em. Grace, Zoe Markham, your friend from the reservation . . ."

"I don't think I should ask what brought you here."

"Not sure what you're talking about."

"I'm not really in the mood for being coy."

He slices the air with a flattened palm, as if to say *no worries, I got it*. "Your father, you mean? Whole thing was self-defense. I saw it with my own two eyes."

"No, you didn't."

"He shot you, Providence. The knife? If you didn't do it to him, what was he going to do to you?"

My head is still underwater, thoughts hazy, but the memory of the knife in my father's neck unfurls with perfect clarity. My shoulders ache from stabbing him so many times.

"You weren't there."

"Oh, I was. Karishma Jadhav called this morning, said you'd be at the liquor store. She was worried you'd get hurt. I got there in the nick of time to see it happen."

"Why are you doing this?" I whisper. "Why are you lying for me?"

"Just doing what we both know is right," he says. "Besides, there was a man outside the store who saw it too. He and I agree we saw the same thing. The one who stopped the bleeding, remember?" Josiah's knees crack when he stands. He inhales through gritted teeth.

"People might ask questions."

"I think it's an open secret no one in Annesville was going to shed a tear when Tom Byrd met the reaper."

My father is in hell. I sent him there. The thought brings the faintest smile to my lips.

"I'd offer a penny for your thoughts, but you never were too hard to read."

"My mother was the inscrutable one."

At that, Josiah smiles. "The preacher promised me he'd work on a headstone for Elissa. It'll take a few weeks, but he's going to put it under the chokecherry tree, facing west so she can watch the sunsets."

"Her ashes are mine now, aren't they?"

"The house and everything in it are yours. I know everyone else in his family is gone, and frankly, your father didn't seem like the type to have a will."

My father starts slurring in my mind, but his voice is already fading.

"Tell the preacher I want her ashes buried," I say to Josiah. "She can be the first Byrd woman buried at the church."

The first and, God willing, the last.

* * *

I am warm from morphine. My body cries out for sleep. Connor tries to see me, but I turn him away. I drift off during Sara's visit, and when I wake, it is Grace in the room with me.

She sleeps on a cot beneath the window, curled up like a wounded fawn. She has eaten the pudding a nurse brought for me earlier in the night. The empty pouch lies on the floor beside her shoes and her backpack. It is scuffed and discolored, bulging with books and binders. Her life should have been so much simpler. We've robbed her of childhood. We've forced her to grow up long before she should have. For all the times she reminded me she was no longer a child, she didn't understand how much less painful her world would be if she was. She should be studying for midterms and buying a dress for prom. Instead, she sleeps beside me in a hospital room, motherless, fatherless, lulled to sleep by the rhythmic tones of the machines to which I am attached.

She stirs beneath the blanket. Her elbows and knees pop.

"Grace."

Every question is about me. Are you angry with me? Can you forgive me? Have I committed the unpardonable sin? Am I evil? Did the world make me this way or is this who I have been all along? Is this my nature, the way a snake must always bite?

My father deserved to die, but my sister did not deserve to become an orphan. I don't know how to reconcile that both can be true. I don't know how to reconcile how I can feel so righteous and so depraved all at once. When I thought of killing my father, I thought of him as just that. Mine. I forget he is ours, mine and Grace's and Harmony's, and even if we all prayed for him to die, I am the one who ended his life.

I am a killer.

I am nauseous at the word, but that's a good thing. Taking a human life is meant to weigh on your soul. This pang of remorse is what separates me from a sociopath.

I will tell myself this for the rest of my life, but I will only believe it some of the time.

Grace cloaks herself in a blanket like E.T. She brings her vape to her lips, but stops short of smoking. I want to crack open our skulls and compare our brains side by side to see if the same defect that made me capable of unspeakable violence afflicts her too. I picture it as a malignant growth spreading across the tissue, turning it from gray to black, and if I find it within her, I will take a melon baller and scoop it out.

"Thank you for staying." I reach toward her. She hesitates but takes my hand.

"You would have stayed for me."

"Is . . ." I swallow hard. It's difficult to speak. "Do you have somewhere to stay?"

"Mitesh said I could stay with him and Karishma for a little while."

"That's kind of him."

She sneaks a tiny pull from her vape and exhales into the blanket. She slips it into her bra like I did with the switchblade. "It's just the two of us now. We're all that's left." She climbs into my bed. We lie forehead to forehead.

"I know about Harmony."

We search each other's eyes for absolution we cannot grant. My sin is unforgivable, and her sin is not mine to forgive. If we fall short of forgiveness, we must pay each other the kindness of silence, now and forever. Grace curls into me, once again the tiny baby I cradled in the linen closet, bringing the crucifix necklace to rest on her bottom lip. Maybe it is not Jesus lashed to the cross. Maybe it is the penitent thief after all.

She begins to tremble. I draw her closer.

"It's okay, Grace. You can grieve if you need to."

29

September 9th

9:43 AM

TILLMAN COUNTY DECLINES to press charges in the death of Tom Byrd. A deputy questioned me while I was still in the hospital—"just due diligence," he promised, "just making sure we got our story right"—but nothing further came of it. Josiah assures me I don't need to worry about a wrongful-death suit either, seeing as the only earthly family my father has left are me and my sisters. "It's all over," he tells me over the phone. "Go home. Live your life. It's done now."

I'm free.

I spend two weeks recovering at Sara's, and that's when I start having anxiety attacks and nightmares. The nightmares are always a little different. Sometimes my father and I are reliving the liquor store, other times we are brawling at the pool hall, occasionally we are fighting in the house, right over the dead spot on the landing. The settings change, but each dream ends with my father pinning me to the floor and driving the switch-blade through my chest like a stake through the heart of a vampire. It never kills me instantly. I gasp for air and struggle against him, but he plunges the knife deeper, twists it, then stabs me again and again between different ribs.

Merely shaking me does not end the nightmare. Sara quite literally throws me on the ground to wake me, and when I do, I am struggling to breathe just as I did when he shot me.

The bullet is gone, but the pain lingers, a persistent, dull throb that aches the same way my reconstructed cheek does in the winter. The doctor wanted to prescribe me Percocet for the pain, but I thought of my mother and declined. Regardless, he assured me it would dissipate in time. The limp would be temporary too. He said the same about my hearing loss, and while I still hear out of both ears, the left will never be the same. Things sound tinny and distant, and I lose words like I'm trapped in a permanent game of telephone. Eventually, only a scar will remain to remind me of that day, a patch of mottled flesh not unlike Mitesh Jadhav's neck, warping my moth tattoo beyond recognition. Kiera was horrified when I sent her the picture.

At my final post-op appointment, the doctor apologizes for leaving such a grisly scar, but I smile and tell him it's okay, I'm covered in scars as it is, what's one more? He writes me a prescription for Valium to ease the nightmares and sends me on my way.

One afternoon, as I am lounging in the sun with Zenobia and my sketch pad, Sara invites me to the annual *wacipi*—or powwow, as she translates—a colorful gathering of dancing, ceremony, and music. It's her favorite weekend of the year. "You haven't left the house in two weeks," she says. She keeps herself busy by cleaning out my father's liquor store. I've given her the deed. She still doesn't know what to do with the building, floating a new idea by me every day, but I know it will be a beacon of hope amidst the squalor of Annesville, the way flowers persist even in the harshest tundra. "You should be among the living."

"It's been nice to have peace and quiet," I say.

"Providence."

"My leg—"

"Leg, schmeg. You're going."

I straighten my afflicted leg out on the picnic blanket and finger the bullet scar, and then the scars dotting my arms. I'm gradually learning how to stop hiding my scars beneath my sleeves. I'm tired of the secrecy and the shame. If I would not hesitate to show people the bullet scar, why should I hesitate to show them the bite mark scars? Both are acts of violence, against myself and against another, but violence nonetheless. I want to leave the shame in Annesville. "Is it appropriate for me to be there? It's your tribe, your celebration. Your people."

She sits across from me and Zenobia, rubbing the dog's nose with her foot. "It's appropriate as long as I'm inviting you."

"I don't know, Sara."

"You've seen a lot of sadness on the reservation," she says. "I know it's hard to see anything else. Shit, I'm all doom and gloom. But you should see the joy too. There's nothing like it."

* * *

And of course, my dearest friend is right. The *wacipi* is unlike anything I've ever seen. In a meadow, inexplicably green and lush despite the brownness of the earth surrounding it, hundreds of people dressed in kaleidoscopic tribal regalia dance to the airs of drummers and singers. Sara walks me through the maze of people cooking traditional Lakota foods. She points out the *wojapi* (and insists hers is the best), the *wohanpi* soup of bison and potatoes and turnips, the *wasna* bars made of jerky and dried cranberries. Artists display handmade jewelry and beadwork in kaleidoscopic colors. Sara buys me a dreamcatcher with different shades of green used for the hoop, net, and feathers.

"I think you're going to need this," she says as she eases it into my purse.

She introduces me to a collection of cousins, one of whom asks what happened to my arms. I tell him I lost a fight with a snapping turtle, and he laughs. A few of them steal looks at my tattoos, but no one else comments. I take a picture of them, Sara standing in the middle, brilliant like a supernova, a woman who is exactly where she belongs.

Eventually, I excuse myself to rest on the nearby bleacher. I massage the scar to ease the epicenter of the pain, but it diffuses down into my calf and my foot. I tell myself when the pain finally goes away, so too will the nightmares, but I know it isn't true.

"Hi, Providence."

It's Scarlett. I could recognize those orange braces from a county away. She ascends the bleachers like a staircase and sits on the row below me. Her lips are tinted from her popsicle, artificial raspberry with a smell sugary enough to make my stomach clench. She sprinkles salt on it from the tiny packet in her hand before taking her next lick.

I scrunch my nose. "Salt on a popsicle?"

"It sounds gross, but it's so good. Like olive oil on ice cream."

"That also sounds gross," I say.

"As my dad would say, don't knock it 'til you try it."

Not long after I was discharged from the hospital, when my days were still just one medication-induced nap after the other, Sara checked Daniel into the rehab facility in Rapid City. I insisted she take the money that Gil gave me to help pay for it. "Pretend it's from an anonymous Good Samaritan," I told her. I can't undo my decision to leverage someone else's addiction for my own gain (that callousness may haunt me forever), but I can play a part, however small, in helping them heal.

Scarlett reads my mind. "I'm not, like, mad at you or Aunt Sara. I'm not even mad at him. I just want him to be healthy. I think it's a disease."

"It is," I tell her as she salts the popsicle again. "My mother had it."

"But she never got better."

"No, she didn't. But she didn't have people in her corner like your dad does."

In the grass, the dancers begin a whirlwind choreography that leaves me breathless just watching. "That's what Aunt Sara says," Scarlett murmurs dreamily, "that the only thing that matters at the end of the day is having people who love you."

People love me. I am lovable.

* * *

Sara is somehow still hungry when we leave the *wacipi*. We pick up a pizza on the way home and eat it on her bed like teenage girls at a sleepover, the dogs pawing at our closed door. Sara consumes her slices crust-first. She laughs when I scold her for eating in a supine position. "If I choke to death on a slice of mushroom pizza," she says, "I deserve it. Just please make sure my headstone says something nice."

"Here lies Sara Walking Elk—sister, aunt, friend, and car thief."

"Car *larcenist*," she corrects. "It sounds more intriguing that way."

"Is my favorite car *larcenist* going to come visit me in Kansas City?" I ask.

"Only if you pay for a five-star hotel room."

"I'm being serious, Sara. I don't . . . I don't think I can come back here ever again. The triggers would kill me."

She sets down her pizza slice to take my hands. My fingers slot perfectly between hers. I've never been a believer in soulmates, but I think that's because I've understood the word all wrong. A soulmate doesn't have to be a lover. It can be someone like Sara, a friend who loves you even during the moments you are impossible to like. "I promise I'll come visit. I'll visit so often, you'll start begging for the days where we only sent birthday cards. It's my honor and privilege to be a thorn in your side, Providence Byrd."

"You're going to make me cry."

"Tell me something happy then. Tell me the first thing you and Grace are going to do when you get to Kansas City."

In less than twenty-four hours, I will be driving back to Missouri, Grace in the passenger seat, whatever earthly possessions we can fit in the trunk and back seat rattling along with us for the ten-hour drive. The thought fills me with as much terror as it does joy. Josiah and Zoe called in every favor they had to expedite the custody process. The court named me Grace's legal guardian in record time.

"We're going out for dinner," I say. "Kansas City barbecue is world-famous. And then I'm . . ."

"Come on, spit it out."

"I'm going to think about enrolling in community college with her next year, as ridiculous as that sounds."

"It's not ridiculous. It's brave," she says.

"There's nothing brave about a remedial math class."

"Sometimes the bravest thing you can do is start over."

A fresh start, for Grace and for me. Two orphan sisters slowly unshackling themselves from their traumatic pasts. We don't have much, but we will always have each other. I think that can be enough.

And the Lord said unto Cain, "Where is Abel thy brother?"

And he said, "I know not. Am I my brother's keeper?"

Happily, I will be my sister's keeper.

30

September 10th

8:46 AM

GRACE PARES HER life down to a suitcase, a duffel bag, and the box of memories our mother left for her. There is nothing else for us to keep. We leave our father's sports paraphernalia on the walls to collect dust, his tuna noodle casserole in the fridge to mold, his clothes in the closet to be nibbled on by moths.

We are the fourth generation of Byrds to live in the saltbox house on Cedar Street, and now we are the last. Everyone thinks I should sell the house. "Other people can come in and make happy memories," Zoe said during her brief hospital visit. But I cannot bear the thought of another family roaming these halls, sleeping in these bedrooms, walking over the dead spot on the landing, cooling their pies on the windowsill. They will erase my existence from this home. They will never know the horrors and the rare moments of joy over a chokecherry pie or a walk-off home run to finish a Rockies game. Our lives will be blotted out by theirs, Annesville writing us out of its story just as seamlessly it writes them in, and though this is as it should be, the natural cycle of moving on, I refuse to condemn us to this fate. This is our house, ours alone. We built it, and so too will we tear it down.

I plan to let it sit vacant for a while, and then I will demolish it. One day, when I'm ready, someone will purchase the land to start from scratch upon our ruins. Our legacy will live on in the family plot at the graveyard and in hushed retellings of urban legends, but no one else will ever live in our house.

Seated atop my car, I soak in the house one last time. Four walls of memories, screams lost in the attic rafters, tears soaked into the floorboards—all of it, left behind. *For dust thou art, and unto dust shalt thou return.* Annesville, left behind. For the rest of my life, when someone asks me where I'm from, I will smile and tell them I'm from flyover country, a wide spot in the road, a paper town. I'm from nowhere.

I once thought no place but Annesville could ever be home, but home is not what you run from. It's what you run toward.

Grace emerges from the backyard with a bundle of orange fur in her arms. "I found Bucket sleeping under the porch."

She presents him to me like a wiseman bringing a gift to the manger. The cat barely acknowledges me before returning to Grace and rubbing his jowls against her chin. I can hear him purring from feet away.

"Can we take Bucket with us?" she asks.

I smile at the cat and then at my sister—my sweet, beautiful, gap-toothed sister. Our world has shifted forever on its axis. It is a triumph and a catastrophe all at once.

"Sure," I say. "We can take the cat."

ACKNOWLEDGMENTS

THERE'S A SAYING that perfectly encapsulates what writing is like for me: "There's nothing to writing. All you do is sit down at a typewriter and open a vein." It remains a subject of debate as to who coined this pearl of wisdom, but the sentiment resonates with me nonetheless. Writing is a very solitary endeavor – until it isn't. While I'm the one who bled all over these pages, this novel would not exist without the help of countless people.

Thank you to my brilliant editor, Holly Ingraham, for truly seeing and understanding this novel, and for all her creative wisdom along the way. She sharpened this book into the very best version of itself that it could be. I also owe thanks to all those I worked with at Crooked Lane Books: Thaisheemarie Fantauzzi Perez, Rebecca Nelson, Dulce Botello, Mikaela Bender, and Cassidy Graham.

Without the dedication of my inimitable agent, Johanna Castillo, this novel might have never come to fruition. I'm indebted to Johanna for taking a chance on a young debut novelist and for keeping the faith through a long submission process – even when my own optimism was flagging. I am also indebted to her assistant, Victoria Mallorga Hernandez, for her invaluable work behind the scenes. I am filled with gratitude to have such a formidable team at my back.

Thank you to my cover designer, Jocelyn Martinez, for her exceptional work and giving my novel a beautiful face to greet the world with.

And now, my family. I appreciate all of you beyond measure for the years of love, safety, and support you've given me: Travis Bruce, Cassie Bruce, Annie Tressler, Steve Tressler, Jody Miller, Travis Miller, Priscilla Banks. Thank you in particular to my mom, Justine Bruce, for keeping my head on straight even when I start to spiral and for always giving me a soft landing, and my dad, Bill Bruce, for shaping me into the writer I am today. I may be a little biased, but I think I have the best parents on the planet.

A special mention to my late grandmother, Ruth Bruce, for every story and every smile. She lived one hundred incredible years, but I'm heartbroken I couldn't have her for one hundred more. I wish she was here to hold this book in her hands. I miss her every day.

Thank you to my future in-laws for welcoming me into their family open arms: Tyler Madden, Rhonda Encinas, Jack Madden.

My circle of friends, old and new, is small but mighty. Thank you to Jessica Hayes, Dante Leventini, and Liberty Broughton for so much laughter and light.

There are countless writers who lifted my spirits during this arduous journey. The Submission Slog Comrades and 2025 Debuts servers on Discord are filled with exceptionally talented authors always looking to fill their fellow authors' cups. To the Small Press Debuts 2025 Instagram chat, thank you for being my people.

A handful of my fellow authors need to be thanked by name: Tracy Hoagland, Melissa O'Connor, Amy DeBellis. Each of these exceptionally talented women allowed me to wear my heart on my sleeve and share my fears and anxieties in our private chats. When I needed a safe place to talk, they were there.

My street team is peerless. I'm eternally grateful to each of you for rallying around me: Kat, Michaela, Nicole, Claudia,

Annie, Deanna, Katie M., Katie P., Madeleine, Elaine, Grace, Melissa, Lindsay, Amanda, Samantha C., Samantha M., Emma, Courtney, Mary, Mary B., Savitri, Laura, Hannah, Molly, Sav, Kayla, and Amy.

And finally, thank you to Hannah Madden, my fiancée, the love of my life, for all things said and unsaid.